to love a monster

A Collection Of
Monstrous Love Stories

A Collection Of
Monstrous Love Stories

to love a monster

Billie Parsons - Sam Trathen - Rachel Radner - LM Wilson
S.D. Hegyes - Katie Commons - Artemed Sullivan

Hounded

Billie Parsons

To my nieces and nephews — because family is everything — love you all.

one

RYLEIGH

The scratching of the bottle I just spun against the hardwood floor grates on my ears. I didn't even want to come to this stupid party tonight anyway but my one friend, Cassie, convinced me by telling me that I 'just have to celebrate' all because it's my eighteenth birthday.

The bottle slows to a stop just to my left: Keith, the one guy at this party that no one wants to kiss. I sigh deeply and start to head to the closet for the allotted seven minutes in so-called heaven.

Just as Keith steps up behind me at the door of the closet, he turns and vomits all over the wall and floor. Stifling my gag by covering my nose and mouth, I throw my hands in the air;

"You've got to be kidding me," I say as I jump away.

"Jesus Keith, get the fuck out of here!" Someone yells from the circle of teens playing spin-the-bottle.

I spend a moment collecting myself then turn to go out the front door when Cassie grabs my hand.

"How about truth or dare instead?" She proposes to the room. Everyone seems in agreement and she pulls me back to the circle.

"Still your turn, Ryleigh," one of the girls says. "Truth or dare?"

After what just happened I choose the safe option, "Truth."

"What does your dream boyfriend look like?" the same girl asks.

Her question catches me off guard a little bit, a couple of the girls' friends snitcher quietly and Cassie throws them daggers with her eyes. I silently stare at the girl and after mentally peeling away the layers of makeup she has caked on, I see who she is: Katherine Holms. She is the stereotypical mean girl: tall enough that her head ends at the quarterback's chin, natural blonde, unshakable confidence, and money for days.

"Umm..." I hesitate.

"Oh c-come on, Ryleigh! You are eighteen and no one h-here has ever seen you even look at a guy like you might like him. Your standards are too h-h-high." One of the guys stammers out from the keg in the corner of the room.

Maybe it's the tone in his voice, the full moon, or the liquid courage I've been sipping on for the past hour. I'm not typically the fighting type. "Just because I don't want anything to do with your nasty ass, doesn't mean my standards are too high." *Oohs* from the surrounding teens brings me back to the circle.

My new found confidence spurs me forward. "My dream

guy is tall, has dark hair, and is from anywhere but Finley." That makes everyone chuckle. "He must be strong–"

At this point, Katherine and her friends start to laugh, full belly laughing. I look around in question and the guy from the keg is also doubled over laughing. Cassie shrugs her shoulders when our eyes meet.

"What's so funny?" Cassie asks for me.

Katherine wipes a tear from her eye and looks at me. "Of course he would have to be strong. She's the only fat person in Finley!" her own laughter cuts her off.

I wish I was phased by her words, but she isn't wrong. I am the only girl in our small town of Finley that weighs over 200 pounds. All my classmates know it and have picked on me for years.

I don't make eye contact with anyone and stand to walk out of the house. Cassie tries to stop me again but this time I just brush her hand away. I don't bother closing the front door when I leave.

Walking home in the middle of the night is never really a big deal in a small town like Finley, being only a couple miles from one end of town to the other there was no need for me to get my license until I leave for college after my gap year. Everything is closeby and everyone knows everyone.

The warm, August night blankets me and the full moon

lights the sidewalk as I start my walk home. The wind rattles the leaves in the trees that rest on the edges of the yards I pass. Dogs bark here and there, and someone honks their horn when they drive by.

Somewhere in the far distance, howling starts, sending a shiver down my spine. It stops me and I look around, trying to determine what direction it's coming from. My focus zeros in on a small path leading to the Dead Forest.

The howling changes, it sounds like the animal is in pain; after only a second of hesitation I turn and continue my journey home.

The Dead Forest has its name for a reason: whatever goes in, never comes out.

two

ARCHER

"She's *here*," I growl at my friend. I can sense her with my entire soul, the hairs on the back of my neck start to stand on end and it seems that something in the air has shifted slightly.

In his whispering voice, Shadow replies, "Are you positive Archer? For it has been a very long time?"

"Of course I'm sure! This is where she was born, where she dies, and so she must have been reborn here! There isn't another option." I shake my head in deep thought. This is where everything has happened. Finley has secrets.

As the full moon reaches its peak, I look up and embrace its light and power. My eyes gloss over so quickly, it is almost like I blinked.

I look over and Shadow is leaning over the edge of the small cliff overlooking the Dead Forest. He doesn't seem to have noticed anything different with me, so I go back to looking up at the moon.

While the moon doesn't really change anything for someone; something, like me; it's a reminder of my freedom. A moon is just one of the many things that Hell doesn't have.

Once again my vision gets glassy. This time, it doesn't disappear. I continue looking up for a moment hoping it will pass when the dogs we passed in the forest start to howl. My head flashes in the direction of their noise.

Suddenly my vision is the clearest it has ever been and through the small patch of forest and across the street, there she stands.

I *KNOW* it is her.

Instincts take over and before I can think about it, I have shifted into my natural form and Shadow is pouncing on me, pinning me to the ground, sharp rocks digging into my side.

"You could frighten her, or worse! Archer... you could hurt her. You need to try and find solace." Shadow whispers to me, his knee digging into my back.

I howl in pain. Emotional turmoil over takes me, I howl until I know she heard me.

Until she walked away.

Away from me.

Even then, I continue howling long into the night.

three

RYLEIGH

My dreams that night are plagued with the painful howls of wolves in the far distance. I chase the sound through a never-ending black forest; past pools filled with red, hot liquid; and over jagged cliffs, always coming up empty handed. I try to run away from the constant noise but no matter how far I go the sound is around me, unchanging in volume.

The next morning, I wipe a tear from my cheek before I roll out of bed and catch my reflection in the small mirror on my dresser, my restless sleep visible. Yesterday's eyeliner is smudged under my eyes. My long, coal-colored hair is frizzy and balled up around the braid that now hangs over my shoulder. I grab my glasses from the bedside table as I head to the bathroom.

And then, I hear it again – in broad daylight – the howls from my walk home last night and the howling from my dreams. It stops me in my tracks and I look around my room at the posters on the wall, the dirty laundry piling up near the door, and my journal on the floor next to my bed; hoping that maybe something in here made the noise. I turn towards the one window in my modest-sized bedroom and stare like the panes hold the answers.

Then it stops.

I sigh with relief, my fear and worry melting away with the last of the howls echoing off of the hills surrounding Finley.

Something inside me knows that the howling is not just some guy's dog in their backyard, this is different, it *feels* different.

～

"Hey sweetie. How was the party?" Aunt Cyndi asks.

I shrug my shoulders and sit down at the kitchen table. Aunt Cyndi was my mother's older half-sister.

My mother died giving birth to me. According to the doctor, nothing would have changed her fate. As for my father, no one knows who he is or where he might be.

My aunt is the only family I have. Aunt Cyndi never wanted children. She never wanted a partner, either. After everything that happened with her parents and her half-sister, my mother; she just wanted to live out her days in Finley, but instead here she is in her late fifties, with a teenager she never asked for.

I'm not bitter; don't get me wrong, Aunt Cyndi has never

given me any reason to think she is upset with how everything turned out. I just wish she could have had the life she wanted. The life she deserved.

"Are you still goin' to Cassie's?" She asks.

After last night, I don't want to do anything. The way that the party and night ended up going still has me asking questions. "I might. I didn't sleep well." I answer.

Aunt Cyndi stops drying a plate and looks over to me, "You OK? You usually don't have issues sleeping, do you?

"Nah, I think the beer I drank last night was bad." I reply, not ready to tell her about the howling, for all I know that could be all in my head. Maybe I'm going crazy.

My grandfather was crazy, said that shadow people took his wife in the middle of the night. When the police showed up nothing was missing other than her body. My grandmother's things were exactly where they should've been: phone on the charger, clothes in the closet, slippers beside the bed.

Aunt Cyndi still insists that her father had nothing to do with my grandmother's disappearance. She said that she remembers them talking for weeks about the shadows: how no matter what, they were always just around the corner; that you could never get away from them or get too close to them.

She doesn't talk about them much anymore. As I got older I learned that Aunt Cyndi just wants to move on from it all–from the pain, from the stares as her father was arrested, and then committed to a mental hospital, and from the unanswered questions.

"Your mom didn't sleep good." Aunt Cyndi says quietly.

"My mom?" I ask, surprised that she is bringing her up.

Tossing the hand towel on the counter, she says, "Yeah, your mom had a hard time sleeping, too. I remember waking up in the middle of the night once and Trista had her hands over her ears and was sitting huddled on her bed. I asked her what was wrong and she said that the voices and the dogs were too loud at night. I never understood what that meant, but as a teenager she always slept with music or the television on."

I tip and shake my head a bit before looking at my aunt, my brain and mouth compete to ask every question that her comment brings up but nothing ends up coming out.

Was my mom hearing the same howling as me?

Why was she hearing it, why am I?

Will it stop?

Aunt Cyndi returns to the dishes like she didn't just tell me that my mother heard dogs at night.

Every. Single. Night.

four

RYLEIGH

I told Aunt Cyndi that I didn't need a ride to Cassie's.

"It's just down the road," but now I wish I had taken her up on her offer.

Something or someone is following me. I keep seeing them out of the corner of my eye. A shadow created by the streetlights, I try to convince myself– until the gravel crunches behind me.

I stop dead in my tracks. I've seen enough horror movies that I know I don't need to see what's behind me to know that I should run.

But this girl doesn't run, not for the P.E. teacher when I was in high school and apparently not when something or someone creeps up on me in the dark.

The thing is, I can't move, even if I wanted to. It's like my legs are cemented to the sidewalk. My backpack starts to slide from my shoulder and I reach up to fix it, but my hand and arm don't move. They are stuck too.

I try to turn my head. Nothing. Without thinking, I scream, Nothing. Again.

I start to panic. My heartrate kicks up about three notches and it's getting harder to take a deep breath. Suddenly hundreds of dark wispy-like men appear to circle me all at once, crowding closer and closer. I squeeze my eyes closed, surprised I can actually do that. I wait for whatever is about to happen.

Deep, nasty, guttural howls, toothy snaps, and barks pierce the air. My eyes shoot open just in time to see a wolf; correction: a HUGE wolf covered in a dark coat of fur , with cropped ears and bright pupils pounce from the trees with its teeth bared .

The wolf's tail whips through the waistline of many of the creatures surrounding me; they disappear into small particles of dust and then they are gone.

The rest of the creatures turn their focus on the wolf and I am flooded with a sense of relief; that lasts only a brief moment before a new concern arises for the wolf deep in my gut. Ear piercing screeches come from the creatures when they all open their mouths as wide as possible.

I wince, or attempt to, as the sound hurts my ears. It looks as though it hurt the wolves ears too because it stumbles to the side and back a few steps.

The creatures turn back to me and quicken their steps towards me. I see the wolf spin and whip its tail again through more of the creatures. Then, the wolf turns to run through those that get in its way until it jumps on the back of one of them right in front of me. The wolf bites down on the shoulder of the creature in a blink of an eye.

Suddenly, I can move again and all the creatures disappear, apart from the wolf and its new 'chew toy' dangling from its mouth. I step backwards and stumble off the curb, falling ungracefully onto my ass. The wolf watches me for a moment before pulling the creature in its mouth into the tree line.

It takes a few minutes for me to get up off the ground and get my wits about me. But once I'm there, I start back on my way to Cassie's just as a man steps from the trees, right where the wolf vanished. Again I find myself unable to move, this time from just from fear.

"Was that your dog?" I ask so quietly that I am surprised when he replies.

"Something along those lines," the man answers sarcastically.

"You did *not* just say I was your dog." Another man slaps his hand on the other's shoulder, a quick look from the first man says, you know that isn't what *I* said.

"I was trying to have a laugh with my lady here," the first man says.

"Ummm... excuse me? What just happened? What did you say? What..?" I ask question after question, not giving either of the men a chance to answer.

"Hold on, my lady, for you need to inhale deeply." The first man says reaching out towards me, concern written on his face.

I try to step back, more cautiously this time so I don't fall again. The fight or flight response is back and I'm starting to think maybe running isn't all that bad after all.

But just as I turn, everything gets fuzzy and I feel myself fall but I never hit the sidewalk.

I fall into something else hard.

five

ARCHER

“**W**hat the fuck?” I ask Shadow as I catch my mate in my arms.

"Why do you question me? I do not foretell what this is?" Shadow answers, running up to my side. "What do you require Archer?"

"Can you get us to the room?" I ask.

"Hold my lady close, Archer," he replies as he slowly transforms into his more natural state.

Shadow is a literal shadow and can move across light quicker than anything man-made. His smoky, transparent figure starts to encompass and lift us and in seconds, we are in our hotel room. I gather my mate closer making sure that our way of travel didn't harm her in any way. Once satisfied that she is not any worse than when we left the street, I lay her on the bed at the end of the room.

"Have you seen them pass out like that before?" I ask Shadow.

"Archer, I have been here a many, many days. This 'passing out' is upon the common." He answers. However, there are many reasons why a young girl might pass out. Perhaps she is ill?"

"You're not making sense, Shadow!" I holler. "I've gone through this situation so many times: I find my girl; we get new rules; we live; and then she dies." I rake my hand through my hair and start to pace the room.

"The amount of times does not mean anything. The present is what to consider." Shadow says when he sits at the table in the room.

I sit across from him and ask, "Any idea why there is a Dali in Finely?"

Shadow thinks about this for a while but ultimately does not have a satisfactory answer; his words, not mine.

It isn't long before my mate's cell phone starts to chime from the side pocket of her backpack. As I reach down and grab it, it lights up the screen and a multitude of text messages begin coming in from someone named Cassie.

My mate has a code on her phone and I don't want to move her otherwise I would try Face ID. I set her phone on the table and flip the small silence switch on the side of her phone. She can check it once she wakes up.

She is going to wake up.

six

RYLEIGH

I wake to my cell phone making noise. The sound seems very far away, almost like it was ringing a long time ago and my brain is finally registering it.

I crack my eyes open to an unfamiliar room and realize that my dream was not a dream; I really was attacked by hundreds of the same dark creatures and saved by a wolf.

That also means that the strange men were real.

I quickly sit up and pull my knees in as close as I can while I push myself against the headboard.

Scanning the room, I see the men that I saw earlier are sitting at a table near a dingy hotel door, two beds with cheap quilts on them, a large window covered by a faded curtain near the door, and a television on the wall above a small dresser.

I rub my eyes because one of them doesn't look real. His face is perfect, not a single wrinkle, perfect blonde hair, and no five o'clock shadow, his eyes meet mine and his face flickers, and I don't mean he has a twinkle in his eye. I mean his entire face seems to glitch.

Even more freaked out, I push myself even harder against the headboard, hoping to just disappear into the wood of it.

The man without a flickering face gets up and comes and sits at the end of the bed. "You sick?" he asks.

"What?" I barely squeak out. The central air in the room kicks on then, blowing the man's scent of campfire and pine towards me.

He repeats himself and scoots a little closer. "Are you sick?"

He is nearly touching me now, I can feel his body heat radiating from him so I pull my feet in tighter, practically a ball of a person at this point and shake my head no.

He rubs his hand down his face and asks, "What's your name?"

I don't answer him. Why would I tell a complete stranger, someone who brought me to a hotel room, who I am?

He doesn't seem upset that I don't answer. Instead his face reads compassion and understanding, like maybe he is tired of capturing innocent girls. Maybe he will be the one I can get through to to help me out of here. If crime documentaries have taught me anything, it's that when there are two criminals, usually one is easier to break than the other.

He pushes himself up from the bed and walks back to the table and grabs something just to toss it near my feet, my cell phone. "Someone named Cassie keeps texting you," he says sitting back down. I don't move right away, why would he give me my phone when I could just call 911. *I should just call 911.*

"Remaining here is not required." Glitch Face says. My head whips up to look at him, questions must be all over my face because he then says, "You may remain our guest, for however long you request."

However long I request? I didn't ask to come over. I snatch my phone of the bed, Cassie definitely is trying to find me:

> Cassie: R U still comin?

> Cassie: Hellooo?

> Cassie: Ryleigh?

> Cassie: Ur Aunt said U left hours ago

> Cassie: Ryleigh! WHERE ARE YOU!

> Cassie: should I call the popo?

> Cassie: plz call or txt me back

Not only did she text me, but she called me eleven times and left three voicemails. Aunt Cyndi also called me once. No voicemail from her though.

I rub my forehead preparing myself for an assault of words when I call Cassie, she is going to lose her shit when I tell her what happened.

"About five hours," one of the guys says.

"Five hours?" I ask looking over to them. The time stamps on the text messages clearly did not register when I saw them.

"Asleep," Glitch Face says.

"I've been here for FIVE HOURS?!" I raise my voice at the end as panic starts to crawl up my spine again.

The man who gave me my phone turns his body to face me, "You're safe."

"SAFE!" I stand from the bed "SAFE!" Panic now in control. "How is being locked in a strange room with two grown men who I don't know, *safe*?!" My breath is coming in and out rapidly and the man stands and walks close to me. "STAY BACK!" I scream at him.

"Look. Couple of things here. One, the door isn't locked. Two, you can go whenever you like. Three, you do know us."

My eyes immediately look them both up and down, "No, no, I don't know who either of you are. If I knew who you were, do you think I would be freaking out like this?"

"You don't remember yet and that's ok. My name is Archibald Carmine but you can call me Archer. That is Shadow." Pointing over his shoulder towards Glitch Face.

"Ry...Ryleigh." I whisper out and sit back on the edge of the bed. A wave of safety washes over me and my breathing returns to normal. "I don't understand..." I trail off.

"Many inquiries?" Shadow asks.

"Yeahhh..." I drag out my response because Shadow's way of speaking is definitely not normal.

Archer looks over to Shadow and softly shakes his head before looking back at me. "We can try and answer all your questions, but first, you need to eat." He hands me a take out container from my favorite burger joint in town.

"How did you..." I start.

"You and your love of beef never changes." He smirks. "Eat. Please?" He stands and starts to look through a book that I didn't realize Shadow is now hunched over.

After eating and texting both Cassie and Aunt Cyndi letting them know I am fine and staying the night with a friend from out of town. While it takes some convincing, they eventually give in and I promise to go to Cassie's tomorrow.

Before I start to ask all my many questions, I mentally dig into my brain.

I don't think I know anyone by the name of Archer, and I definitely have never met someone named Shadow. These men are strangers and I just told the two people in my life that care that I am safe.

What the hell is wrong with me?

"So?" I ask and both the men turn to look at me. Shadow's face continues to do its strange flickering thing and it's very distracting; I can't help but stare.

Archer playfully smacks Shadow on the shoulder in a bro kind of way, "I thought she was my mate, maybe we were wrong, huh?" A darkness washes over Shadow's face for only a moment before he straightens himself.

Something Archer says peaks my interest "Your *mate*?"

"That is just part of a much bigger question, my love,." Archer answers.

"And that question is...?" Shadow and Archer share a look. "What?" My voice pitches upward when I ask. "All I have are questions. Nothing's making sense. All you guys do is answer in riddles or with more questions."

"Perhaps a story?" Shadow asks and I just shrug my shoulders in defeat because it's not like they have truly answered my questions so far.

"Let me." Archer says. Shadow tips his head to Archer in agreement.

"A very, very long time ago there was a woman born from the fires of Hell, cursed to live the life of a mortal human over and over again with little to no recollection of her previous lives. She was destined to lead the dead to the gates of Hell alone. Every twenty-fifth birthday she would be visited by a hellhound and reminded of her duties. The woman learned that the only way for this to happen she would need to meet with the King of Hell, Lucifer, and he would promise her a soul.

"When the woman faced Lucifer, she begged for solace, for some sort of peace among her never-ending lives. Now, something she didn't know was that Lucifer takes requests very seriously and very literally. Lucifer knew that new souls were being sent to Hell everyday, but he gave her the soul love of a creature he despised the most, of a creature that shapeshifted, from a human to a hellhound.

"Lucifer making them soulmates made the creature cursed to lose his mate over and over again; punishing them both for eternity. The creature now searches all the planes of existence looking for his mate, only to lose her once again"

"That," I stop and think about his story, "that is really shitty." That makes Archer and Shadow both chuckle.

"It's more than shitty, Ryleigh." Archer says quietly. "It's real. That creature is me. And that woman is you." He says looking in my eyes.

I can't help the laughter that escapes me. *You've got to be kidding right?* These men have lost their minds, or maybe I have, either way this is the most far fetched conspiracy I've ever heard. Archer stands and grabs my hands so he can hold them in his. A pulse runs up from my hands to the center of my chest as his eyes meet mine. "It wasn't a joke." Seriousness laces his words.

His tone gets my attention and I see the honesty and pain in his face.

He must *really* be crazy though. There is no way he is a, what did he call it, a hellhound; no way I am the woman in his story, I would reme...

I guess I wouldn't remember, would I? In his story, the woman hardly ever remembers anything, does that mean that sometimes she, I, we, do remember?

"Archer, perhaps my lady requires a moment of isolation?" Shadow says while flipping through the book again.

I pull my hands from Archer's and he sits across from me again. He doesn't say anything else, he just watches me. I look back at him and from the corner of my vision, Shadow flickers again.

"What are you?" I toss my chin Shadow's way. Archer looks over at him and then back to me. All of this is absolutely batshit crazy, but if you're going crazy you might as well embrace it.

Archer questions, "What makes you think he isn't a human?"

With only a side glance towards Archer, "The flickering," I answer.

Archer stands and walks back to the table, grabs the book from Shadow's hands and quickly flips back and forth through it. Shadow also stands and takes a seat where Archer just was.

"What? He does flicker, right?" Or maybe I hit my head when I fainted.

"Humans are not privy to my deficiencies," Shadow replies.

"Your deficiencies?"

"Only other creatures of Hell may see the truth of beings," he says.

"If I am what you think I am, then I am a creature of Hell. Right?" I say.

"You are who I *know* you are." Archer says from the table. "You are human?"

Getting uncomfortable and shifting myself on the bed, "Was that a question? Of course I'm human. I was born here in Finley. My mother died giving birth to me eighteen years ago."

"The mystery remains on how you see my being. Explain further," Shadow prompts.

"What else do you want me to say? I was looking at you earlier and it was like your face shifted very fast. I thought it was because I had just woken up, but it is still happening. It isn't constantly moving, just here and there." I try to explain. Shadow nods his head and joins Archer, leaving me again without any answers and even more questions.

Defeated and confused, I rest against the headboard of the bed.

seven

ARCHER

I found her.

I sneak a glance over my shoulder to see she is back asleep.

I know it is her, I've never been wrong about her before.

But this doesn't make sense. She has never been able to see Shadow as anything other than another human. How is she seeing him now, after all these centuries?

Shadow and I continue to look through the Creaturnarium, hoping to find an answer as my mate sleeps. Our story is written in the pages of this book, descriptions and tales of all the other creatures among the planes of existence are in this book. The answer is here, somewhere.

Loud pounding starts on the door, making me and Shadow look up and then to each other. I look back over my shoulder and see that Ryleigh is now awake and clearly a little freaked out. Shadow pushes his chair back from the table, the large window shatters inward, throwing glass into the room and all over us. I pounce in front of my mate, preventing any glass from hitting her. Scratching sounds come from every direction, loud enough to make Ryleigh physically cringe.

"SHADOW!" I holler, wrapping my jacket around Ryleigh.

"Shant we disappear, Archer?" Shadow replies while tossing me the book and Ryleigh's backpack. I grab Ryleigh and even though she fights me for a moment I pull her close into my chest. By the time I stand Shadow is next to me already returning to his shadow form. I push Ryleigh's face into my shoulder and whisper to her. "Close your eyes and hang on tight." She doesn't have a chance to say anything before we are just mere particles once again. I feel her fingernails piercing into my chest as she grabs my shirt tighter in her small fists.

Within seconds we are back on the cliffside over the Dead Forest. I softly set Ryleigh on her feet, a small laugh escapes me once she is on her feet.

"That was funny?" she argues and playfully smacks my chest.

"Not at all." I answer.

She turns around with a huff, taking in our new location. "Wha--"

I interrupt her, "--you're so short this time." Ryleigh tosses me a mean glare over her shoulder.

"Seriously?" She asks.

I step up next to her and she looks up at me, she has to physically tilt her head to look in my eyes. She sighs deeply and looks forward again in defeat. "Where are we?"

"Dead Forest." Shadow answers.

"You brought me here to kill me, didn't you? Oh my god, *I'm going to die!*" She starts to pace and chew on her thumbnail.

"No one is going to hurt you, ever. I promise you, my mate." I try to pull her closer to me but she stops me with a hand on my chest.

She is angry now, her eyes scream confusion and hatred. "Stop calling me your mate! If I was this *woman* you think I am, then I am going to die, nothing you can do about it." Ryleigh walks away from me, right up to Shadow. "If you're not human, what are you? How did this just happen?" She demands, gesturing to where we are.

Shadow looks to me as if I should be explaining it. I turn away, as a signal for him to answer her. "I am a Shadow."

"I know your damn name!" Her irritation is evident in her stance.

Shadow shakes his head, "Ryleigh, I AM a Shadow."

"His real name is long forgotten by most and the few who do are very, very special, when we met he said to just call him 'Shadow.'" I clarify, Shadow nods his head in agreement.

Ryleigh looks between us and throws her hands up. "I am crazy. I knew it." She then plops herself down on a large rock near the trail, drops her head a bit and stares at her hands.

"Your mental status is not in requirement of concern." Shadow says.

"It's a good thing you're not a child of a Gorgon. Shadow would've turned to stone from the look you just gave him." She then tosses me the same look. "Look. Ryleigh. You can trust us.

You are my mate, no question. Shadow is my companion. We've known each other for eternity. We have no reason to lie or to hurt you." I try to comfort Ryleigh using my words.

"You may not lie, but you also may not be *real*," she confesses.

eight

RYLEIGH

Archer and Shadow are just figments of my imagination.

I am going to wake up in my bedroom, this will have all been a bad dream, it has to be. There is no way that these men are creatures of another world and they are here for me, and me alone. None of this makes sense. Frustrated, I turn my body and adjust myself on the rock I'm sitting on in order to look at these men again.

Shadow's face still flickers while he is talking to Archer. He is good looking, pale skin, shaggy blonde hair, tall, and thin. Archer, now, my brain has created a work of art. Archer is well over six feet tall, he clearly works out, his brown hair is cut close to his head, clean shaven, emerald-colored eyes, and naturally tan. He peeks over at me and I feel embarrassed that I was just caught gawking at him, whether or not he is real.

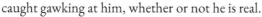

"If Shadow and I aren't real then explain this:" Archer waves his hand around just like I did not long ago. I shrug my shoulders to answer him by not answering.

Archer walks up to me and drops to his haunches in front of me. "Sometimes. Sometimes things in this world just don't make sense. We have to live with that."

I look into his eyes, "Prove it." I can see he doesn't understand what I mean. "Prove to me that I'm not crazy," I plead.

Archer reaches up and wipes a tear from my cheek.

"My love. You ARE NOT crazy, I don't know how to prove to you that I'm real. That we are real." He says gesturing between the three of us. "I know you are confused and skeptical. We will figure this out. I promise."

It's not that I don't believe what he says. It's just hard to be alright with believing him when I think he is a figment of my imagination.

"For it is very late Archer. Perhaps we slumber?" Shadow asks. Archer shakes his head in agreement.

"We have to go somewhere they can't find her," Archer retorts.

"Who?" I ask.

Archer straightens to his full height, grabs my backpack from the ground next to me, and reaches out for my hand. "Honestly my love, all of them."

"All of them?" I ask, he doesn't respond, instead he looks over my head to the Dead Forest. His hands clamp over his ears and he crouches down, trying to get away from whatever it is that he hears. I stand to turn, looking out the same direction he was. I don't see anything, I don't hear anything either. I start to turn back around when I hear it. The screeching from earlier in the night, when they saved me, it's back. Far away but loud enough that I hear them and they are getting closer by the second.

"We have to go, *now*."

I grab my bag from where Archer dropped it when the screeching started. Shadow leans down and whispers something to Archer. Archer shakes his head a few times and Shadow keeps whispering, he places a hand on Archer's back and then backs away, he turns to me and as he opens his mouth to talk, shreds of cloth fly through the air.

In a blink of an eye, Archer's clothing is in a shredded pile at the paws of the large wolf that saved me only hours ago. The wolf isn't a wolf though, now that I am closer I see that this creature is not of this world. His head alone is twice the size of a normal wolf, his paws end with claws that look razor sharp, and his ears are cropped like one of those domesticated dogs. The tail on this creature is much longer than any animal I've ever seen and it looks similar to a whip: frayed on one end, his short fur the color of mud. When the creature's eyes meet mine, I see it.

This is Archer, the bright green irises of the man are manipulated but they are the same of these creature's. Before I can say anything, Archer trots over to me and rubs his head, which reaches my waist, on my hip and then starts to circle me while whining. I cautiously place my hand on his head, he settles just long enough for the screeching to be heard again. I look over to Shadow. He doesn't seem to hear it, but Archer and I do. I exchange a look with the beast next to me.

Shadow grabs a hold of us once again and we are transported to yet another strange place.

nine

RYLEIGH

Archer doesn't shift back to his human form once we arrive. He runs out of what I assume is the front door of this place and vanishes.

Shadow shows me around the modest-sized home. Dark, hardwood floors with light-colored furniture throughout.

"Safety is guaranteed here," Shadow says.

He shows me a bedroom where he says I can sleep and leaves the door cracked open when he leaves. I assume he does that so I know that I'm not stuck in here, not to try and peek in if I were to change my clothes.

I quietly close the door and look around the room. The hardwood floors are a nice contrast to the light gray sheets and comforter, floor-length blackout curtains cover what I assume are the windows along one wall, paintings of red and orange marks hang above the bed.

I peek into what ends up being a large closet and then into a bathroom. After everything that happened tonight, a shower is all I want now, more than sleep. I grab the change of clothes from my backpack. I guess it's a good thing I had planned on crashing at Cassie's place tonight. The steam from the shower starts to billow out of the bathroom door, inviting me in.

I dip my head under the water and the hot water cascades down my back. I close my eyes and think about everything that has happened. I almost convince myself that when I open my eyes I'll be in my bathroom back home, all of this just a passing thought. When I do open my eyes, the glass enclosure and bright white lights remind me that no, this really is happening. I look around the shower and see a bottle of shampoo I gather it up and pull it close to my face so I can read it without my glasses. It isn't just shampoo, but it is my shampoo, the same one I used just this morning. The same brand and scent at least.

There is no way that either Shadow or Archer went into my house and saw what brand of products I prefer. The conditioner, bodywash, and the razor on the shelf are all mine. Just as I was starting to feel normal, this happens.

What the fuck is happening?

Once dressed in a pair of sweats and a tank top, I walk out of the bedroom to the kitchen where I hear Shadow and Archer talking. When I enter the room, they stop talking and turn their heads toward me. Archer takes his time looking me up and down, lingering on my chest and hips. It makes me uncomfortable so I wrap my arms around my midsection, trying to hide my body from him.

Placing his hand on my arms he says just above a whisper,

"Please don't hide your body from me." I pull away a little. What man that looks like he does would want to look at a woman that looks like me? "You are the most beautiful creature to ever cross my path."

His words make me blush a deep red that spreads to my chest.

"Where are we?" I ask. Archer continues to caress my body with his eyes when he answers me.

"Home."

"It's beautiful." I say as I walk along the kitchen cabinets feeling the cold granite counter with my fingertips.

"*Our* home." He corrects.

"I figured you guys lived together." I reply. Shadow half coughs into his fist, a huge grin on his face. I look between the men and it finally dawns on me. I place a hand on my chest, "*I* lived here?"

"This is our home. No one can hurt you here," Archer says.

"This isn't in Finley, is it?" I question, looking around again. There is nothing like this in Finely, nothing this nice, nothing this comforting. Aunt Cydni's house doesn't even feel this safe and this much like home.

"No. This isn't in Finely, Ryleigh." Archer answers as he moves closer to me. I give him a questioning look. "We are in Hell."

ten

ARCHER

"Like literal Hell?" Ryleigh asks.

I take her hand and walk her to the front door. "Would you like to see it?" This is my favorite part.

Most people think of Hell and picture dark caverns full of lost souls lit up by the pools of lava. When Ryleigh tentatively nods her head yes, I can tell that is exactly what she too is picturing.

I squeeze her hand in reassurance, then I turn the knob and swing the door open. I hear the gasp that falls from her lips.

Hell does have the lava pools but instead of being surrounded by jagged rocks and broken souls, they are encompassed by fire flowers: beautiful shades of red, orange, yellow, and sometimes blue. The pools light our world alongside the lights from the modern overworld.

Hell has everything the overworld has: power, water, internet, grocery stores, and even weather. Huge fields of crops cover the hills near our home. Large black trees with black leaves grow along the sidewalk. Children and pets run in the yards. A car passes by honks and waves to us.

"It's like home. Just a little different." Ryleigh says as she turns around. "How did you know what products I like?"

Out of everything she is seeing right now she asks me about her shampoo? Not the child that looks like a lizard playing with another child with a missing wing? Nope, she wants to know about her shampoo.

"You almost always use the same scents," I start, grabbing a small piece of her hair and pulling it close to my nose so I can inhale the scent. "I took a guess on the brand, my nose is pretty good at finding what it wants," I say teasingly while looking in her eyes.

The eye contact becomes too much for her and she turns to go back inside. I touch her arm to stop her but I can't think of what to say to her. So much has happened since she was in my arms last. Wars have been fought. Friends have come and gone. The only constant was my love for her.

"When was I here last?" Ryleigh asks, looking at me.

"One-hundred and eighty-one years ago," I answer honestly. Her eyes get large and she stops breathing for a fraction of a second. She then takes a really deep breath.

"I think I need to go to bed." She says walking back in the house and straight to our bedroom. I hear the door click shut before I can even get the front door closed and locked.

"My lady will soon understand all." Shadow says from the

couch. I walk over and join him. He hands me the Creaturnarium pointing to a passage:

Dahi - The Duplicator

The Dali is a creature from the Underworld, known for its ability to duplicate itself thousands of times at will. With long limbs and glowing white eyes, this creature is most terrifying for a mortal to encounter and most do not survive.

   Dali can only be summoned by a powerful being of deception:; shattered souls, shadow creatures, and Lucifer himself. There is no way for Dali to leave the Underworld unless summoned and requested to go to a different realm. Dali are loyal creatures and will do whatever their summoner requests, without question or hesitation.

"Are you trying to tell me that you did this?" Anger laces my voice as I reread what the book says.

"Preposterous!" Shadow snaps. "My affection for my lady. My affection for you." He shakes his head in disbelief, unable to finish.

I slam the book closed and toss it on the table, my anger quickly diminishing; "I thought...I. I don't know what I thought."

Shadow shifts himself and as he talks he slams his finger into the cover. "The words you read are the same that I read. The Dali are very dangerous. They are after my lady, your mate. Another being is trying to determine her whereabouts, Archer."

"All these lifetimes and we have never had our own hunting us."

The Gods tend to get together and establish some new rules for us and they have their lackeys hunt us down to deliver the news. To have someone or something from the Underworld looking for us, trying to hurt us, specifically Ryleigh.

This sets me off. My hound stirs under the surface, wanting to be released to protect my mate. I mentally tell my hound to calm down, that we are safe here.

One of the unspoken rules of Hell is that no one is hurt here, *unless they deserve it*. Almost always those that deserve it did something during their mortal lives that warrants the punishment or they personally went against Lucifer.

Shadow retires to the spare bedroom to rest. Immortal creatures like us don't need sleep, food, and water as often as a mortal. We can go years without food before we start to get hungry. Water is optional, and every creature needs sleep at different intervals. I tend to rest and sleep twice as often as Shadow.

I look around our home and can picture a new life with Ryleigh here. I can picture her in the kitchen with nothing but an apron on; her plump ass out for me. When she turns around her large breasts are barely contained under the apron and she looks at me with her glasses slipping down her nose just to get flour on her face when she pushes them back into position.

A door creaks to my left and wakes me from my dream of Ryleigh, I didn't mean to fall asleep. I sit up straighter when I see it's her.

She is trying to be quiet and I don't think she knows I'm on the couch. I hear a cabinet open and shut, then another, the sink faucet turns on and the sound of a glass being filled rushes to my ears.

My hound has also woken up to the sounds of my mate just simply living, her soft breathing, a small yawn, the sounds of the water running down her throat.

Neither my hound or I can take it any longer, so I rise from the couch to head to the kitchen.

I look at Ryleigh when I enter the room. She doesn't hear me walk in, giving me a chance to look at her, to watch her. I step up behind her and softly brush my fingertips on her arm. Her body tenses before she relaxes against me a bit. I dip my head to place a small kiss on her shoulder. I move her long locks from against her neck and leave a trail of kisses up to her ear. A small growl escapes my lips when I hear a sharp intake of breath from her.

"Ryleigh... my girl... my love, my mate," I whisper to her when I run my nose along her cheek.

eleven

RYLEIGH

My breath catches when Archer's lips graze over mine. I want to lean into him to take more, to give more.

As if he read my mind he turns me so we are facing each other. He cradles my face in his hands; his thumb caresses my cheek and he rests his forehead against mine. I reach up on my toes and fit our lips together.

I'm not a prude by any means. I've made out with a few guys and done some oral things, but I am still that cliche virgin girl that everyone in highschool thought I was.

When Archer's hand falls from my face to wrap around my back to pull me in closer to him, my breasts press to his hard chest. His tongue swipes across my lower lip asking for permission to go further.

Before I have a chance to protest, Archer bends down enough to lift me up onto the kitchen counter. I pull my face back enough to catch my breath and say, "I don't really know what I am doing here." gesturing between us.

"How many?" Archer asks. I tilt my head to the side a fraction in question. "How many men, baby?" He clarifies, running his fingertips along my collarbone.

"None," I say quietly. The emotion in his eyes is overwhelming but before I can say anything else, he smashes his lips on mine again, growling into my mouth. He wraps my arms over his shoulders and once again he is lifting me. This time, he holds me as close as he can and walks to the room I was just sleeping in. Archer gently lays me on the bed before he steps back to stare at me.

"You are perfect."

He leans over me slightly and softly touches my lower lip with his finger, "Your lips." He stops his sentence when he bites his own lip. His finger moves over my chin and down to the cleavage of my breasts, "Your tits." Another growl escapes him when he palms both of them through my tank top. "Everything about you is just so..."

Once again he cuts himself off. My breathing quickens when his fingers rub the soft skin of my belly just above my sweatpants. Nervousness stops me from saying or doing anything other than stare back at him.

Archer crawls over me and starts to kiss and nip at my lips, neck, and chest again. Our hands explore each other's bodies; his hand reaches into my shirt and one of mine rubs at the bulge in his pants. He runs his sharp canines along my jaw and down my throat.

A burning sensation starts when he crosses the top of my breasts, making me wince. His tongue slips from his mouth and he licks at the blood that oozes from the cut he created. With my blood on his lips he presses them against mine again, the distinct taste of copper and salt blend with the taste of Archer, making me moan and arch into him.

A knock on the bedroom door makes us scurry away from each other like we are just some teenagers about to get caught by their parents.

I look over to Archer. The smile that spreads across his face makes me chuckle into my hand. His bright white teeth are showing, his canines still elongated and extra sharp digging into his lower lip that is smeared with my blood.

"This structure does not prevent sound from traveling," Shadow says from the other side of the door, making my chuckle turn into a full laugh. Archer stands from the bed and straightens his clothes. He walks to the door and before slipping out, he sends me a wink over his shoulder causing the butterflies in my stomach to implode on themselves.

After cleaning myself up and getting changed into fresh jeans and a t-shirt, I join the men in the living room. They are looking through the book they had at the hotel again.

"What is that?" I ask, pointing to the book.

"This is the original Creaturnarium, written thousands of

years ago by a very powerful woman." Archer answers while showing me what passages they were looking at.

Some of it is in a language that I don't understand, pointing to it I ask, "what language is this?"

"Shawin. Language of Shadows." Shadow answers proudly. "A significant portion of this text is scripted in Shawin."

"Was the writer a Shadow creature then?" I ask them.

Archer flips to the first page of the book that has a description of the author, most of it is written in the Shawin language, but what I do understand raises even more questions.

"Why do you appear perplexed?" Shadow asks me.

"Veronica Spear. That was my grandmother's name. But that doesn't make sense. You said this was written thousands of years ago, she went missing twenty years ago, there is no way..."

"Ryleigh? My lady? May I read this to you?" Shadow asks and I hand him the book.

"Written and spellbound by Veronica Spear upon her return from the mortal world. King Robert, leader of the Shadow people, saved her from a tragic end by returning her to his homeland in the Underworld. Veronica was born into powerful magick and many wanted to harness that magick by capturing her and forcing her to perform rituals and summonings. Veronica used her magick to keep this book full of the most updated and accurate information to help those that find themselves needing to defeat, defend, and befriend creatures of all of the realms."

"My grandfather was committed to a mental hospital because he said that his wife was taken by Shadow people. This is... I don't know. He wasn't crazy? He didn't kill her? Wait though, the timing..."

"Time can be changed and manipulated by powerful witches, and it seems your grandmother is one of them." Archer says in way of an answer.

I nod my head in understanding, even though none of this is making sense. Since these guys saved me last night, my entire world has been tossed in the air.

I gently place my hand on Archer's forearm when I say, "Archie. I need to go to my aunt's house. I need to go see Cassie. All this is a little too much right now and I need something normal."

With a satisfied sigh, he says, "Haven't heard that nickname in years." I blush because I didn't realize what I said until it was over, it just felt so natural for me. "It isn't safe in Finely."

"Is it really safe anywhere? I need time to adjust. Time to figure things out," I beg.

"Security is of utmost concern, my lady." Shadow adds.

"We will go with you. We will wait for you at the cliff. All you have to do is say my name and I will come to you." Archer closes the book and starts to gather his things to leave.

"All I do is say your name? What, are you Beetlejuice?" I joke.

He points to his ears and through a small chuckle, "Ears of a hound, remember?"

twelve

ARCHER

L eaving her at Aunt Cyndi's house alone is one of the hardest things I've done in a very, very long time. There is so much uncertainty going on, all my interactions with Ryleigh are different than any of the other times in my long life that I got to have my mate. I think Shadow sees it too.

Something is different about my mate.

Finely looks different from the cliff in daylight. The cars are lining up at the coffee shops and the two street lights control the drivers. School buses are traveling the roads, picking up children for their first day of school and a police officer pats down some guy downtown.

From the corner of my vision a large creature moves down the middle of the road unseen by the mortals. With a distorted face and abnormally long limbs that drag along the road, it stalks closer to Ryleigh's home.

My hound is out in an instant. Shadow follows as I run past the trees and bushes of the Dead Forest. We break the treeline just as Ryleigh steps onto her porch and comes face-to-face with the creature.

Behind me, Shadow flips through the Creaturnarium trying to determine what this is, even after all of our years in existence neither of us know what is staring my mate in the face.

Ryleigh stops in her tracks on the porch when she sees the creature in her yard.She whispers my name. The creature turns its head towards me and Shadow; he knows we are here.

Turning its head back to Ryleigh, it leans in close to her and whispers in her ear. I can't hear what he says for some reason, but I can see its lips move. When it backs away, Ryleigh nods her head in agreement to whatever it said and it walks away.

I run to her still in my hound form and she looks around to see if anyone will see me. To the mortal eye, my hound looks like a normal dog; so to them it just looks like a pup running to his owner and not a Hellhound running to his mate.

She pulls me and Shadow inside just to slam and lock the door. Before she turns around, I return to my more human form and grab the throw blanket from the couch and wrap it around my waist. When her eyes land on my bare chest her train of thought seems to have completely halted, that only lasts a few second before she starts yelling.

"What the fuck was that?" she asks, throwing her arm behind her.

I shrug one shoulder and then ask, "What did it say?"

She holds her pointer finger out and says "You don't know

what that was? How the hell is that possible? You literally live in Hell and the one monster I could confidently say is from Hell, you don't know…"

"My lady? He spoke to you." Shadow says.

Ryleigh runs one of her hands through her hair, "It said King Robert requests my presence, now. Or else. What else could there be? I've had a thousand copies of one guy surround me. Someone tried to break into your hotel. And they chased us through the Dead Forest! That is just the tip of the iceberg when it comes to crazy shit happening to me, isn't it?"

She storms around me to sit on the couch, tossing her glasses on the table, and wiping tears from her cheeks.

"I know you wanted some time to process. But we don't have time for that. If the King wants to see you, we go." I say and Shadow nods his head in agreement.

Letting out a sign and replacing her glasses, "Ok."

thirteen

RYLEIGH

Shadow takes us back to the house in Hell so that Archer can get clothes before we see the King.

"Any advice?" I ask Shadow, remembering that he said King Robert is the leader of the Shadow people.

"King Robert is controversial. Years past, my king began to dabble in the darker arts. Many followers have attempted to overturn him, this is a difficult task when you consider we are immortal."

"So, watch my back. Cool. *Cool.* " I try to seem convincing but I'm sure that Shadow sees right through my facade.

We travel to the land of the Shadow people the way most of our travel has occurred so far. But Shadow explains to me that within the limits of his homeland particle travel is forbidden, that it is seen as a waste of each Shadow's energy and power. This part of Hell is much darker than where we came from, there are less creatures milling around and the only noise you hear is quiet whispering.

Shadow leads the way up to a dark building with Shawin text above the door.

I lean to ask him what it says but he beats me to it, "Home of your king."

I shake my head at the words. This King is really self absorbed, so much so that he labeled his home.

I walk up the few steps to the door when it swings open to reveal a huge man. He fills the doorway as he looks us over. He steps to the side. But as Archer passes him, the man says under his breath, "We really should have a no dog policy."

I spin on him, his eyes going wide clearly not expecting any of us to do anything. Archer and Shadow both stop me from saying or doing anything further than staring this man down by grabbing upper arm and hand, so I send him my meanest look and even stick my tongue out at him when Archer tosses me over his shoulder.

Archer carries me through the long, barely lit halls until we come to a huge ornate door, silver and red weaved into the design of the wood. He sets me back on my feet as another guard opens these doors.

My eyes take a moment to adjust to the lower lighting in the small room. Once they do, I see a man around Shadow's age sitting on a throne surrounded by naked women made of mist. They are more transparent than Shadow in his natural form. They have silver and red bands around their ankles and wrists. I instantly get a bad feeling about this situation and take a small step back just to hit the chest of the guard from the door.

"Is that him? He seems young to be King," I whisper to Shadow.

"They stop aging at twenty-five mortal years." Archer answers.

For some reason that actually makes a lot of sense. Archer said they both were immortal and were created thousands of years ago. I don't know why I was picturing some old guy with a large belly and gray beard.

"Shadow. Welcome, my disciple." King Robert says reaching his hand out, Shadow drops to one knee and places his forehead on the King's hand.

"Archibald. Didn't expect to see you so soon. I thought my friends would've stopped you." The King's words make my stomach turn.

Archer steps in front of me and says, "You summoned the Dali? Why would you do that? And your messenger..."

The King holds his hand up to silence Archer. "Ahh, you mean my Nolli," as he says this the Nolli steps in from a door behind the throne dragging its long limbs behind it. "The Dali, they would never hurt her; you on the other hand..." he lets his words trail off.

King Robert stands from his throne and walks towards me, he pushes Archer to the side as he looks me up and down. King Robert reaches a hand out high as if to put it around my shoulders.

"Ryleigh. Welcome home, my daughter."

—THE END, for now. —

The taste of Forgotten Flowers

Sam Trathen

For Carol, my one and only Wow.

The Taste of
Forgotten Flowers

The snows had finally stopped and a warm, wet spring was blowing in when Lio's horse finally turned her snout into the woods. Everything smelled wet, smelled alive. Freesia and sweet pea, sweet alyssum and peony. He could name them all. Wisteria. Moonflower.

And he did in his head as he rode. Not out of pedantry or the desire to please himself, but because he had to. He had to distract himself from that which was coming.

Usually, the petrichor mixed with the scent of the spring woods brought him relief. Another hard winter survived, a hot and moist summer on its way. Spring was a time of relaxation. Time to take a breath. That was how it had been when he was young. He was cityfolk, after all. There was no planting season in the city.

But it didn't feel that way this year. For some reason, Lio's belly was unsettled. It wasn't his real name, Lio. And this, this pain and grief, it wasn't a new feeling. The uneasiness had been with him last autumn, even subtly before the end of summer.

By winter, it kept him up at night. By the longest night of the year, it had become untenable. Like an itch behind the eyeballs.

But there was a certain heaviness of the heart that persisted, too. Like even if he got as comfortable as he could, even if his body felt better, he'd still be restless.

"The Wildwood," his mother had told him, flickering her wrinkled, sun-speckled hands like she was conducting a harvest festival band. "Go to the Wildwood. The Fey have healers the likes of which we could never measure up to. But you must be so *very* careful!"

So he'd gone. Left in the middle of the night, when no one would see him go. When no one would know. He didn't even tell her he was going. It was embarrassing enough already, wasn't it? He was newly a full-grown man. He didn't have to tell his mother where he went, right?

He'd rode a night and a day through the mundane part of the wood, seeing only foxes and deer, the occasional rabbit, and once a wolf's tracks through the mud.

If you see a wolf, it is because it wishes to be seen, his mother had told him when he was small, the first time she had taken him into the woods beyond the city. *It can kill you before it knows you are there.*

But he was trying not to think about wolves.

He was trying not to think about a lot of things.

～

T here was a keep within two days ride of the Wildwood. Everyone knew it was the place to stop and rest before making the final part of the journey. Lio had accepted their hospitality, had forced down their food even though he had almost no appetite. Had lain in their beds even though he could not sleep. Had sat next to their lady even though he had no head for conversation.

She must have once been a warrior for the size of her. Probably back long before the war across the sea. Long before Lio was even born. But she was well-muscled and a large woman, even with her greying hair and the cane that hung on her carved, wooden chair. She sat up stout and strong and conducted her court as lively as if she were in her prime. And she treated Lio as a long-lost friend.

"The thing about the Fey," the Lady told him, midway through her fifth mug of mead, the long pipe between her fingers twirling smoke to the ceiling like a sprig of switch grass, "is they are kindly and giving folk. People don't realize that because they think of them with *human* minds. But they aren't human! And they don't *think* like humans. And they don't *act* like humans. You know the hand-tongue, right?"

"Yes, I do," Lio signed back to her. The old woman laughed.

"Can't tell you how many folk come into me own keep and try and tell me they never bothered to learn the hand-tongue!" These words, she signed, and yet somehow, they still carried the woman's brash humor. It was some kind of respite for Lio's dreary mood. "How good is yours, eh? Or did you only learn how to ask your question and nothin' else, like some of 'em?"

"My mother was born deaf," Lio signed back. "It was the only tongue we had in our house when I was small."

"Well, you're a luckier bastard than most folk who come through here then," she returned to using her smoky voice. "No ears," she strummed her fingers up and down her dark throat. "They couldn't hear you even if they wanted. And they've not got much in the way of vocal chords, either, eh?" she clapped Lio hard on the back. "But you'll do well then!"

But you'll do well then!

The words seemed to echo in his ears, in his temple as the woods turned darker, the canopy of trees nearly blotting out the sun over his head. The strange lighting made the trees seem purple and far taller than he was sure they were in real life. They also seemed to be growing closer and closer together. It was making him feel like he was being watched.

He left his horse to graze just as he was certain night must be falling beyond the woods. The landscape had grown too steep, the bracken slippery with rain.

She had been a gift from a friend who had gone over the sea and she was a spirited, funny, little thing, unlike any horse he had ever known. Really, it was a shame. He'd never owned his own horse before. He had tended those in the King's stable since he was small though, had always dreamed of the day when he would own his own. What she might be like. How strong her legs would be, how fast. But a horse was a frivolous cost.

Even this one had cost too much to keep. Too much to feed. But he hadn't been thinking about things like money lately.

Lio had never named her, and he had never learned what she had been called before.

All he had was the memory of pink lips pressing into her velvety forehead, dark hair tumbling as seagreen eyes turned his way, as the last dredges of golden light before twilight dappled over a freckled nose...

But he wasn't going to think too long about that.

"I hope I'll be back," Lio told her. "But if not, go back to the keep. That kind lady will take you in, I'm sure of it."

She wickered at him but went back to rooting through the ferns that covered the forest floor for rare grass and dandelions.

Lio slung his saddle bag over his shoulder, wondering for a moment if he should leave some of his things behind too. His mother had insisted that he bring a sword, *"Just in case!"*

But the Lady of the Keep had laughed at him for having it. *"What could you even do with that, eh? You're skinny as a cattail! If there is something to fight, it will kill you before you ever see it. Before you even know anything is wrong! Promise."*

"And what about the Fey?"

"What did I just say?"

He had brought his lyre. Another frivolous expense his mother didn't care for. He wasn't much of a player, but he hoped it might pass the time on the road. Or maybe that it might bring him heart when the road got long.

Lio strapped the sword back to the horse, but kept the lyre.

And then he continued deeper into the heart of the woods.

But you'll do well then!

~

"And what about the name thing?" he had asked the lady of the keep.

"What name thing?"

Lio frowned. "Everyone says if you tell them your name, they keep it," he insisted, but the quiet of the woman next to him was suddenly making him feel very stupid and self-conscious. His cheeks burned and his eyes felt itchy but he kept his hands on his knees. "They say you mustn't ever tell them your real name. Say you shouldn't even travel to this keep without taking a fake one, on the off-chance you encounter one alone the road in secret."

"In secret? Well, now there's a laugh! Trust me, love, you would surely know if you encountered one." And she did laugh. So did the people all around her. "Let me guess: Lio isn't your real name?"

"It's not," he admitted, cheeks burning, staring at his lap. Someone far beyond, the lady snorted. Lio didn't even look up to try and see who it was.

The lady of the keep made an impatient noise, but then

reached out and grabbed his chin, tilting it upwards until Lio looked her in the eye.

"Well, it's a good thing to travel under an assumed name anyway. On the off-hand chance you meet unsavories." She wriggled her fingers and bounced her grey eyebrows up and down. "Nothing to be ashamed of, traveling smart. As I said, you'll do well out there.

"So it isn't true? About the names?"

"Nah! Never heard of it before!"

"Strange that you know so much about them and yet you've never heard that," Lio mused, his frown growing.

"Either way, it's hogwash, isn't it? Most of those stories are. Folk sure are fanciful. There's a new tall tale every single year. S'hard to keep up with them is all," said the lady of the keep. "One day it's names, the next day they'll steal your baby and replace it with a fake one, then the next day you can't accept gifts from them. Or is it you can't *give* gifts to them?" she asked the man sitting across from her.

"I heard one where they came from the moon!" someone further down the table laughed.

"The *moon!*" cried the lady, spitting wine on Lio as she broke into furious laughter.

He had been trying to count the hours.

Surely, the moon must now be quite high in the sky.

Surely, he should've stopped to take some rest.

Surely.

And yet he kept going, one foot in front of the other, watching each and every step.

He did so half because he was worried he might turn up an ankle and half because the woods had gone from a twilight lavender to a deep, rich purple as the night grew later and later.

And something about them-- the woods around him, the Wildwood as a place, as a thing, as a living *being*-- was beginning to terrify him. Not just unsettle, not just worry! But everytime Lio turned his dark gaze up and out at the closely-grown, infinitely-tall trees, every time he pushed through an over-grown fern or stepped neatly around a mushroom circle (*"It's not magic; it's just something dead and rotting under the ground!"* his mother always used to say), he felt he was being watched.

And yet he hadn't seen a living animal since... since...

...Well, he couldn't very well be expected to remember that, now could he?

At one point, hours ago it seemed, he had pulled the lyre from the strap on his back and started to play it with sweat-drenched fingers. But the sound echoed oddly around the bark of the trees.

They don't like it, the words had come to him as clearly as if they had been said aloud. *They don't like it. Stop!*

He'd put the lyre back on his back and continued walking.

"...It's these fools who come in with big notions that have a hard time. Folks who want to take a faerie bride, or steal their gold. Folks who think they can conquer the Wildwood. As if it were a kingdom they could conquer! As if they could even comprehend!" She leaned in real close to his face. Lio drew back instinctively. "None of *those* folks ever come back, you know? The Fey, they're quite happy to give. That's what good neighbors do for one another, they say. But you gotta be humble. You gotta be respectful and gracious. They don't like to be taken advantage of." She looked him up and down. "What is it you've come to ask of them, anyway?"

"I am... unwell," Lio said, looking away from her again and blushing for all that he was worth. To his great relief, she did not laugh or repeat his words to her friends. Instead, she leaned in close to him and dropped her voice into a low whisper.

"Well, my dear, you are far from the first to come here seeking respite from an illness. And you know something? Most of them are easy fixes. I'm sure yours will be too."

"They are?" He met her grey eyes again as she patted his hands atop his knees.

"Yes, they are." And then her voice picked up in volume.

"How many times has a man, woman, or child come here as a last resort, on death's door, barely able to make the journey, only to come back after their visit with the Fey, whole and healthy?"

"I don't know," it seemed like she was waiting for an answer.

"Too many! Well then, do you know the rules?" He shook his head, ponytail flipping over his shoulder. "You know all those things about names and gifts but you don't know the rules?"

"I'm sorry."

"No apologies needed, dear boy. Listen, it's quite simple: You're to write down what you need on this paper," she pulled a role of parchment out of her waistcoat and handed it to him. "And then you go ahead and leave it at the gate. You'll see where you have to put it when you get there; that part is very easy. The easiest! But the next part is important: once you leave your note, you're to turn around and come straight back here. Do you ken that?" she arched an eyebrow at him.

"Yes," Lio said, nodding his head.

"No matter what time you get there, you turn right back around and come here. Don't wait. They won't like it when folk wait. They appreciate privacy when they conduct their business." Here, her words had a strict gravity, and he could see, suddenly, how it was she had come to rule an entire keep all to herself. "But someone from the Fey guard will come along, collect the note, and bring it to the Conclave. If your desire is something they can grant, they will signal to me to return you."

"How do they signal?"

"That's for me to know and you to never worry about ever again," she winked at him.

Surely, it must've been morning by now.

Surely.

Now it was that refrain's turn to take its position between his eyebrows and inside of his temple, thrumming like a powerful, painful drum.

But the Wildwood had not gotten brighter. No, indeed, the shadows seemed even longer than ever before now. Lio wished he could step around them or over them, like that game folk back in the city played where you couldn't step on a cracked cobblestone unless you break your mother's back. But they persisted, crawling towards him every time he stumbled into anything consisting of a clearing.

Defeat crawled into his heart.

"I should rest," he said aloud, just to convince himself he hadn't lost his hearing. The darkness ate the words, swallowed them like they had never been there in the first place.

And then, with the next step, he saw it, not too far away: a rocky outcropping in the side of the hill. Perhaps a formation that might provide shelter for the night?

Well, it seemed better than nothing.

His aching bones thanked him with every step he took closer and closer to the rock and he could already feel his body

slowly sinking into his bedroll. All he needed was a little
momentum to get there. He breathed in slowly through his
nose and out his mouth, stepping over gnarled tree roots, over
more rocks, over the desiccated body of a wolf that must've have
lain there for weeks.

"A cave," he said numbly, when he was close enough to
realize it wasn't just an outcropping. Something primal inside
of him felt sated: cave meant shelter. Cave meant den. Cave
meant safe sleeping.

The only branches around the cave were too wet to light,
and he barely had the energy to collect them. But he did light a
match so he could see through the back of the cave, could make
sure nothing big had already chosen it as a home.

And then there it was. As if it had always been there. At the
back of the cave, carved out of copper. Thin and sparkling in
the flickering match light.

A gate.

It was as if it had grown out of the slate cave walls. Just
propped up. Braced against nothing but more rock. Guarding
nothing but more than rock. No fence connected to it, beyond
the walls of the cave.

It was just there.

Lio touched it to be sure it was real, and then sniffed his
fingers. They smelled like blood.

"Well," he said, to no one in particular, "all those stories and
yet no one said it was going to be *inside* of a bloody cave!" No
one laughed at his joke, and yet he still felt like someone
ought to.

It was finely wrought though, with artistically swooping curls and filigree unlike anything he had ever seen before. And as his eyes got used to the darkness of the cave, he could make out the friendly shape of plants. There was the star of a wild geranium. Here was the large, flat leaf of a creeping liana plant. A fiddlehead fern spiraled there. A huckleberry bush grew fat with berries near the bottom. He could name them all.

Next to a begonia leaf, there was a copper basket, bedeviled with tiny sprigs of copper yarrow.

"The easiest," Lio said, remembering the lady of the keep's words. He took his note from his pocket and lifted the lid with two fingers, and then dropped it inside, unceremoniously.

It felt like there ought to be some kind of fanfare. A horn blast or a whistle. A round of applause. But there was nothing.

Lio had half expected that dropping the note within would make him feel better immediately. That somewhere, within the Fey lands beyond the cave, someone would see his request, find him, and pluck the curse from above his head with invisible fingers, like snatching a spiderweb out of his dark hair. That the pounding in his head would cease and the deep anxiety in his belly would dissipate.

But that didn't happen.

He stepped out of the cave and looked around, tossing the burnt match into the wet bracken.

The darkness was oppressive, heavy. And the quiet was even worse. He could see the wolf skull, just vaguely on the ground back the way he came. Could see the remains of the pelt, the sharp tooth sticking up into the air like a threat.

He had to go all the way back... now?

Suddenly, his bones felt too weary to move, his heart too heavy to breathe. His ribcage was a burning prison around his organs.

"Ah!" he dropped to his knees, clutching his chest.

Something was out *there*. Something horrible beyond his wildest imaginings. Something that had killed the wolf! Something dark. Something so old, he could not even comprehend it. Any second, it would make itself known; would scuttle soundlessly into range of his eyes, smirking lifeless eyes and yet somehow, still horribly alive. Something that wanted to hurt him.

It was too much.

Lio edged back into the cave on his knees, toppling backwards as he did so. He crawled over to the gate and the wall beyond it. Somehow, it almost felt safe just touching it.

They are gracious and giving people.

They would understand, wouldn't they?

They'd know surely that all he needed was some rest. Just enough to forget the terrors. Just enough to bring a bit of light into the cave.

Surely.

Just a bit of rest. Just a few hours. Just to knock loose whatever these haunting thoughts were that belabored him so. Just until the sun came up and a teensy, tiny bit of light could creep in beneath the canopy. Surely such things didn't exist in the light. *Couldn't.*

He set the lyre down, careful not to twang any of its strings as he did so. Then he unrolled his bedroll and blanket, laid them out carefully as if he were having guests. As if his mother were going to come and inspect it. (*"Nothing clears a mind like a made bed and a clean room!"* she used to say.)

Lio sat down on the bedroll and interrogated his body. What do you need? Food? The lady of the keep had given him a neat little roll of rations: some bread, a fine cheese named something fancy that he could not recall, a flagon of elderberry and rosehip wine. A jar of mushrooms seasoned with wild garlic and spring onions. He took them out and examined them, pulling the jar close to his eyes to make sure he didn't miss a single thing. But the sight of the mushrooms floating in brine turned his stomach.

No, it was sleep. That was what he needed. Foolish to think anything else.

He put the mushrooms back, took a long swig from the flagon until it poured down his chin, and covered himself in the blanket.

~

The sharp smell of grass and the heat of the summer sun blared first into his consciousness. Following that, the smell of sweetness drifted by, lazy as a leaf on a river. He sniffed, trying to grab the scent, trying to keep it for as long as he could. To savor it.

Cold, soft curls brushed along his neck, and then the familiar weight of arms around him. Arms he knew. Arms he cherished. Lio dug himself into them, wondered how to keep them. How to wear them around himself for forever.

It seemed a foolish thought to go without them ever again.

And yet--

They withdrew sharply, suddenly. He gasped for air from the cold that engulfed him, from the searing pain in his chest, the tightness in his thighs. If only he could squeeze them so hard, they would fall right off. If only they would die and leave him in peace.

"No, no, no!" he whispered to himself, the words cloying in his throat. "Please, no! Please!" His voice cracked. "Please come back. *Please!*"

But there was nothing except emptiness around him. Inside of him. And such a great emptiness still somehow left no room for anything except for grief.

No. Not this time.

He forced his eyes open, pushed himself up. There was the smell of salt now instead of sweetness. Of brine. A smell so strong, it seemed vulgar.

It was too late.

Yes, he lay in grass, but it wasn't the grass of the hill behind the stables. It was the grass above the cliffs. The cliffs that overlooked the ocean, that hated beast, and the treasure it bore on its waves. And that treasure would be there, tiny and helpless, just as it was in every dream.

Lio looked out over the vast sea until he found it, nearly to the horizon. Green sails. The King's color.

He watched it chase white-capped waves until the horizon

swallowed it, and then, despite knowing it would accomplish nothing, he wept.

∽

S omeone was tugging on his arm.

No-- someone was touching him, softly.

Lio jolted awake, grabbing the hand, feeling the glove of it beneath his fingers. The face before him wasn't so much a face as a shapeless being, covered by a heavy cloak, the space where a face might peek out of the cloak sewn with soundless, copper bells.

(*"Don't ask about the bells,"* the lady of the keep had warned him. *"Trust me, you don't want to know."*)

The cloak itself was a deep purple, so dark that it reminded Lio of the woods, yet it spangled with copper embroidery.

She was enormous. Taller and broader than any man Lio had ever seen in the city. And yet there was something lithe and graceful to her stance that made her seem impossibly small. Lio knew logically if he stood, he would come up to her breasts, maybe? For she had breasts, and that was why he called her 'she' in his mind.

And yet, he somehow felt strongly that she would be shorter than him. He could tell that her waist was twice the thickness of his, but she *seemed* so impossibly thin.

But the most alarming thing was the antlers.

They were as white as human bone and as smooth as quartz. They rooted out of holes cut into the cloak's hood, spiraling up towards the ceiling, sleek and beautiful. Lio felt himself transfixed by them, his mouth falling open.

He had seen paintings of the Fey, of course. And the costumes that the traveling mummers wore at the midsummer festival-- yes, those had antlers too. But they were the same antlers of a roe buck, those cast off for a spring rutting.

They didn't *glow*.

The creature waved a hand at him, and there was a curtness to the movement. "Hello?"

Lio raised a meek hand in response and made the sign of salutations.

"You *do* communicate," said the creature, flexing their gloved hands in the gesture of a jest. "I thought you were one of the speaking ones for a moment there."

Lio made the motion of apology.

"No, no, no. I woke you. No apologies. You may call me Yarrow," she said.

"Yarrow?" he managed to gasp with a dry mouth, and then remembered, belatedly, to make the shape of her name with his hands. That wasn't her real name, of course. It would be something like Yarrow-Blooming-Through-Fierce-Spring-Rain-Despite-The-Seasons-Changing. Something far too long to sign. And they didn't share their full, real names with people. Not unless they cared for them.

At least that was one of the stories he had heard. He had forgotten to ask the lady of the keep about that one. Perhaps it was true.

"Yes," she signed, patiently cocking her head.

"I go by Lio," he spelled it out with one hand.

"Lio," she returned, soundlessly making the shape of his name with her own, unclasped hand, spreading out her thumb and pinky to do so. "But this is not your full name?" These words left her fingers in a strange, incomplete sort of way, as if the gestures were lazy or half-finished.

He released her hand, realizing slowly that she was asking for its return. "No." He said the words aloud as his hands flitted the sign. He always did. Couldn't help it. It used to annoy his mother even though she couldn't hear him. "I was warned not to tell you."

"Oh! That's just a tall tale!" she signed deftly, with an air of cheekiness to her long fingers. It was easy for her-- she had one more knuckle on each finger than he did. "Surely you do not believe it?" The pose she adopted was one of a parent scolding a child for silliness.

"I don't know rightly what I *should* believe," he signed back, frowning.

"And who warned you?"

"Just about everyone I met on the road here, when they learned I was going to see the Fey." She was circling around the cave like a lioness patrolling a downed prey, examining his things. She even lifted up his boots, one by one, held them to her nose and sniffed.

"Well, they are wrong. But I shall still call you Lio if that is the name you give me," she signed, after setting down the boots. "Why are you here? You are not supposed to sleep in the cave, you know. You are *supposed* to leave a message for supplication and return if you are signaled to return." She signed it very slowly, like she was speaking to an imbecile.

"Yeah, I know," he said with his hands, scratching the back of his head. "I'm sorry, I just... I don't know what came over me, but I couldn't go back out there."

"Into the Wildwood?" He nodded. "I see. You were causing quite a commotion out there."

"I was?"

"The wood is effected by strong emotions. It seems yours are *very* strong." She spread her hands out wide in front of her chest. "You are unwell? There is deep grief in your heart."

"I am unwell," he agreed. "In a way I do not know how to heal." She was intended to infer the rest: *and you are a healer. Or so I am told.*

"I am a *guard*," she corrected slyly, then turned slightly so he could see the bow on her back.

He made the gesture of apology again.

"No, no, no! No more. What have I said?" Her hands were moving so quickly, so deftly. Lio was considered very good at the hand-tongue for someone from the city. But he was having trouble keeping up. "Perhaps I can help."

"I left the note, like the lady of the keep told me." He pointed to the basket. But she waved a long hand and reached inside of her cloak hood, revealing the scroll of paper. She shook it at him, a gesture asking for permission. He nodded and drew his legs out from beneath him, sitting flat on his bottom.

She held the paper before her masked face. Lio couldn't tell if she read it-- or if she could read in the first place. But after a moment, she pulled it down, rolled it up, and tucked it back into her cloak hood.

"You were dreaming when I arrived," she signed, squatting down next to him and sitting carefully on her heels. Even sitting, she still towered above him. "I could see some of it."

"You could *see* it?!" He didn't know why it came as such a surprise. Dreams were the land of the Fey after all. Or so he had been told.

"Yes." She said it without any embarrassment of her own. "But it made no sense to me, out of context. Perhaps you would like to share with me what it was about?"

"It's not worth sharing. It's just... something feels very wrong all the time. But moreso when I sleep. If I *can* sleep."

"Tell me," she adopted the pose of the listener, sitting down softly on the ground, crossing her legs, and laying her palms facing upwards on her knees.

"I... well, I fell in love at the midsummer festival last year."

"I saw his face in your dreams. I know him."

"You *know* him?" This surprised Lio. She signed the boy's name to him and he nodded.

"His father was Fey; his mother a human," she signed, as if it were no matter at all in the world. "He walks between both worlds. Fey-touched." She made the sign of indifference, arching her broad shoulders. "It's more common than you'd think. He passed his summers at the keep not far from here, but his winters, he came to us and learned our ways."

Lio's jaw dropped open.

"He never said anything about that!" he signed in disbelief, fingers jumping over his chest. "He looked perfectly human."

"Humanesque phenotypes are dominant in first-generation offspring," she was back to signing so quickly he could barely keep up. "Often, they are born deaf or with ill-formed ears! And frequently, they are completely sterile. But not always. Usually there is some sort of tell, though."

Lio tried to keep up. "Pheno...?" he tried to spell it out, tired fingers stumbling over the letters.

"Most offspring look human," she translated. "It's an easy mistake to make. And you're hardly the first to make it."

"Do you not look--"

"Continue the story, please." Her fingers were snappy now.

"I'd never met him before. He had come to the city in search of work, he said. Said he was uncommonly good with animals." And he had been. The horses at the King's stables looked at him like they were smitten, came running down along the paddock like slobbering, lovesick fools whenever he whistled. Lio had never seen them act that way-- not even when they were being bribed with apples.

And Lio? Well, he had been smitten too.

"He stayed all summer, and then, when the squalls quieted in the fall, he went with the King's delegation across the sea."

"You did not accompany him?"

"I..." he frowned and worried his lip. His mother's voice: *you cannot give up all you've ever known for a fling! I have seen it in the petals! You will go over the sea and you will never return.*

"...I think I made a mistake." His voice cracked as he said the words aloud, even though only he heard them.

"You protected yourself," she signed, patiently. "A season is a very short time, even for a human."

"But..." She nodded at him to continue, the bells shaking and shivering soundlessly in the place where her face should've been. "I can't eat. I can't sleep. I feel so miserable all the time. I worry constantly over the stupidest things. And I can't focus on my tasks. The stables let me go after the King's son's stallion broke loose this winter. Even after I tracked him all up and down the city!" In the cold, with holes in his boots and everything!

"You miss him," she signed patiently.

"It's not *just* that. It can't be. I've missed a lot of people in my life. I've had my share of lovers. But never has it been like this. It's never been this," he looked up at her, drawing his lip in between his teeth, "painful. All the time. At first, a dull ache. And now, it is like a constant thunderstorm in my mind. Why is it like this?" Lio asked. "No man or woman has ever made me feel this rotten. Why must it be so hard?"

"Do you want the answer of the healer or the answer of the heart?" She made a gesture of tenderness, but there was something else in the way that she posed which he did not understand completely. Something stronger.

"I want both. I want *anything*."

"Very well. There is a chemical compound in the sweat of the Fey that triggers strong emotions. Humans are particularly beholden to it. In your people, it produces euphoric effects.

But! There also a high chance of addiction." She made a gesture of indifference, akin to a shrug but still off. "You slept with him; he sweated on you. And now you are addicted. That's all it is, sweetling." She reached out and took his hand and squeezed it, then signed with the other, "You aren't dying."

"And what is the answer of the heart?" Lio asked her, looking away.

She tilted her head in a fashion that was so reminiscent of his mother, it nearly startled him.

"Oh, my dear. Let's not kid ourselves." Lio frowned at her affectionate gesture and took his hand back, folding it against his body. "Look. There is an easy, but temporary fix to this."

"There is?"

"As I said, you are hardly the first to jump into bed with someone of Fey blood and not know it." She paused a beat and then continued, in a sheepish sort of stance, "Do you think he will come back to you?"

"He said he would. He *did*." Lio's words were declarative and sharp. The implication being, '*Do not ask me further on this matter.*'

She signed the shape of agreement with her hands. "But you don't know when he is due to return?"

"No."

"Then you must find a source elsewhere."

"A source?" Lio signed.

"Someone else with Fey blood to supply you until he returns. Why, even *I* could offer you comfort."

"Comfort?"

"I could lay with you," again, she spelled it out very slowly as if he were being stupid. "My secretions would feed your high for a time." Lio blanched. The idea was not necessarily enticing when phrased that way. She made the motion of offense but he shook his head rapidly.

"No, no, I meant-- I couldn't ask that of you."

"Ah, then you have pledged fidelity to him and he to you?"

"No," he said, frowning. "He said that was unfair."

"To him?"

"No, to me. If he... if he didn't come back. He didn't want me to wait for forever." He stopped, feeling a blush creeping up his neck. "I mean! He said he *would* come back to me! But something might happen to him and I..." he didn't know what else to say.

It was all sounding very stupid now that he said it aloud.

She lowered the mask from the top part of her face, exposing wide, almond-shaped eyes. Wider and larger than any human's, the skin around them black as pitch, blotting out any other visible features to her skin. Those eyes had no irises, no pupils. Instead, they were filled with a deep, midnight blue, and dotted with silvery specks, which seemed to glow in the light of her antlers.

"Lio," she signed his name while leaning back in the tender pose, arms wide from her body. "I do not seek to replace him for you. Only to give you respite. I have known your love since he was a child. He has always been a restless wanderer, but he is earnest. And I know his heart. I do not think he has deceived you. Truly. He is not that type. But he would not like to see you suffering."

"And what do you get out of it?"

"Pleasure." Her fingers danced over the blatant word. "And the knowledge that I helped a friend when he needed me." Lio smiled ruefully. Her vacuous eyes glimmered like the light of a thousand stars. But she continued. "In truth, your emotions hurt the Wildwood. What happened last night cannot continue to happen or it will cause serious damage. And my job? Is to guard and protect the Wildwood."

He reconsidered.

"Is it.. is it like it is with a human?"

"We're not *dis*similar, biologically speaking," she signed back, her tone neutral.

"No, I meant like, ah--" She made a sudden gesture of understanding.

"Not like your love. I have an orifice. Like a human woman."

"Oh," he said, lamely. "Well, that's good, I suppose."

"It was my understanding from your dreams that you have no preference when it comes to sex," she said. "If you would prefer someone who--"

"No!" Lio said, blushing. "You're right. I don't have a preference. But am I *your* type?"

Yarrow made a coy gesture. "I happen to have a predilection towards humans."

"So I'm not your first one?"

"I am over seven-hundred years old." And then, despite the

fact that it didn't need to be said, "You are not my first. As for type, most Fey are like you. Biological sex is slightly more complicated for us than it is for humans," Yarrow said, with the tone of someone being very forgiving. "Like you, we trend towards having no personal preference but focus on the person themselves." Lio frowned as her strange eyes ran the length of him. "You are a shapely and handsome creature. You are young and your body is strong. I taste your pheromones in the air and they taste sweet. Yes, I find you attractive. Is there any need to say anything more?"

"Actually, sex is a bit complicated for humans, too."

"*Lio*. Will I suffice?" She touched the robe wrapped around her body. "I will display myself for you if you wish to make an assessment?" The Fey only showed themselves to their lovers. That was another one of the stories that he had heard. It had always sounded like such a romantic notion to Lio. Far more romantic than doffing someone in the back of the stables. For some reason, it seemed unfair that she would offer to show herself to him. But then he realized that if they slept together, he would see the whole of her anyway.

"You don't need to do that," Lio said, blushing and looking away. He couldn't remember the last time someone had made him blush. "If you truly wish to. Yarrow, you mustn't feel obligated to lay with me."

"Why? Are you bad at the technical aspects of sex?" The gesture she made for the word was vulgar. He snorted.

"No! I mean, I don't know." He signed. She made the sign of humor. "I've never had a complaint, I guess."

"You guess!" She repeated the sign of joy and humor. "Well then, I do not feel obligated," she returned simply, and stood up.

She unfastened the clasp on her cloak.

She was strange.

Stranger than any person Lio had ever seen.

Stranger than any creature.

Now that he could see the whole of her face, he realized that the blackness around her eyes was merely decorative kohl. It smudged when she pulled the rest of the mask off her face.

She was right, though. She wasn't dissimilar from a human. At a distance, someone might even think her one.

A very far distance.

She had long red curls that had been braided to hide beneath the cloak, the plait thicker than the span of Lio's hand. These, she untied and carefully freed one-by-one and permitted to hang around her body.

Her cheekbones were high beneath her eyes, and her nose was flat like a spade, tipped with a dark dot of coloring which Lio's eyes lingered on.

Her skin was starkly pale, but made dun by the light of her glowing antlers and eyes. And she was dappled all over, like a rare pony, with dark splashes of color. Only her belly was free of that coloring.

The muscles of her legs were thick and strong. He could

THE TASTE OF FORGOTTEN FLOWERS

make out their definition even in the dark, particularly those of her thighs. Something about them made him salivate.

A thin trail of red hair ran from the center of her belly to the middle of her legs. Thicker hair than a human might have there, but plush and soft. Lio's fingers twitched.

He stood up to see her better, but also to get a new sense of her size, for he still couldn't shake the feeling that he was misjudging her. But no, she was taller than him by a head and a half, broad and thick, especially in her hips. Now that she was disrobed, her breasts seemed small for her size. Small and lovely. Lio's eyes lingered on them--perhaps a little too long--before he startled and looked away. To her bare hipbone instead and then down her thighs again.

"Everything alright?" He caught her sign out of the corner of his eye.

"You... you look like him," he signed, feeling suddenly weak in her presence. "In ways I didn't expect. You have the same freckles," he dared himself to touch the patch on her smooth, hip. Her skin was cool to the touch and slightly dewy with the moisture in the air. His love had them there, too. Lio had spent long hours kissing each one. "And he's tall too."

"We are cousins," she reminded him with a casual flick of her wrist. "In a way." The way she moved her palm told him it was meant to be taken as a light-hearted joke. "It is alright if you wish to think of him instead of me." Now, she cocked her head. "I will not take offense."

Her head.

"They're *real*," he said, in astonishment, saying it aloud

before realizing he hadn't signed it. She inclined her head to him and he signed it very quickly. "Your... your antlers, I mean. I thought they were decorative." She smiled at him.

"An additional sense the humans do not possess. They are very sensitive." Her eyes pulsed wide when she said this. He was meant to infer her invitation. "Our version of hearing, perhaps."

"May I?" he asked, still. She nodded. He reached up and caressed one with his thumb, right down the front of it, finding odd delight well up in his belly when her cheeks flushed at the touch. It was strangely cold. "Do you feel vibrations with them? Like sound?" he asked, pulling his hand back to form the words.

"You are a little scientist," she responded, spelling the last word out.

"I don't know what that means."

"Someone who looks at the world with eyes open and curious." She lifted her top lip in a smile. They didn't smile naturally. Another story. It was a learned behavior. It looked fake on her. "Even when they are supposed to be focused on other things."

"You're right." He swallowed and trailed his hand down to her cool hip.

~

S omehow they had started kissing. Perhaps she had been the one to take the initial plunge. Lio didn't recall.

All he knew was the sweetness of her wide mouth, the force of her tongue, the cut of her sharp teeth into his lips and cheek. He was dimly aware, somewhere, that she had put her arms over his shoulders to pull him close, to pull him atop her. She smelled like the morning, like dew, like catmint, like lemons.

But her *mouth*.

It *is* a drug, he thought, somewhere in the furthest recesses of his mind. He could feel it now. Heavier than alcohol, more pleasureable than smoke. All the anxiety in his belly evaporated as his tongue sought out more of her. More. More. *More*.

"I want to taste you," he gasped, when she finally pulled away to take a breath. "I need to taste you!" His fingers translated the words in a clumsy hurry.

"Then taste me," she said, firmly, biting his bottom lip one final time and catching his flesh on the corner of a fang, before nudging him with a brow down the length of her body.

He trailed down her carefully, enjoying the anticipating, savoring the strange withdrawal from her mouth as his body thrummed greedily. More, more, more. He kissed each of her breasts, then the ridge where her ribs met, then the soft hollow of her belly, the top of the dewy fur there. Trailed his own cheek through that lushness just to memorize the feeling of it against his skin, just to smell her musk.

She did look something like a human woman. Not

dissimilar, he thought as his eyes lingered on her strange, slick sex.

And then he kissed the subtle swoop of her mound and parted her gently.

She tasted like sweetness. Like new summer melons. Like fiddlehead ferns. Like a deep, fresh breath.

"You taste like *him*," he signed as her thighs tickled his ears. But he continued the motions of his tongue. She *felt* like a human woman; she reacted like a human woman when he licked this spot and that. "So *good*."

She made a noise like a breathy laugh, clasping her breasts to her chest like a brace of pigeons.

Lio jerked up. "I'm sorry! I shouldn't have compared you," he signed quickly.

"No, no, no! What you shouldn't do is stop," she returned with one hand, thumb rubbing across her nipple. But her hand seemed to be waving back and forth, seemed almost to dance. And he found his eyes fixated on the rosy nipple, his body seeming to drift like a cloud.

"Fuck," he said aloud, "I *am* high."

She put her palm on the top of his head and pushed him back down, making her point very clear.

"You're a gracious lover," she signed, her chest rising and falling more slowly now. He had eaten her to completion once, twice, three times until she was satisfied. Until he was.

"Do human men not normally...?"

"No. They tend to prefer their pleasure to that of others. But don't feel too bad for me. Human and Fey women both do. Fey men *delight* in it. I do not go unsavored for long." She bit her lip, and he saw the edges of a fanged canine tooth poke out from the side of her lip. "Perhaps you have some Fey in your pedigree, too?" She rubbed her thick legs together eagerly, reminding him of a cricket. He grinned.

"Perhaps."

"Shall I return the favor?" The idea was compelling, but that sharp, little tooth was niggling in the back of his very foggy mind. And there was the weight of his unsatiated hunger, too.

"No. I..." he sighed deeply. "That was enough. That was what I needed."

"What you needed," she replied, "but we could go longer? We could do more."

"No. I will not take more than I need."

When he awoke, he was in cool arms.

But his head was clear. And light was trickling in through the cave's entrance. Not much light, but better than it had been. He blinked blearily as he sat up, feeling her long arms withdraw from around him and slide down his back as he turned over.

The cave walls weren't slate. They were amethyst. The sparse light made them glitter lavender and the copper gate shine like a new coin. Lio rubbed his eyes.

A hand on his lower back brought his attention back to Yarrow.

"How do you feel?" she asked. This little bit of light lit her up too, far beyond her glowing antlers and the specks of silver in her eyes. Now he could make out the true pallor of her skin, the iodine darkness of her freckles, the red of her long curls, nearly like molten copper itself.

Lio took assessment of his body.

His head no longer ached. His limbs and chest no longer seemed to bear the brunt of gravity. His joints had stopped pulsing, and his belly... well, *no*. The weighty anxiety was still there. Still bitter and nameless. Still quivering.

"I feel better. Quite a bit better, actually," he said with some degree of earnestness. She touched him on the leg, offering her take on a smile. Actually, he was finding it kind of endearing now. Or perhaps that was her secretions still working its way through his blood.

But still. Better.

"Does the addiction ever go away?" he asked with his hands.

"I'm afraid not," she signed back, drawing her hands up from his thigh.

"I don't get it," he said, looking down at the rumpled blankets between them. "Was it all just the withdrawals that made me feel so strongly? Or do I actually care for him?"

"How do you feel about him now?" She stretched out like a large cat, the strange bones in her dappled back moving beneath her flesh.

He closed his eyes and sighed, then covered his eyes with both hands. "Worse, in a way. I miss him more." The pleasure of their entanglement felt empty without him. It seemed cruel to say that to her though, especially when she had just been so gracious.

"If it were just the addiction causing your feelings for him, then you would feel sated now," she said, with a knowing look in her eyes. She reached out, taking his hand in her own and squeezing it. "It is alright to feel this sadness, my dear friend. But you *must* feel it, not ignore it. You must stand in it, appreciate it for what it is, and then you must act to cure it."

"You've done so much for me, and now you offer me wise counsel too?" he asked, smiling at her. "You are indeed a good friend. The lady of the keep told me you would be."

"Who?"

"The keep. A two-day ride back towards the city?" he frowned. Why couldn't he remember the woman's name? Even her face was difficult to recall for some reason.

"Whoever she is, she must have my measure," said Yarrow,

simply. "I try to be a friend to all. Sometimes, I am more than friendly." She winked at him, but it looked strange, as if her eyelid didn't close all the way. Another affected human gesture.

"This is not the first time you have provided this particular service to someone?" he realized suddenly. He was surprised that he didn't feel jealous about it. He had gotten that way with lovers before. Had resented those they knew before him.

"No. And it is not a service. I have not charged you any gold, have I?"

"Why do you do it? What do you get from it?" He had asked this last night, but for some reason, her answer didn't feel legitimate then. Now, after everything, perhaps she would be truthful.

"Pleasure," she said, with a cock to her head that screamed satiation. "Honestly. What is so wrong with that? There are people in the city who exchange pleasure for coins."

"I feel as if I should give you something more though. Something more than pleasure, more than coins."

"Some people feel that way sometimes," she made the gesture of indifference, still reminding him somehow of a large, lazy cat. "Lio, you are under no more obligation than I was."

"Still. You gave more me than you were obligated. And simple pleasure seems like nothing in comparison to what you have given me."

She smiled at him, and for a moment, for the first time, it almost looked like a human smile. "Then you may gift me with whatever you see fit to leave behind."

"Heliotrope," he said, finally. She made the gesture of

confusion. "Heliotrope. That's my name. Heliotrope, son of Millet the flower seller. You can have it."

"*No!* I told you! That is just an old, tall tale!" she admonished, her gestures sharp and declarative but still, she was still smiling toothily at him. Yes, he did rather like her smile, even if it terrified him for some reason.

"Still. It's yours."

She made the sign of gratitude her galaxy eyes glimmering as a particularly bright sunbeam made its way into the cave. "I will treasure it."

He picked up his bag. "And well may you keep it. I have decided what I must do about the sadness: I am going over the sea."

"Oh sweetling," she signed and her demenor changed so suddenly as she rolled over on the blanket. It was such a sharp and distinct change that it unnerved him: she seemed sad. "But how will he know you without your name?"

"What do you mean?" someone asked.

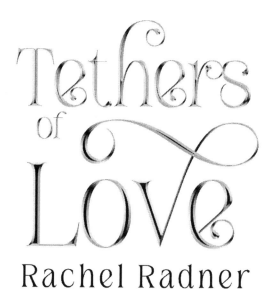

Tethers
of
Love

Rachel Radner

one

Dark, brooding eyes stare back at me from the photo mounted on the wall.

In the image, I'm hanging on his arm like a lost puppy, looking so tiny compared to his muscular, large build. Black hair splays around his face and reaches just below his ears. Hair I dreamed of interweaving between my fingers. He's staring at the photographer—his mother, the brilliant senator Lana—a whisper of a smile gracing his thick lips.

He was seventeen in the image; I was twelve.

I was already in love with him. He viewed me as a little girl.

It was eight years before, well—

I can't will my mind to go there right now. I just can't. Not when I'm staring into the eyes of the boy I once loved deeply. I can't look at him and think of any of it.

As I'm gazing into those eyes, it feels as if his hand gently lands on my upper arm. I sense his warmth. Sense his build standing beside me. The ghost of him.

Except, he's still in the living, out there somewhere. At least, that's what I hope.

No, no, no, no. Not again, not again, not again.

Have I genuinely gone mad?

"Aelia." Clifford's deep voice rips me away from the past, and I blink away the raw emotion welling in my stomach. The presence I've imagined fades away into oblivion. It's just me and Clifford now.

Turning from the framed picture, I catch the stern eyes of the man who's been a constant presence in my life ever since I met him right here, on Lana's estate grounds, as a little child. His hair has grayed since our first meeting, and there are more wrinkles on his round face than before. Otherwise, he's the same as ever, standing in the arched doorway with his thick arms crossed over his suit vest and white dress shirt. A pocket watch sticks out of the breast pocket.

"Hello there," I say, voice tiny. I'm so out of sorts that my former English accent almost sneaks back in, but it's a hybrid of an accent, mixed with the Southern California tongue I've long adopted.

My face flushes, and I feel like a child that's been caught red-handed doing what she ought not to be doing. I sink into the wooden bench beneath the picture, glancing around at the familiar, rustic features of Lana's mudroom. These, too, I have known since I was a child—from the Emser tile flooring to the wooden shelving meant for footwear to the walk-in bathing area for rinsing feet and washing off Lana's dogs before reentry. The space, like most others in this house, feels familiar and comfortable.

"I keep telling Lana to take that picture down." Clifford's scowl of disapproval hits me directly in the gut. "That man is a menace to society. He should be forgotten, not remembered."

"I'm sorry, I..." I pause, recalling all the times the boy who formerly held my heart consoled me while on babysitting duty and I'd woken up from a nightmare. Can people like that truly grow into adults capable of murder?

Murders, I correct myself, adding the *s* to ensure my mind emphasizes the plural.

"Even now, I keep thinking there's been some mistake," I continue. "Is it possible they got it wrong?"

Clifford's hard look softens but only a little. "Anniversaries have a way of making us think silly thoughts, dear."

I bite my lip, a million questions, questions I've asked myself countless times before, wandering into my head. Like Lana's home, the thoughts have become familiar—too familiar for my liking, but another way of coping with the unfathomable.

"Need I remind you of what he did all those years ago?" Clifford asks. "What that monster has yet to pay for."

I press my eyes shut for one quick moment.

He doesn't need to tell me. I wasn't there, but I imagine the events unfolding every night as I'm drifting off to sleep, imagine them as if I were actually there. I hear the gun firing in rapid succession, and the screams of the people as they take their last breath by the pool. I see the glint and pain in Adam's eyes, pain I had seen so many times on him throughout the years I knew him. And then, my brain envisions the finale—the terror in his father's eyes as Adam points the gun directly toward his chest.

My brain has conjured these images, as this is what we've all been led to believe based on one sole witness who lived to tell the tale.

Yet I can't believe the testimony or the movies my brain has concocted in my heart.

"Do you need reminding, Aelia?" Clifford asks again, the eagerness in his tone nearly begging me to say yes, so he can recount the tragedy of that day, lest any of us in his orbit should ever forget. His own daughter was killed—one of the victims taken. It's part of what drew Lana and Clifford together after everything happened, although Clifford had pined after Lana for many years prior.

"No," I muster the courage to say. "I do not need to be reminded."

Clifford's lips slip into a slight curl, the closest thing he ever does to a smile. He opens his mouth to say something else—after all, this is one of many times he's caught me here, in this very spot. Like always, I expect to hear him recount the events in full detail, regardless of how I answer.

Instead, his phone rings.

Clifford's face contorts.

Reaching into his pocket, he produces the device and glares at the caller ID.

"I've got to take this," he says. "But remember this next time before your brain misfires inaccuracies: evidence isn't wrong, and the innocent don't *run*."

As he steps away, he assumes his pleasant, kind tone he uses with his potential clients, and he begins to talk investment and other financial jargon lost on me.

Once he's far from sight and in another room, the tension in my stomach releases. I've never especially liked Clifford, but I've also always loved Lana enough to respect her choices. She sees something in this man—she's always seen something in this man, even before her husband died. Therefore, there must be something redeeming about him.

Or so I constantly tell myself, despite the voice in my mind that warns me again and again that Lana has not been in the greatest headspace for all these years. And what if she made a mistake?

What if there has been one grave mistake after another grave mistake after another?

Stop, I internally warn. *She's an adult capable of making her own decisions. This is Lana. Strong, former senator Lana. She always knows what she's doing. She always has the answers. And Adam...*

"Adam is a monster," I exhale, voice hardly more than a breath.

My uneasiness only grows as I find my garden shoes in one of the wooden cubby holes. Slipping them over my feet, I head in the direction I intended before the photo caught my eye and I had a run-in with Clifford.

Lana's in the garden, and I need to be there with her today.

Today of all days.

two

"Do you think the blue is off?" Lana asks, taking a step back from her painting. We're in her garden, an oasis of green plants and red roses and the scent of honeysuckle. A row of orange trees greets us to the left, and on the right, fig trees. The sun shines down brightly, and we're only in April, so everything around us is lush and in full bloom from all the winter rain.

Lana's hair is entirely grey these days, wrapped in a loose bun on the top of her head. Her left hand cradles her opposite elbow, the attached arm reaching up toward her face. A thoughtful finger presses to her lips. Deep wrinkle lines surround each side of her mouth. With her pale blue eyes, darkened now by years of pain, she studies the acrylic on canvas: an image depicting the green mountains behind her lavish estate.

"I think it looks just right," I say, a chipper smile on my lips. And I mean the words, too. Lana is a person who always give 110%. Ever since her retirement five years ago, she's focused all her efforts on her artwork. She puts her heart and soul into her paintings, including the one now. Then, she sells each painting, donating the money to various charities—all of which somehow relate to victims of abuse and violence.

"I don't know," Lana muses. "Something seems off."

Ever since her husband died and she lost her son, she's said this about everything.

Not just her artwork.

"I think it looks quite realistic," I say. "You've matched the blue to the sky precisely, and you've managed to differentiate it from the greyer blue of your roof."

Lana sighs, and I know that truly, this has very little to do with the painting. She inhales a deep breath, then waves a hand in the air.

"I think I've been staring at this too long. I could use a break," she says. "Care to join me for some tea?"

"I would love that."

We venture over to the iron, latticed table with the matching chairs. Lana hobbles more than walks, pain radiating through her face with each step. I hold out my hand, but she shakes her head, refusing my help, as always.

A teapot awaits us, and there's already two cups on saucers. A container of honey rests next to this with a spoon sitting on a small plate. This isn't a surprise. Lana, who knows we both enjoy a warm cup of tea, always has it ready for us around the time I come to visit—typically, every Monday afternoon once I'm through with work. Today, of course, is a special visit, given the anniversary, and I've come to visit her on a Friday.

Since the incident fifteen years ago, I've made it a point to visit her frequently, the woman who is like a second mother to me. I've known her as long as the woman who adopted me, after all, and they've each showered me with love and affection from the beginning.

We're seated now, and she's already pouring me tea. I never try to offer anymore; she always insists that I'm her guest, and she'll do it herself. Lana values her independence. With her independent wealth, accumulated long before her days as a senator, she could have people waiting on her hand and foot. She's never used her money for those purposes.

"I miss him," I freely admit as I've done on countless occasions in the past, cutting to the chase as we do. All the while, I'm staring at Lana sadly. This is the nature of our relationship: we can be open and honest with one another, a promise we made after Adam's fall. "I don't want to miss him, but every time I see our photo in the mudroom, I don't see the man he's become. I see the boy he was."

"I miss him, too," she chokes out, staring at the kettle as she serves. "Even now, after what he's done."

"Does this make us terrible people?" I ask, a question I've never asked before. It must be Clifford's conversation from the mudroom. He's gotten into my head again, and I haven't had a chance to process it before my get together with Lana.

She shakes her head. For a second, she's silent, collecting her thoughts. Then, she takes a breath, and her next words come out slowly.

"No," she says, voice scratchy. "It makes us human."

"Sometimes I still feel his presence," I tell her, afraid to admit I mean this very literally. I've almost told her the full truth for years, but how on earth could I ever explain that? While we made a promise to be honest, I have never found a way to broach this particular phenomenon. It's all in my head, after all.

Lana places a hand over her heart, a kind, yet broken, smile on her face.

"He's always right here," she says, her eyes beginning to well with tears.

Adam is the only time I've ever seen her cry.

Reaching for her hands, I take them in mine, hoping that this poor woman can find solace in my presence. I also know, from prior conversations throughout the years, that she's blaming herself right now.

"It's not your fault," I stress.

"What if I had been here more?" she asks, and not for the first time. "Worked less? I should have been a better mother. I never should have let anyone talk me into sending him away to boarding school. I could see it in his eyes how badly that hurt him."

"You were and *are* an incredible mother," I say. "You were always here for him when it mattered most, the same way you are always here for me."

"Girls are different," she jokes, bringing levity into the conversation. "Molly and I never had to worry about *you*."

I can't help but laugh. Molly is my mother, the woman who adopted me—and of course, they've never had a problem with me. Molly found me in the foster care system: an eight-year-old girl who had one dream. To find her parents. While I had not found my birth parents, Molly rescued me from sheer loneliness and despair. I would have followed any rule she had given me, not that she had many rules to give, just for her to keep me and continue loving me.

There's always that fear in my heart that the love people have to give me will run out.

That I am still the very same child who, at four years old, screamed after her parents as they dropped her in an alleyway and took off, never to be seen again.

My hurt breaks all over again when I think of that night in the dark. Of being an abandoned child with nothing but her teddy bear, the one with the missing eye, to guide her through the damp night in London.

But Lana, Molly, and Adam—they are the three people who brought me back to the light. Who chased away the nightmares brought on from that terrible time. Which is why, even now, I wonder where Adam is, and how he's doing, and I hope that he's alive. Even if he did, in fact, kill close to fifteen people that day. I can't dissociate the man from the monster—I still need to know.

So, as Lana as I finish our tea, a terrible idea strikes me.

A terrible idea I know I will have to execute on.

three

I t has been fifteen years since Adam walked into the Montecito Yacht Club with his father, Henry. Fifteen years since they shared what would be their last meal together in the restaurant. Fifteen years since they stepped out by the pool and shared a drink at the bar. Fifteen years since Adam and Henry got into a heated argument over a subject unknown.

Fifteen years since Adam allegedly reached into the interior of his black cargo jacket, pulled out a Walther semi-automatic pistol, and shot and killed all the guests within the vicinity before shooting his own father in the heart. I say allegedly, because the case never went to trial.

Adam escaped while in prison. One minute, security cameras showed him in his cell.

The next, he was gone.

In a red dress reserved for fancier establishments, I walk through the main entrance of the club. Something which I'm afforded to do because Clifford has remained a member, and as a kind gesture he once made it a point to tell me he added my name to the list of family members. As I stroll through the reception area, at dinnertime on a random Friday, I take in the faces of innocent people and their families. For a place once the setting of a crime that became a media sensation, no one here seems to remember. Or maybe they simply no longer care.

Perhaps it's a whisper of a time long gone. Although, it's only been fifteen years—which is both yesterday as well as an eternity.

I enter the restaurant part of the club, and patrons chat amongst themselves. Glasses clatter. A group of men in polo shirts laugh at the far end of the room. I do a slow spin, taking them all in, shutting my eyes for a second. Trying to envision that night, that final meal between Adam and his dad. I'm not very intuitive, and certainly no psychic, but something told me to come here tonight. That I might find some answers.

Instead, as my eyes reopen, I'm assaulted by a rush of memories. Adam holding my hand during my first visit here, when I was only nine, and helping me find the restrooms. Me as a preteen running to him after this kid bullied me by the pool, and leaning into him as he hugged away the tears, consoling me with words only he knew how to use with me.

A final memory works its way into my head. That time, the summer before the murders, when I'd nearly kissed Adam by his car, but we'd been interrupted before I had the chance.

Had I almost been about to kiss a future murderer?

Or was Adam a man wrongly accused?

The innocent don't run.

Clifford's word from earlier replay in my mind, right as I feel *it* again.

It's as if an invisible hand has taken my hand in his. Pulsing my fingers, I swear I feel resistance, like there's flesh against mine.

Fear runs through me.

This is nonsense. I'm not feeling him or anyone else.

I jerk my hand away.

Moving forward, I work through the club and out to the pool. Although it's evening, the sun has yet to completely fall from the sky. From where I'm standing, I look out, beyond the swimming area, and I see all the boats docked in the distance. I've been on a yacht a few times, with Molly, Lana, and Adam. One time, Molly and Lana chided the two of us for spending the time on our gaming systems while we were out at sea. A smile tugs at my lips, remembering the two-player quest game we were so desperate to beat. It took us weeks, but when we finally defeated the last boss, we went out for ice cream to celebrate, just the two of us. He was sixteen and had just gotten his driver's license, and I pretended it was a date.

"Miss Grimaldi, what a pleasure to see you here."

The familiar voice pulls me to the left. Franklin, the manager of the club, emerges from the shadows from behind the pool bar. He's dressed in a bespoke black suit that fits snugly over his rotund, short body. The same sort of attire he's worn every time I've seen him here, and all the many times someone interviewed him on TV. As the sole witness of a mass murder, Franklin Murdock's name became a known one.

"Hi, Franklin," I say. "How nice to see you."

"What brings you in tonight, ma'am? Shall I have one of our hosts find you a seat at a table in the restaurant?" He glances around as he asks this, and he's looking over his shoulder, like he's ensuring no one is listening. Is this the price to pay for surviving a mass murder? Or is he paranoid for another reason?

The skirt of my dress ripples in the breeze. "Actually, no. I'm here to, well, simply reminisce, I guess."

"Ah, I see."

"It's been a hard fifteen years," I say sadly.

"That it has been, ma'am." He stiffens, and I'm not sure if it's because he hates talking about that day, or if it's because there's something about that day he doesn't want anyone to know. I've often questioned why the authorities would go off of one man's word, not that I've ever had a reason to doubt Franklin. He seems honest, as far as I can tell. The sort of man who pays his taxes and abides by the law.

"I'm sorry to bring all this up," I say.

Franklin's gaze directs to the ground. He's silent for a moment, but then his eyes slowly pan up and something that cuts me to the core.

"You really should not be here, Ms. Grimaldi."

I swallow, deciding to push forward. "Why? I'm technically a member of this club by proxy."

He raises both brows, his voice low, repeating what he's just said. "You should really not be here."

I tilt my head. "Why? What do you know?"

"Nothing," he says quickly.

"That sounds like something," I push, driving forward without a care. I need to know the truth. "I often can't sleep over what happened here. I still can't believe he, umm, well, Adam, would do what he did. But you saw him? You saw Adam with the gun?"

He quickly nods, still not meeting my eyes.

"Yes, ma'am. Yes, I did. It was him."

"You're sure?"

He'd only said it five hundred different times on the news, the news I was glued to, despite Lana and Molly's reservations. Still, I want to hear Franklin tell me to my face.

"Adam Kantor shot me here," Franklin says without hesitation, pointing to his upper chest. "And here." He points to his abdomen. "And here." He points to his thigh. "I'm not sure how I survived. The whole thing is a blur. I only know that I'm a very fortunate man. A fortunate man amongst so many other unfortunate ones."

Another memory lurches into view before I can stop it.

I'm twenty, and Adam's twenty-five—mere days before the shooting, and we're throwing around a potato in Lana's kitchen. His smile is bright on the outside but masking all the pain on the inside. And he's egging me on, telling me I'm going to drop that damn potato, and I'm insisting that he's wrong. We're adults, but still children, goofing off in one of my absolute favorite ways.

"Don't mess with me," I warn. "I'm a Black Belt!"

To prove my point, I jump into my best defensive Taekwondo stance with my arms up, ready to catch that potato. The stance that only took my years to perfect. It's a wonder I got my black belt at all.

"You're a Black Belt in what *exactly?" He smirks, as if he's forgotten. He hasn't. "You look like you're asking for the big kid to come and steal your lunch money."*

He swings his arm behind his back and chucks the potato my way from his opposite side, a big grin on his face.

His comment causes me to laugh, and as I catch the potato once more, I stumble. He stops me from tumbling, his chest flush against my back as he steadies my shoulders with his two big hands.

Glancing up at him, our eyes lock in a way they've never connected before.

The potato drops to the ground.

I realize we're no longer smiling.

And then, he scurries away.

"Ma'am?" Franklin asks, breaking me away from the memory. "Are you alright?"

I open my mouth to say something to Franklin, but I have nothing of value to say. I'm not alright, will probably never be alright, and coming here was a mistake.

"If there's nothing more," Franklin says, "then I insist, for your own safety, you really must leave. He already knows you're here."

"What?" I ask. "Who's *he*?"

"That's all I'm at liberty to say, and I've already said too much."

His eyes are wide with fear, and it's then that I know the

threat from all those years ago has never left. Whether Adam committed those murders or not, Franklin knows something else. Anxiety rushes through me.

"Nice seeing you again, Franklin," is all I have to say, acquiescing to his request.

Without another word exchanged between us, I take my exit and head toward my car.

four

My keys jingle as I insert them into the lock.

Entering my apartment, the first thing I notice amiss is the sound of the television, blaring through my entire studio. I'm typically diligent about shutting it off before I leave, so the noise causes my nose to crinkle.

"Hello?" I ask, scanning my accommodations. It isn't much, but it's home, and up until this moment, I've never felt a sense of dread upon entering.

Everything in my apartment has been turned upside down. The sheets are bunched together on the floor. The pillows have been destuffed. Every shelf in my dresser opened. My pink jewelry box, the one Lana gave me the first time we met, has been opened—and the little, enchanting jingle is playing. My teddy bear, the one with only eye, remains perched above on the shelf above my bed, unscathed.

I take another daring step forward.

"Who's here?" I ask, my limbs trembling. While my body inches forward, I assess the situation, desperate to find something that can be used for the sake of defense. I'm a Black Belt, yes, but I can't remember the last time I attended a Taekwondo class. To say I'm rusty would be a fair statement. However, something on the floor by my feet catches my eye. Something I can use.

The toilet flushes, and every limb in my body tightens.

Slowly, and with purpose, a man with a sunken face steps out to greet me. He's tall. Lanky. Eyes that are glazed. Reflexively, I start to move backward, but I step right into the rough hands of another man, who holds my shoulders with a firm grip, restraining me.

"What is this?" I grit, mustering the courage to speak. "Who are you? Why are you in my apartment?"

"Why were *you* poking around the club?" the man asks, his voice gruff, scratchy.

"I'm family friends with Clifford Astor," I say. "My name is on the list. I'm a patron. Now, I'm going to ask that you please go, before this turns into a mess you'll regret."

"Oh, what we gonna do?" the man behind me asks, laughing; I pick up on a slight New York accent. "D'we want to reconsider, boss?"

They both start chuckling.

"'Fraid not," the man in front of me answers, his laughter abruptly cutting short. He pulls a gun from his pocket and slowly raises the weapon, pointing it directly at me. "Sorry, love. This ain't personal."

The millisecond before he fires, I kick up a decoration knocked down from a nearby shelf, the item I noticed earlier.

It's an ornamental, small tree-stump with the words "welcome" written on the one side. Big enough to hopefully help. The bullet flies through the air and sticks directly into the stump, which I've shielded over my chest.

I swing around and slam the wood into the man's head behind me, rendering him unconscious.

The "boss" grins at me, his weapon still raised. "That's cute. I've got more than one bullet, y'know. And what do you have? A piece of wood."

He's right. I'm done. It's over.

The man fires, and I clamp my eyes shut, hands still up. Holding the stump.

Bang.

Bang.

Bang.

Bang.

I'm shaking as I reopen my eyes, expecting that I'll be bleeding out, even though I feel absolutely no pain. The man in front of me now stares with widened, petrified eyes. A thick, translucent image has formed in front of me. It's a man, or a ghost, or something else. He's standing with his back toward me. But not a ghost, since the bullets, in their regular, non-translucent form, are lodged deep inside this thing, this being.

The ghostman, as I've already named him in my mind, starts to lose some of his translucency. Reaching into his opaque body, he pulls each bullet out. His hand, that I see through his body, flicks the bullets away. Like they're minor splinters.

As the apparition moves toward the shooter, his body

solidifies into something more human—and I see a tall man with a long, cargo jacket and boots who is also wearing a black cowboy hat.

The shooter continues to stare at him, a look of horror on his face. "W-what a-are y-you?"

There's no response.

Instead, the ghostman towers above the man, stoically. Silently. Then, in one swift movement, he reaches his hands around the man's neck and jerks. A loud *snap* sounds as the man slumps over on my carpet floor.

A rush of nausea surges through me, but I blink it away.

I search yet again for something, anything, to ensure this creature does not do to me what he's just done to this man. I'm not sure who he is or what he's doing here, and there's no guarantee he's on *my* side. All I know is that my heart is racing, my veins are pulsing, and every part of my body has gone into panic mode.

The ghostman slowly turns from the dead man on the floor. A silver, metal mask covers his face, which only serves to make him appear even more emotionless. Even so, I feel him staring at me from where he's standing. Studying me. Like he can sense the fear in my heart.

"Am I next?" I choke out, still scanning my room for something and trying to buy some time. Not that I'd have anything to harm a creature that can survive a bullet.

But perhaps harming him isn't the key here.

Surviving is.

The ghostman in the mask cocks his head slightly to the

right. His body has lost all of its translucency now, and he appears no different than any other human. I know better.

"If you understand, blink once," I deadpan, my heart pounding.

"Blink," he says—although his voice either sounds robotic normally or his mask has some sort of modulator.

"At least he has a sense of humor," I say, so nervous that the English accent of my youth has returned. If Adam were here, he'd laugh and say my British-ness was showing—which I'd always respond in kind by reminding him my ancestry is actually French, not British, I simply spent my earliest years in London. As it is, however, Adam's not here, and I'm standing next to a tall creature who's staring at me blankly.

"Well," I continue, accent and all, "how will it be then? I have no means of defending myself against you. The best I can do is try to run, but you'll outrun me, won't you?"

Instead of answering me, he returns his gaze to the dead man in my apartment. He touches his hand to the man's forehead, and the bodies slowly vanishes, fading from our sight. Then, he moves along, brushing by me and inspecting the other man—the one still unconscious from my ornamental stump. Once more, the ghostman presses his hand to the man's forehead. The same thing happens; the dead man vanishes from sight.

The ghostman draws closer and lowers his face so that the metal of his mask nearly touches me. I try to swallow, but every part of me has grown too stiff to do anything.

"What did you just do to them?" I murmur, fear coating my

words.

"Try to get some rest," he says with the same robotic voice as before.

I let out a nervous breath, not trusting any of this. "Sleep? I'm sorry, but have you seen what just occurred here today? Unless... is... is that some sort of sick fetish you have with women? You want to kill me in my sleep?"

Ignoring me, he brushes by and slumps down by the door.

"Sleep," he says, drawing out the word and motioning slumber with his hands, placing his palms together and pretending they are a pillow for his masked head.

I narrow my eyes. "Are you just going to sit there?"

"Yup."

"Why? I'm strong enough to defend myself. I almost had that guy."

"Did you? Mea culpa, then."

"Yes, I did, and if you're not going to kill me, you're free to go. I'd like to have my apartment back."

He cocks his head to the right for the second time since he's been here.

"Would you *stop* doing that," I say.

He cocks his head yet again.

"Oh, I see. *Fine.*" I groan, opening my mouth, ready to restress that he needs to leave. Except, after walking into an apartment with two men who just tried to kill me, do I really want him to go? He might plan on killing me in my sleep, but if he leaves, I sense there will only be someone else who shows up in the other guys' stead.

So, either this ghostman kills me.

Or someone else.

I'm trapped.

Grumbling, I start to pick up the carnage that has become my apartment, all the while the ghostman remains on the floor by my door, glued in place. I can't tell for sure whether he's watching me or not, based on the mask, but it *feels* as if he is. I'm running through options in my head of what to do or who to call, but I'm worried that reaching for my phone in my dress pocket will only set the ghostman off. And I'd like to live for as long as possible.

It takes me a solid hour to return the apartment back to—somewhat—normalcy. Some of the shelves need to be replaced with new wood, and I'll need a new stand for my TV. But otherwise, my space looks close to normal, and I let out a deep breath. The one I've been holding in since this whole ordeal began.

The ghostman has faded into the background—which isn't hard for him, considering he's resumed a nearly translucent state.

"I'm going into the bathroom to change into my pajamas," I say, uneasy and reconsidering the attire change. What if attackers come again, and I need to move in the middle of the night? Even so, I move forward, pajamas in hand, and add, "If you follow me, you will regret it."

He cocks his head again, and this time, I nearly laugh, despite the discomfort in my stomach, and the pressure in my head.

In the bathroom, I glance toward the door, paranoid, while slowly pulling my phone out. I decide to send a group text to Molly and Lana. At first, I whip up a paragraph that goes into full detail of the events, ending my paragraph asking them to tell the authorities, that I'm trapped in my apartment, with a weird, uh, robotic creature who can make himself invisible.

Except it dawns on me that texting them might only bring murderers to their doors. Or them to me where the killers might end up flocking.

Guilt bites at me. I can't involve Molly or Lana. Whoever that ghostman is out there... he's the only choice I have to survive right now.

Instead, I delete my message to the two women who deserve my complete and utter transparency, and I do something I have never done. I put my phone away, and I withhold information from them.

As I leave the bathroom after my wardrobe change, I'm deflated. Defeated. Nestling under the covers, I stare at the masked creature sitting by my door. I'm both angry and afraid.

"Need a pillow?" I ask with some sarcasm, cautiously watching him—an unsettled pang working though my gut. I'm still trying to process all of this, and his presence simultaneously fills me with dread and makes me feel relief.

"I'm not sleeping," he says.

"That'll make two of us," I say, as a thought dawns on me. "What are you, anyway? Do you even need sleep?"

He's silent for a beat. Then he nods and says, "Yes."

"Choosing to ignore my first question, I see. So, what

happens when you fall asleep, and I take off your mask in the morning to determine my own answers?"

"I won't fall asleep, and you won't take off my mask."

I throw a pillow in his direction, ignoring his sleeping comment. "Why were those two men here? You must know if you showed up. Unless there's some sort of crime radar us mortals are unaware of. Or are you simply a human being with a fancy scientific cloaking device and super human strength?"

He grabs the pillow and sits on it. I wait for an answer, but there is none.

"You're a man of many words," I dare. "Or are you a ghost or, uh, spirit?"

"You talk too much," he groans, the robotic tone sounding especially annoyed. He reaches into his pocket, and I brace myself. When he pulls out a phone, my nerves settle.

"Can you, uh, announce what you're about to do next time?" I ask. "Kind of would be nice after having a gun pointed in my face."

"I'm not here to hurt you, Aelia," he says, typing something into his device.

"You know my name." And he's said it as if it rolls easily off his lips—an uncommon name that is common to him. Like he's said it a million times.

"I'm not the only one." He lifts from where he's sitting, resuming more of a solid form, and he places the phone, face up, on the mattress. I'm half tempted to look through it to find out more about him, but I don't dare test him. Not when he could break me like a twig. Instead, I respect his property, and I look at only what's up on the display.

He's on some app I've never heard of before, and there's my picture, with my full name. The name I was born with as well as my current name, as if they needed to be overly thorough.

Aelia Luce and *Aelia Grimaldi.*

And there's a hit on me.

It was posted two hours ago. Right after I finished speaking with Franklin.

My face scrunches. "A million to kill me? Because I went to Montecito and spoke to Franklin? *What* is going on?" As the anxiety inside me starts to grow, I begin speaking rapidly. "Very few people seek me; I'm the girl who was left, not the one sought after, not the one people even notice. I'm no one. Why do people want me dead from an innocent conversation?"

He tilts his head again. This time, there's nothing funny about the gesture.

"Why are we still here if people have found me?" I ask, still full of panic. "Shouldn't we move?"

"No. Not just yet," he says. "I've placed a protective perimeter around the complex; no one will see you here for now."

Before I can say anything else, to ask him what the hell a protective perimeter is, our phones buzz back-to-back. And since we're pulling devices out now, I have no shame in reaching for mine, tucked away in my pocket.

The headline at the top of my phone from one of my news apps makes my stomach lurch.

FRANKLIN MURDOCK, SOLE WITNESS IN MONTECITO MURDERS, FOUND DEAD IN CAR.

"What?" I breathe. "I just... no... he can't be dead."

Another headline pushes through in notifications from another news source.

HAS ADAM KANTOR RETURNED?

"Adam did this?" I ask no one, maintaining my focus on my phone.

"No," he says. "Adam Kantor did not do this."

"How do you know?" I spit out, a mix of emotions welling inside of me, every part of me out of sorts from this night.

There's a long pause.

Then he finally breathes, "Adam Kantor is dead."

Dead?" I ask, numb to the words. "*No*. Adam's not dead."

The ghostman simply stares at me, his mask a blank state of nothingness. In his metal face, I see a reflection of myself, and the way the anguish has consumed me. My hair is in disarray, wild and unruly and flying in every direction; my eyes make me look like a madwoman, about to claw someone's heart out.

"He's not dead," I grit, the tears welling in my eyes. "You don't know. You don't know *anything*."

I start to hyperventilate; my breathing becomes belabored. I'm trying to calm myself, trying to take deep, soothing breaths. But my vision grows blurry, and the anxiety attack continues to climb. The ghostman inches closer to me. Then, he takes one of his gloved hands, and he presses it to my neck.

"Like I already said," he urges. "*Sleep*."

In an instant, the world around me grows dark.

five

"When are you going to straighten up your life?" Henry asks, his tone laced with disapproval as he speaks to his son. "Your mother and I are so worried. We're scared for you, the sort of people you're associated with."

I'm walking into the kitchen, holding a set of empty plates from dinner, and I abruptly do an about face. I can come back later.

"See? Look at Aelia," Henry says. "Aelia, come here a second?"

I halt, discomfort washing over me. "Actually, I should probably get back to—"

"She's graduating high school a year early," Henry says with pride in his tone. Pride that simultaneously makes me feel special and makes me hate myself in this specific context.

Adam's on the other side of the island, his head down.

"She's already been accepted to Yale," Henry adds. "Yale, Adam."

Adam huffs loudly. "So, if I go to Yale, that'll make everything better for you both? Right. I'll get on that now."

"No, son," Henry says, sadness in his tone. "We just... we just want you to stay out of trouble."

Trouble?

I take a quick breath, not wanting to be part of this conversation at all and hating that Henry's comparing me to Adam. Whatever is going on here, I shouldn't be part of this.

"I'll never be good enough for you, will I?" Adam asks, so much pain etched in those words. "I'm twenty-two; I'm not going to college. And if it isn't college, it's something else. From the hobbies I enjoy, to the careers I'm interested in, to even the women I choose to date."

I wince at that last line. Adam has had his share of girlfriends, none of which I've particularly liked—but I have vastly different reasons for that than his parents.

"Son, calm down," Henry commands. "We're trying to keep you safe."

"Calm down? Keep me safe? Look he's talking. You're gone half the year. Maybe if you'd been around, things would be better." Adam's on the verge of tears; I hear it in his voice. All I want is to go somewhere with him privately, so we can sit and talk all this out. I'm on his side, whatever this is all about. I always have been. The same way he's always been on mine.

"I'm trying to have a heart to heart with you," Henry says. "We all love you."

"You do? You've got a funny way of showing it," Adam says, as the two continue arguing back and forth. My feet remain glued to the floor, and every time I try to sneak away, Henry pulls me right back into the conversation.

Finally, their arguing morphs into screaming, and they parry back and forth.

"I'm not a child!" Adam cries.

"You'll always be our son," Henry says, softer now.

But Adam's fists are clenched, and he storms away.

Not for the first time, I see hate in his eyes. Anger that cuts right through to his soul.

I let out a loud gasp as I wake.

I'm slung over someone's shoulder. I'm wearing my black peacoat jacket, pajamas still on underneath. The world slowly sharpens around me, revealing a black sky. Damp streets reflect neon lights above. A dank smell of sewage and blood swirls around me. Creatures of the night that look like werewolves and centaurs and bipedal birds probably taller than me swarm around trashcans and heat rising from the drainage. As I'm being moved, the creatures all stare at me, like I'm a being of grave interest.

My head thumps.

I feel the ghostman's metal mask against my arm as he carries me.

That's when all the events from my apartment rush back into my brain.

Adam Kantor.

Dead.

No. It can't be.

"Put me down," I grit, regaining my strength, squirming in his arms. His tight grip over me restrains me, but I'm determined to shimmy free from my confinement. To find my own answers.

"I wouldn't recommend you walking this street alone," he says sardonically. "Or fighting me like this."

He presses a hand against the back of my neck, and I instantly feel my body fall limp, unable to squirm or move or do anything. As I deliberately blink my eyes, I realize the only thing I can still control is my face.

"What—" I start to say, fortunately able to speak.

"Sorry," he says. "But it's their dinnertime; they're always famished, and if you'd kept moving like you had been, you only would've drawn attention to us."

I let out a sharp breath, my paralysis scaring the hell out of me. "You took me here, why? To kill me. I knew it. God, I shouldn't have been so stupid."

"*Calm* down," he says. "You're not here to die. The people who are looking for you are human. I took you somewhere they wouldn't dare venture."

"Oh, wonderful. To a place with creatures who want to eat me, with a masked ghostman who can paralyze me with his touch. Damned if I do, damned if I don't, aren't I? What is this, anyway? Some sort of underworld? Or maybe I ingested something bad, and this is some sick nightmare, and none of this is real. Adam's not dead, after all, so this must be a dream."

"Just keep your head down and ask questions later," he says, as if to taunt me—because clearly, I can't move my head.

"And who are you, exactly?" I ask. "*Why* are you helping me? And on what grounds are you claiming that Adam is dead?"

"I'm someone that no one will mess with as long as we keep our heads down, business as normal. No one here is going to attack us if they think you're *mine*."

I roll my eyes at the way he's stressed the word *mine*—and the fact he's ignored my other questions. I've enough experience with him to know he isn't going to provide any further information, but I need him to understand certain things— whether he plans on killing me or not.

"I belong to no one," I stress.

"Never said you did." He huffs, the noise sounding especially gruff with the digital tone.

"Oh, I'm simply spelling it out. I don't know why you're helping me, but there isn't anything like *that* in it for you at the end of the line. You might as well kill me now if there is. So we're on the same page."

The ghostman starts laughing, but it's the sort of laugh that is hollow, dead. Weighted with something else, some hidden pain.

And not helping to assuage my fears.

"I have people who care about me," I say, desperate. "If you so much as touch—"

"No one is going to touch you," he says. "Myself included."

Sighing, I try to trust his words, although, truthfully, I can't. Even so, I do as he requested earlier, for now, and try to take a deep breath that helps settle my nerves. My body may be paralyzed, but I can still feel everything. The way the heat around us is so thick it's palpable. The sweat beading on my forehead. The putrid smell of sewage as we step through an underpass.

Creatures shrink into the shadows, glowing eyes pointed at us.

Watching.

Waiting.

My heart continues to beat rapidly inside my chest, and my head is tight. I take a few more breaths, and some of the tension subsides. It's only then, once I've calmed myself, that I notice the way the ghostman's arms are gingerly holding me. One cups around my legs. The other presses against my back. I might be dangling over his shoulder, but he's holding me like I'm of some value to him, handling me delicately. Whoever wants me, whoever he's working for, must want me alive.

And if this all stemmed from my visit to the club...

Is Adam involved somehow? Despite the fact this creature insisted he was dead?

"Why do you think Adam is dead?" I ask again. The pain from earlier rushes through me all at once, imagining Adam dead. Imagining the light in his eyes gone for good after being shot and left for dead on some street.

"Please," I add, my voice cracking. "He meant, er, he *means* a great deal to me. He was my..." I stop, trying to assess the nature of our relationship. Too overwhelmed to think of anything else, my words trail away.

"Your what?" the ghostman asks. "As I understand it, Adam Kantor wasn't much to anyone. Sounds like a, uh, how do people refer to him? Ah, yes. A monster."

"You're thinking of the Montecito murders," I say.

"Yes. Seventeen dead."

"Seventeen," I agree, as we start to move into slightly less grungy territory. In place of the sewage smell, a blast of fresh air fills my nostrils. We're passing into what appears to be a park in the middle of a massive city. High rises abound, surrounding the perimeter of the park.

"You think he did it?" the ghostman asks. "Killed all those people."

I swallow. "I don't think it matters what I think. The people who do matter believe he's guilty."

"That's not what I asked."

"Oh, so, I'm required to answer all your questions, and you're not required to answer mine? The double standards here are incredible."

He's silent, and there's nothing, save the sound of his feet crunching through a stretch of grass in the park, as he crosses through to the other side.

Maybe it's the fear causing me to be a little less tight lipped, but when I open my mouth next, the truth spills out.

"I don't think he did it," I say, and I realize it just might be the first time I've ever said that aloud. Even to Lana, I've never been so direct, simply because up until this moment I've never let myself answer the question that the ghostman has just asked me. Answering it would have been too painful, and even saying the words now fills me with hope I don't want to feel.

"You don't think he did it, but...?" the ghostman asks. "I'm sensing there's a but here."

I sigh. "Oh, there are many buts. One of which is that my opinion isn't viable as it's a biased one."

"Biased how?" he questions.

"I grew up with him," I say. "A fact I'm sure you already know if you're involved in all this. You must know a lot about me. With your abilities, you can probably watch anyone you'd like."

A shudder works through my body, as I wonder how long he's been in my orbit, this stranger with the mask. He says nothing, something that's becoming all too familiar. And in his silence, something harsh dawns on me.

"You're the one I've been feeling." The words come tumbling out, weighted with pain and despair, highlighting how silly I've been. How could it have been Adam? Why was I so ignorant to think something like that? It was this ghostman, following me around for reasons he hasn't yet revealed, during his own reconnaissance.

I'm greeted with his silence.

I shut my eyes for a moment, trying desperately to compose the emotions welling in my chest. But the anguish is building, pressure behind my eyes causing my entire face to flush.

"Of course it was you and not him," I say, as the tears start to roll down my face. Tears I can't even wipe away or try to hide, because someone else is controlling my body. Droplets plunk from my face to the back of his jacket, and I watch with horror as my own tears coat a tiny section of his clothing. Which only makes me cry more. And then, I'm full on ugly crying, and hating myself for being so emotional. I'm a strong person, not a wreck, not someone who cries in front of strangers. Not someone who cries in front of anyone.

The ghostman must notice, for he abruptly stops walking. He touches his hand to the base of my neck, and then he places me down onto the grass beside him. With all feeling in my limbs restored, I sink down to the grass and roll into a tight ball, burying my face in my hands. Shielding myself from the world, I try so desperately to stop this crying.

All at once, my brain transports me back to various memories of my life. Crying in the alleyway, screaming for my parents. Waking up alone in various foster care living environments thereafter, crying in hushed tones, for fear of making my foster parents angry—even in the situations when they had been kind people. All the times I cried in Adam's arms as a child. All times he knew, even when I was a teen and an adult, when I was about to cry even before I started.

"I'm scared that anyone I get close to might leave me," I admitted to Adam one time, bawling my eyes out to him. It was after my first semester at Yale, during winter break when I'd returned for the month between semesters. We were in his room as I recounted how lonely I'd felt being away—and how much I'd missed him. Phone calls periodically hadn't been enough.

"I'm never going to leave you," he said. As I leaned into his chest, he wrapped his arms around me. "You'll never be alone."

"Do you promise?" I asked, like the little girl I was still, deep down, on the inside. The scared girl afraid of winding up in that alleyway again, watching as the people she loved simply left her, like it was the easiest thing in the world. More tears fell, and he wiped them from my face, gazing at me with soft, caring eyes. Eyes that looked upon me with genuine care. Eyes that made me feel safe. Made me feel loved.

"I promise you that no matter what happens, I will never leave you," Adam said, his fingers softly brushing against my cheek.

The ghostman slumps down next to me on the grass. He's so close our knees touch. I return to the chill of the present, far away from a memory that warms me, that keeps me going when all I want to do is wither away. I'm not a social person. I may be friendly, but I'm terrible at making friends. I'm even worse at keeping them. It's in my nature to retreat, and there are few people I trust.

I trusted Adam.

When he got out of that jail, no matter how he did it, he never once came to find me. Never once dropped me a note or a hint or anything, to let me know somehow that he was still here. I would have believed him if he told me he hadn't committed those murders. I don't think he's capable of it. But I was never given the chance to hear his side or to even know whether he was alright. Because he simply *left*. Vanished.

I've been alone ever since, even with Lana and Molly. Because the one person who truly understood me has been missing in action.

It hits me how alone I really am.

And right now, it's just me and the ghost.

"Here's my dilemma," I choke out. "Adam either died, and you're right, and that means I'll never see him again. Or you're wrong, and he's alive, but I lose, anyway. Because he's been gone fifteen years, no matter how it is, and he's never coming back, so he might as well be dead, even though I really don't want him to be. Either way, I lost the one person who made me feel the safest."

Not for the first time, or so I assume, the ghostman places his hand over mine. It causes me to look up. Through my tears, I see a blurry masked man staring at me, and I imagine a person beneath the mask, gazing at me with pity. There's no fear from his touch, nothing that makes me hesitate. And maybe I'm mental, but I allow him to keep it there, touching mine.

"Aelia..." he starts to say, and there's that familiarity again. That flawless pronunciation. The way my name rolls off his lips like he's said it his entire life.

Something rustles in the bushes. Every hair sticks up on my body, and I become hyper aware of our surroundings. Something else has scurried around us. A snake-like creature hisses in the not-so-far distance.

The ghostman leans in and places his arms around my back, lowering his voice as he speaks. "You are not safe here. We need to go."

"Go where?" I whisper.

"I..." He hesitates, glancing around, as if to ensure we're

alone. "I have a living accommodation. Here. In the realm of the dead."

Before I have a chance to ask him one of my million questions, he's lifted me up and propped me over his shoulder, the same way as before.

Except this time, I let him without putting up any fight.

six

Inside the skyrise apartment complex, the ghostman carries me into a lobby that looks no different from any other I've seen before. The ceilings are high; there's a chandelier at the center. A man wearing traditional bell boy garb stands behind a desk, thumbing through a book. He's the first human I've seen here.

As we pass, the man waves and smiles, as if nothing is amiss. "Morning," he says.

"Morning," the ghostman says back right before we turn a corner and head down a hallway. He presses a button, calling the elevator.

Once we're inside the car, he places me down.

"The realm of the dead?" I whisper. "This feels like New York."

"Not New York," he says, still staring at me. "And that guy? He's an AI, in case you were wondering. A sort of joke to mock the living. Otherwise, we only see your kind when, well, they die, or one of us has gone to collect their soul."

He's being more forthcoming than before, but I'm not about to ask why. Instead, I decide to pry for more information.

"Is that what you do?" I ask. "Collect souls?"

"Yes," he admits, nodding. "But only the bad ones."

"So, presuming I'm not considered bad—"

"You're not."

"Then, why am I on your radar?"

"Reasons."

The elevator lifts us to the top floor, labeled PH. With a loud ding, the doors open, and he exits, taking my hand and guiding me down a series of hallways. It's here that I notice the laws of gravity have been defied—doors overlay other doors and walls seem to be stacked one after the other, like looking at an art print with shapes copied and pasted, one after the other.

"It threw me for the first time, too," the ghostman admits freely.

"What are we looking at?"

"Individual apartments with no need for separation," he says. "Dimensions work differently here. There is no sense of organic space, not really."

Once we've turned down the third hallway, he presses his hand against a wall, which then causes everything around us to shift. A door appears that wasn't there before, and he takes us inside, before we then walk through another hallway.

"You really could kill me if you wanted," I muse, this time with some humor laced in my tone. "No one would ever find the body."

He tilts his head the same way he did in my apartment. This time, I can't help but laugh.

"Really, though, it hasn't been about murdering me the entire time, right?" I ask.

"Eh, I'll most likely kill you in the morning," he teases.

I arch a brow, my lips spreading into a sad smile, as I pick up on the reference immediately. *The Princess Bride*—a movie I know well. I must've seen that movie hundreds of times. It's a film I used to watch with Molly and Lana all the time—and sometimes, Adam, although he always pretended to ignore that it was on, texting or playing on his computer on the sofa while the rest of us were glued to the TV. Every so often, I caught the smirk on his face, and the way his eyes lit up with joy during some of the scenes. So, I knew the truth.

At the end of the final hallway, the ghostman stops and presses his hand to a red door. Expecting to step through, I inch forward, but he holds out a hand to stop me. The scene around us morphs, and we go from an empty hallway to a high rise, swanky, city apartment that might as well span the entire floor. All the lights are off, but there's light from the window that spans along the left wall. I'm instantly drawn toward it, catching a river of lights twinkling. Skyscrapers fill the landscape below, and we seem to be cast higher than the rest.

"Is this view real?" I ask in awe, touching my fingers to the glass. While I've spent most of my life living with a woman who is relatively wealthy, and I've seen my fair share of cities, I'm still the poor girl at heart. The one easily impressed.

"It's real," he says.

The entire scene is silent, although I imagine that in the day, even here, the events below bustle with activity. I see him in the reflection of the glass; he's watching. Not taking his eyes away from me.

It's in this silence, and the way he's watching me, that my brain pieces things together. Everything starts to snap into place. Like a sudden *aha* moment. A lightbulb flashing above my head.

My mind begins to process the events of the evening. A ghostman with strange abilities, who seems to know me, shows up in the nick of time to save my life—when he's in the business of collecting the *bad* people. The way he's been speaking to me, I know he wasn't there for those two men—those souls were an afterthought. I should never have been on his radar. If he were working for someone, I'd be dead. If he were in it for the money, he'd have collected. If this were simply a job, he'd already be on his way to the next gig.

Then, on top of all that, there's *the Princess Bride* reference.

The way he carried me with care.

The way he says my name.

My eyes widen at my own harrowing realization.

"Your space is nice respite from *collecting* souls," I say, trying to calm myself down. I might be wrong—but I'm probably not. "Was soul collector on your list of prospective career goals as a child?"

"No," he says.

"No, I don't remember you ever mentioning that among your interests."

I turn back to look at him. He's standing a few feet away, in the shadows. He's crossed his arms over his chest, and I notice the familiar way his thumb is gripping the index finger of his opposite hand. My eyes stare at his gloved hands a little too long, and he abruptly stops the movement.

"Do you need your mask to breath?" I ask, taking a large step toward him and bridging the distance between us. Studying him more closely now.

There's some hesitation before he answers. Then, "No."

"Can you speak without it?"

He waits until I'm next to him before he answers, a soft "yes" escaping his lips. My heart beats faster than before, because now, somehow, I'm certain my gut is leading me in the right direction. Taking one of his gloved hands, I hold it in both of mine. The shape of his hand is one I know well, even though he's only ever touched me platonically. I trace my thumbs against his palm through the latex. The ghostman flinches, but he does not pull away.

"I'm not the only one who wondered what happened to Adam," I say. "They had armed security around his cell. A security camera pointed on him at all times." Gingerly, I slip my finger under the sleeve of his jacket. Once I feel skin, I keep going, searching. He doesn't stop me. I continue, "You're a man, or perhaps a ghost and a man, capable of hiding and slipping through places. Care to shed some light on how you think a human might have vanished in those conditions?"

"You sure they were watching the shower floor in his cell?" he deadpans.

I smirk. "I'm positive. Besides, Adam hated small spaces. He wouldn't have made it through a tunnel like that."

"People change, Aelia."

"Only some aspects. Other things never change. They're constant at someone's core." My hand has reached halfway up his lower arm. Touching soft hair and muscle, no different from before, I continue searching. "Just like some scars never fade."

He's silent.

When I find it, my body tenses. The area of the skin is rough; it's the scar from that time we were playing in an abandoned treehouse, and he stepped on a piece of rotted wood and fell through to the ground.

"I remember when you fell. I used your phone to call Lana, and they had an ambulance come for you, with a group of people who found us in the woods. You were unconscious for an hour," I said, rubbing the patch of skin. "I was only ten, but the idea that you were dead petrified me. But in the end, you lived, with nothing beyond a broken arm that mended, and the scar still on the underside of your arm." I lift on my toes and bring my face up to reach his mask. "Take this off, Adam."

"I already told you. He's dead."

"I have a feeling you've been with me the last fifteen years," I breathe, reaching for the metal. Knowing full well he has the ability to paralyze me, to put me to sleep, to stop me at any time, I lift the mask.

His flowing hair spills out in layers as I push up the mask, the same raven black he's always had. First, I see his strong chin and full, pink lips. Then, his long nose. Lastly, his eyes, darker than ever before. A hue once brown, they now appear black, no longer shining. The only indication so far that he might actually be, as he claims, *dead*.

He takes the mask from me and lets it fall to the floor. The metal lands with a clang.

"Is this what you wanted to see?" he says in his real voice—Adam's voice. The voice I've known since I was eight years old; the one I've heard morph from scratchy pubescent teen boy into the deep male vibrato he grew into. Except now, his tone, once full of variety and liveliness, rings with a dull monotone I've never heard from him.

He stares at me blankly—so different from the man who, last I saw, stared at me with care in his eyes.

I place a hand to his cheek. In place of warmth, he's like ice to the touch.

"Adam's gone," he adds, words empty. Hollow.

"You're not gone," I murmur. "You're still here. You're with me. You *saved* my life."

"I've broken every rule," he says. "When they find out—"

"Who's they?"

"Demons," he says, fear in his eyes. "Those who invoke order here. Fraternizing with humans is forbidden, even when I'm in your realm."

"Our realm," I say.

"Your. Realm."

"You're human, just like me."

"I was human. Millenia ago."

"Montecito only happened fifteen years ago. What are you even saying?"

"Time works differently here."

"I don't care. I feel your flesh. Whether you've been gone fifteen years or fifteen hundred, you don't belong in this place. How did this even happen? What did they do to you in the jail?"

"Not the jail," he grits. "I was already dead when they brought me there."

"Dead?"

"Dead," he confirms.

"You were one of the victims," I say, filling in the blanks without him even having to tell me. Something vile bubbles in my stomach. Anger blooms in my chest. "Who killed all those people? Who killed *you*? Why did someone try to place the blame on you? How did you end up in jail if you were already dead?"

"The more you know, the worse this will be for you."

"I don't care."

"*I* care," he says. "I wanted you to move on. Not mourn over me. Not mourn the monster."

I flinch at the way he's thrown my own words back at me. I did say this to Clifford on multiple occasions, not considering what was in my heart. So full of fear of the unknown that I let the media and people around me get into my own damn head. Even so, what else was I supposed to think?

"That isn't fair," I say.

"You're right. It's not."

"I've missed you all these years, and I would have believed you if you had only come to me and told me the full story."

"It took every ounce of restraint for me to not visit you and tell you everything."

"You should have listened to your gut."

"And you should have made new friends and dated people," he says. "Gone out more. Tried to find someone to spend your life with. You deserve a full life, not a half one."

Hurt ripples through me. "You know none of that is easy for me."

"Maybe because you're too caught up on the past, Aelia. You need to let it go and move forward. Learn to trust people again. Learn to trust someone other than me—who I once was. You're a beautiful, young girl who is letting her life pass her by."

There's a quick flash of pain that flickers across his face as he says this. But then it's gone, as if it never happened, and I'm too upset to analyze what I've just seen. It's not that he's wrong exactly—anyone else might have said the same things to me. It's simply that the Adam I knew never spoke to me like this before. Not once. He'd never been anything but understanding, always acted like he was on my side, while offering his advice in a much gentler, kinder manner.

"Is that all I've ever been to you?" I ask. "A young girl?"

"No, wait, I—"

"There isn't going to be anyone else. Don't you understand that? You might very well be the only man I ever could have trusted."

"Well, that's something I'd advise you remedy."

"Advise I remedy?" I ask, especially heated now. "How dare you? You. The person with two parents who always loved him. I'm sure if the roles had been reversed, and I were here, you'd have had no problem forgetting about me. But I'm not you."

"I could never forget you," he says. "You're not hearing what I'm saying."

"You're clearly not hearing *me*. I can't simply let someone new in. I know what love does—it leaves you stranded, broken on the inside, when the other party decides they're done with you."

I swallow, a sharp pain working down my throat. I'm about to cry again, and this time, I don't want Adam to be around when it happens. Inhaling a deep breath, I compose myself—but I see it in his eyes he knows the emotions needling inside of me. The way he would have known before. Except, he's done nothing but insist that things need to be different now. And maybe he's right. So, I can't let him see it as my heart is starting to break all over again.

I plaster on my most fake smile. "You know what? It's been, uh, one emotional evening. I'm not going back home for a few days, yes? Paralyzing me temporarily on our walk here seems to have stressed that. I'm also too frightened to go back out into what *that* is with creatures who want eat me. I think I'm going to find a sofa or something and just get some rest to clear my head. Can we reconvene at a later time?"

"Yes," he says, the same pain in his eyes. "Anything you need. There are multiple bedrooms here, too, if you don't want the couch."

"Great," I say. "I'll find a room then. Catch you in the morning. If that's even a thing that exists here."

I don't give him a chance to respond. Instead, I seal my heart, blocking that dam that threatens to break, to contain all the pain. I can't let the emotions out. Won't let it out. Not until I'm out of his sight and in a more private place where I can deal with this.

Adam doesn't stop me from walking away.

seven

Rain patters against the walls of the bedroom I'm in as I snuggle against satin sheets with thread count that must be through the roof. My arms wrap around the softest pillow ever. If it weren't for the seedy creatures outside, I might wonder if this were heaven and not hell. There's a balcony in this room; two French doors open to the outside.

Adam's on my brain as I drift away into a state of half sleep. A collection of our "best of" childhood memories play on repeat in my mind's eye. A million visits to get ice cream on a warm night. The movies we went to see together and would talk about for hours. The way I'd find him sulking over something he didn't always want to talk about, but in the end would share every detail, and we'd end up bonding over whatever it was. Each time we shared something new with the other and further cemented our bond.

Most of all, I keep seeing his gentle, kind eyes—the ones that used to smile at me.

The active memories fall away as sleep consumes me. In their stead, dark images of creatures with horns and demonic faces flicker. Panic eats at me at my core. I hear someone laughing maniacally. There's someone unwelcome, who I can't see, standing behind me. Their presence sends a chill down my spine and brings an onslaught of unwelcome, dark emotions.

"Who do we have here?" the presence snarls; I hear it lick its lips. Thick, stubby fingers with claws reach for my neck. All the while, I'm transported back to London, watching four-year-old Aelia scream out for her parents. That old, harrowing pain jostles my system. Makes me nauseous. Sucks the life from me until all I want to do is curl into a ball and fade away.

"Ah, an orphan," the voice croaks. "Parents didn't want this one. No one does."

The claws apply more pressure around my neck, and my airway restricts. I gasp for air that does not enter.

"St-st... stop!" I choke out, reaching my hands up to my neck. I try to pry the fingers away, the screams of my former child self drowning out my own adult voice. But the claws dig into my skin, piercing me. I'm desperate, struggling to rip the offender away. But I'm failing, and I feel myself fading, and I start to accept that after all this, now might be my time to die.

No.

Not today.

With the last of my reserves, I grip the claws around my neck, and I rip them off me. Blood trickles down my neck as my eyes snap open. Jerking upright in bed, I reach for my skin. The area in the middle, where the claws had been, feels tender.

No, no, no, no.

I'm reeling. Feeling the full effects between a strange spirit or demon or whatever strangling me combined with the image of myself crying for my parents as a child. I squeeze my eyes shut, with no intention of ever going back to sleep, and let out the feral cry that's been bubbling to the surface.

Each of my hands fist into tight balls, and I squeeze my eyes shut.

Parents didn't want this one.

The icky presence from my dream surrounds me, and I feel myself suffocating all over again. Feel myself fall into a trance, as if someone else has taken control. My head grows heavy; there's anguish and melancholy swirling around me, starting to eat me from the inside out. Suddenly, like a heavy weight, my soul seems to be holding me down. I feel too uncomfortable for my own skin. I want out.

Consumed by these emotions, I let my body guide me. I hop out of bed and walk toward the French doors leading to the balcony. The metal of the handles is cool to the touch. The doors swing open with ease, and I'm stepping outside.

The endless drop seems as if it might bring me peace. A way for me to feel nothing. To let go of all the pain.

Leaning over the edge, I shut my eyes. Welcoming what will be imminent darkness.

A strong hand grips my shoulder, forcing me to snap out of my haze.

I feel the icky presence flee.

"*Aelia,*" Adam says firmly.

Reality rushes forward. My trance crashes and burns. Fully alert, I stare at the drop below, and my heart jumps into my throat.

"What..." I stumble backward, and Adam catches me. His arms are strong and firm. I sink into his touch, my heart pounding. I'm in shock, at a loss for words.

He lifts me up and carries me through the French doors, using his foot to shut them after we've entered. After placing me in bed, he climbs onto the mattress, facing me. His dark eyes somehow look even blacker, and I notice his fists are clenched.

I'm shaking, finding it hard to breath. In utter shock. Finally finding my voice. "Adam... I'm not... I wouldn't... that... what just happened?"

"It wasn't you," he says, voice tight. "You were being manipulated. That's what demons do here. They find what triggers beings the most, and they toy with them."

"I thought this was a safe space?" I ask.

"Dreams are no-man's land."

It's then that I watch his eyes navigate to my neck. If his eyes appeared hateful before, now they flash with pure rage.

"They *touched* you?" He's clinching his fists, nostrils flaring.

Subconsciously, I reach a hand to the area where the demon strangled me in the dream, and I bite back bile as I feel the cuts from the nail.

A shudder works through me.

Adam fades from sight.

Jerking up in bed, I lean against the headboard, eyes wide as

I can only assume where he's gone. How Adam knows which demon is beyond me. I swallow, still shaken from the events of the dream, and the trancelike state that led me to the edge of the balcony. For the moments he's gone, I feel genuine fear, and I wonder if I'll ever be able to sleep again.

A demon found me in my dreams.

Would this happen for the rest of the night, like some sick Freddy Kruger situation?

Adam reappears at the foot of the bed before I have a chance to start worrying about him. There's a dab of blood on his lip—seemingly his own blood, which perplexes me—and he's panting heavily. I crawl over to him, while wondering about the blood. I'm about to take his hands in mine, when he pulls me in to his chest. He holds me there tightly, pressing his nose into the crown of my forehead. I feel his heart racing in his chest—a *heart*, still beating rapidly, pounding so hard it feels like it might break through.

"I will incinerate the soul of the next demon who so much as looks at you," he grits into my hair. "I will *destroy* them."

His fists are clenched; he's vibrating. He's still fuming, anger dripping off his person in waves so thick it's palpable.

I pull back from him slightly, so I can see his face again. His lips quiver. His eyes are still full of so much venom. I need to calm him down. I need to do *something*. Placing my hands on his cold cheeks, I lift up on my knees, and I pull his mouth to mine. His body stiffens as my lips find his cold ones, but I don't waver.

He doesn't kiss me back, even though I feel the tension in him begin to dissolve. His body slackens. Then, he brings a hand to my hair, the way he would have in the past, and he runs his fingers through it. His touch settles my nerves, and I take in a calming breath, still unnerved by this entire situation but finding solace in his comfort.

"You kissed me," he deadpans.

"You took multiple bullets for me," I fire back.

"You *kissed* me."

"Yes, it is a thing that people do sometimes."

"Before this, you had kissed approximately zero people in the last fifteen years."

"Approximately zero isn't a thing, Adam," I say, smirking. "And I'm not sure whether to be flattered or scared by the fact you know this. Especially given that you told me earlier this evening I should have moved on with my life. Maybe you need to follow your own advice?"

"I said what I said because I hate seeing you unhappy. You still have a life to live."

"And you don't?"

"My life ended a long time ago," he says. "There's nothing left. What remains of me is nothing but a hollow, empty soul."

I raise a brow. "A hollow, empty soul that whisked me away to the underworld to save my life."

He doesn't respond, and I feel in my gut that we've yet again hit a wall. Instead, I move forward, hoping to find practical answers.

"What happens if I fall back asleep?" I ask. "Will anyone try to kill me again?"

"I'm sleeping here tonight. On the floor," is his response, voice still on edge. "I'll sense the next one if they show; it's how I knew to come in earlier."

"Don't sleep on the floor," I sigh. "We're adults, and it isn't like we've never shared a bed before."

I think of the summer between my freshman and sophomore year of college. Some girl had broken up with Adam, some girl he really cared about—which both upset me to see him so out of sorts but also filled me with a secret relief. The relief part made me feel especially guilty when I found him crying in his room, alone. In the process of comforting him, we'd fallen asleep together on his bed, fully clothed.

Adam lets out a soft breath. "I don't feel pain the same way any longer. It's of no consequence to me whether I sleep on the floor or on a mattress. That's the irony of having items that formerly brought comfort. They haven't been provided to us for our benefit but rather to mock us, like most things here."

"Then, sleep on the bed because it will make me feel less afraid."

Adam searches me, staring at me with question in his eyes. I can tell he's mulling this over, weighing my request in his head.

"Okay," he says, as he's slipping off his shoes. "To better protect you, I'll remain in the bed."

I can tell in his tone that the idea of being right next to me has calmed him down. He already seems less worried. As I lay back, I take him with me, and it's the most natural thing in the world for me to curl up in his arms as we settle into the mattress.

"I missed you," I admit, voice gentle.

"You know I know." He plants a soft, tender kiss against the crown of my head.

"Sometimes, I swore I felt you."

"Did you?" Half of his lip slightly curls. The closest I've seen him come to smiling.

"Unless, of course, it was you." I take one of his hands in mine, and I begin to trace my finger along each of his.

He's silent for a moment. Then, he says, "I made a promise to you once. I don't break my promises."

His fingers wrap around mine, and our eyes connect.

"And this is why, before tonight," I say, "I've kissed approximately zero people."

There's unresolved longing in my heart as I stare into his dark eyes. Somewhere in there, I know Adam still exists. He's there, and I will never let him go.

Leaning toward him, I brush my lips against his once more. Cool lips remain frozen, unmoving, once again not kissing me back. I kiss him again.

"Tell me to stop," I say, "and I will."

He's silent. But desire flashes through his eyes, and that's enough for me to keep going. So, I persist, planting yet another soft kiss—hardly kissing him at all, more grazing his mouth than anything. His eyes flutter shut, and I swear I feel his face increase in temperature. His ice cold lips warm slightly. It must be my heightened emotions, or the fact I know our time is limited and I haven't seen him in forever, but I roll on top of him. Snaking my arms around the back of his neck, I lean down to meet his face. Then, I place another soft kiss against his mouth.

"Tell me what happened to you," I whisper against his lips.

"Tell me why you're doing this. This isn't like you."

"Do you really not know? Has it never been obvious?"

His eyes search mine, confusion at their core.

"Tell me what happened," I repeat.

"What difference does it make?"

"I want to know. And you're clearly not dead. Between the blood and a beating heart. So, what are you really? Half dead? Mostly alive? Somewhere in between?"

"Somewhere in between, I guess, in a body with heightened sensory perception," he murmurs against my mouth, lightly sucking on my lower lip as he does. "Now, tell me what's going on here, before I start acting out all my fantasies."

"I'm not sure I'm following," I say. "Fantasies of whom?"

He arches a brow before throwing my words back at me, "'Do you really not know? Has it never been obvious?'"

My heart races, and I let out a sharp breath. His hands begin to play with a button on my pajama tops. But then his eyes snap open, and he abruptly halts.

"Shit." His voice hitches. "This... I can't do this."

"Yes," I say, "yes, you can."

I fall into this moment, slipping my hands beneath his shirt, as I remain on top of him. My fingers trace the skin above his belly button, feeling abs that have been defined since before Montecito. Between the times I'd seen him in swim trunks and the times I'd accidentally walked in on him shirtless in his room, I know his chest well.

I plant another kiss on his lips, and I feel his body relax, sinking into my touch, contrasting from the way he seems to want to fight against this.

He swallows, his jaw clenching. "I'm not supposed to want this."

"But you do?" I ask, hoping with all my heart that he answers in the affirmative.

In response, he works his hands up to my face and gingerly cups my chin. My limbs loosen, and I'm like puddy in this man's embrace. He's staring into my eyes, torment raging through him, laced with both terror and desire.

"I need you to help me stop," he says with a controlled voice, "while I still can."

"And what if I don't want you to?"

"You should," he says. "I'm no better than anyone else here now. I've taken countless souls. Sent them places that, if you knew the half of, you'd never speak to me again."

"Bad souls," I say, starting to unbutton his shirt.

"Bad souls," he echoes, his eyes gazing at my hands on one of the buttons.

He lets out a low moan as I begin to grind against his lap, his erection growing. His opened shirt reveals his chest, and he slips out of the top. Adam cradles me in his arms and lifts me up. Before I know it, we're against the headrest, where he straddles my body, now on the bottom, his covered erection pressed against my clothed groin. A rush fills me, and I can't help the slight smile that tugs at my lips.

He drapes over me, pressing his nose to mine.

"Is this what you want?" he asks huskily.

"Perhaps without the clothing."

He grins. Then, helps me slip out of mine first, the top and the bottom. While I'm pulling off my underwear and bra, he's shimmying out of his pants and boxers. And then he returns to me, crushing his lips against mine passionately, finding my lips with a fever I've never seen from him before. Our mouths hungrily meet, in a rapid succession of sensual kiss after sensual kiss. My core loosens, grows wet for him, begs for his touch.

Stradling me once more, he lets out a shallow breath.

I guide him inside of my body, expecting him to feel cool, like the rest of him. It's only then that I notice his entire body has warmed, and it is heat that fills my insides. Only then that I notice that the blacks of his eyes have morphed into something closer to their normal state, the way he was before. His soft browns gaze down at me with a mixture of longing and care, the way they have at certain times in our past, as his moves up and down. I'm gyrating my hips against him, and we're both breathing heavily, gasping for air.

His forehead touches mine as we move together, pleasure caressing my core.

"I've missed you," I say through another moan, "with all my heart."

He leans in and kisses me passionately, his tongue exploring my mouth as we continue to move in a rhythm like we're two souls that are really one. As our bodies become more entwined, I can feel my heart racing with a mix of excitement and fear. We've never been together like this, and I worry this will be the first and last time.

But as his lips travel down my neck and his fingers dig into my hips, my worries fade to the background. His touch ignites a fire within me that can't be quenched, and I won't ever be able to shake him from my core. Whatever happens next, I know that much to be true.

He pulls me in close as we reach the peak of our passion. I feel him let loose inside of me, squeezing my body as he releases. My mouth opens into an *o*, and I'm right behind him, the explosion causing my body to stiffen momentarily.

His arms snake up my sides, and he holds me in his arms, nibbling on my nose. Slipping under the covers, we naturally wrap around the other, our legs threaded.

Adam presses his forehead to mine, his soft brown eyes looking at me with longing.

He smiles, his lips turning up at the corners as he leans in to kiss me again. It's a slow, tender kiss, filled with all the love and longing we've been holding inside for so long. I haven't seen him smile like this since we've reconnected. Somehow, it feels like the real Adam's returning. The one I've loved for most of my life.

I reach my arms around his neck, pulling him closer.

"Adam," I breathe, my smile wide. "You look... human again."

His eyes fill with uncertainty. "I don't know what's happening... I... it's like all this weight has lifted from me."

With a playful grin, he rolls us over in the bed, so that he's flat on his back and I'm in his arms. He tugs me to his chest, running a soft hand through my hair as he gazes upon me with great care.

"Do you see now, why there could never be anyone else?" I whisper, my heart swelling with love, as tears prick my eyes. "I never wanted to be apart from you. I... I've always loved you."

I squeeze my eyes shut, tasting my warm tears as they silently slide down my face.

His gaze softens as he collects my tears. "I had no idea. All those years?"

"Almost all of them, yes."

He smiles, lips brushing against mine softly. "I wish I had known."

"You know now," I say, the harsh reality of our circumstances hitting me hard. "Even though I could fall asleep at any time and a demon could come and kill me."

"You know I will not let that happen to you, Aelia," he says, planting another kiss on my lips. "I love you too damn much."

As if to prove his retained abilities, he fades from view, and I feel his entire essence wrap around me.

"Any demon that tries to hurt you will face my wrath," he says.

He returns, his physical presence reappearing.

Then, he kisses me once more as I sink into his embrace, not sure of where we go from here. But knowing full well that no matter what happens, from now on, we would handle the future together.

Rogue

LM Wilson

Never turn your back on a wolf in love.

BLURB

I hate him. I want him.

Byron MacDire, aka Mac, is the bane of my existence. He's the guy who drives me crazy. The guy who makes me want to be a better person. He's the guy I want to kill. Preferably while having a hot make out session... Okay so I spiralled, but can you blame me? The guy is a walking contradiction. He's hot as sin, got a body that belongs on a god and he's a freaking goodie-two-shoes. A nark. A suck up, who will do anything to get on the good side of teachers, my dad, everyone.

Well, everyone except me. The guy is an... Okay, okay, I'll wind it back a bit.

Mac and I have a history.

Not like that!

We've never even kissed. Eww... No, our history is far more complicated than that. You see, my name is Nina Hart, I'm the bad girl who wrecked his million dollar car. I'm the girl who stuffed his locker full of spiders on a dare.

How was I to know the jerk was afraid of spiders?

The guy hates me, so why does he follow me?

What secret does he hide that makes him so intriguing to me.

He ruined my life and yet, I can't stay away from him!

He's a monster, yet I'm falling for him. I blame it on the tropical island paradise.

prologue

MAC

I've been trying to figure out how to get myself out of this mess for two years - not only is the girl I'm in love with going to be my stepsister, but I can't even tell her that she's my mate. If my father ever found out that my mate is a human, he'd kill us both.

What do I do? I bully my mate and drive a wedge between us, of course.

Father set me up with his pick of girls after I refused to tell him who my mate is. All shifters are unable to shift until they meet their mates, it's the only reason he knew I had found her. He doesn't even care who she is, just so long as the next Alpha has a mate and will be able to continue the bloodline. The hardest part is that I can't stand the spoilt girl he set me up with. Kara Phillips is the kind of girl who will do anything for power. She treats me like I'm her ticket to the big time. She's always dragging me around and demanding I do romantic things at school. She throws the biggest tantrums if I refuse her PDA and sleeps around with more guys than I can count when I refused to hang out with her outside of school. She's only supposed to be a scapegoat, a way to keep my father from breathing down my neck, yet she acts like she owns me.

My father didn't help matters either, the moment he heard that mother was remarrying, he used his Alpha authority to force me into sabotaging her relationship. He even went so far as to have me investigate who she was marrying and try to mess with his family.

I'm starting to wonder if Father knows the truth about who my mate is.

I have to protect my mate, even if it means making her hate me forever.

one

NINA

Mac struts through the halls of Drace Hart Academy like he owns the place. He wears perfectly tailored suits, coifs his hair to perfection and is always surrounded by a gaggle of giggling girls. He is handsome and wealthy and has an aura that screams smug entitlement that drives me crazy.

He stands a head above the rest of the crowd with his glossy dark hair falling into his eyes and framing his face. His wire-rimmed glasses perch on the bridge of his nose, accentuating his striking green eyes. As he scans the room, those same eyes seem to draw people in, offering an almost irresistible promise of kindness and understanding.

He's not kind though. He's a monster.

Word to the wise, never trust a guy who is smart and good looking.

He's an asshole. A complete and utter douche canoe with

perfectly formed lips and shaggy hair that flops into his eyes. I just don't understand what everyone sees in him.

I mean, he's not *that* good looking. He has a toned physique, washboard abs, and biceps that bulge beneath his tight-fitted shirts. He often sweeps his girlfriend off her feet with one arm as they embrace passionately, her tiny frame suspended in the air. Standing at an impressive six-foot-five, he towers over everyone.

In school, Mac and his girlfriend are the envy of everyone. Everywhere they go it's as if no one else exists – he drapes his arm around her shoulders, she tucks her hand into the pocket of his jeans and they' share quick, passionate kisses in the hallway. But the school day ends, and the real story begins to unfold. She has late night meetings with other boys, while he keeps to himself; never once does Mac acknowledge the whispers of infidelity or bring up her suspicious behaviour. It's as if he's wearing blinders when it comes to her.

I should know, I've spent the last two years living next door to the asshole. Every day after school he runs home and spends his waking hours holed up in his bedroom or lounging by the pool in his backyard; swiping his phone with one hand and sipping Redbull with the other. *Not that I've been keeping an eye on him or anything.*

Nope, I can't stand the jerk. Mac is nothing special. Not to me anyway.

∾

My name is emblazoned above the entranceway, engraved in gold and staring back at me.

Drace Hart Academy is my grandfather's legacy, when he passed it was placed into a trust fund that will release to me when I turn twenty-one. Boy, did that piss my father off. He thought for sure he'd end up owning the school.

Although it is unfamiliar territory to me, I can already tell that running a school isn't something that will come easily or without challenges. For my grandfather's sake, I will take over the school, but that doesn't mean I have to like my father being in charge right now. He took over running the school until I turn twenty-one, the age I'll legally be able to take control of it.

I'm known as the 'bad girl', which isn't entirely accurate. Sure, I played some harmless tricks on the school bullies and I may have gotten a few tattoos, but that doesn't make me a bad person.

I never used to be this way. Until the night my mother was killed, I was a model daughter and student – diligent with school work, quiet, never touching cigarettes or alcohol, and didn't use more than a few swear words. But that all changed when she drove down that road. The car accident happened too quickly for anyone to make sense of it – according to the investigators, she hadn't stood a chance.

Dad had promised to pick my mother up so she wouldn't have to drive so late at night, and instead she died in an instant.

My mind is brought back to Mac, who's dressed in a neatly pressed shirt and khakis today, he's the picture of absolute perfection, but the sneer on his face tells another story. His eyes dart around the room, taking in every detail of the people around him as if he's looking for someone to accuse or tattle on.

He's a two-faced snake - all charm and politeness at first glance, but a cruel heart underneath. Every time our eyes meet in the waiting room, I feel my stomach knot up with anger and resentment.

My shoulders tense, and my eyes burn with frustration. I've been waiting for Mac's girlfriend to finish telling her lies to my father. She's never liked me and has made no real effort to hide it. Every time our paths cross, she stares daggers at me, like I've committed some unforgivable crime. But I've never done anything to her, so what is her problem?

I sigh heavily, my breath catching in my throat. When I shoot a questioning look towards Mac, he avoids my gaze, his expression as unreadable as ever. Just like always when we're in school, he refuses to meet my eye or answer any of the questions that simmer on the tip of my tongue.

I don't know what I ever did to piss him off. To make him hate me so much that my discomfort amuses him, but it's been like this for two years. Two years of torture at the hands of a guy everyone else thinks is a good guy.

He's not. Byron McDire is an asshole.

He fidgets in the seat next to me, and my skin tingles when our arms brush together. I can feel the warmth emanating from him, radiating through my clothes. With that single moment of contact, my body betrays me; Tingles race up my spine, causing goosebumps to erupt across my flesh. The worst part is, the reaction doesn't stop there. No, I'm tortured with butterflies in my stomach and a throbbing between my legs. But why do I desire something from someone who despises me with a fervour that eclipses all other feelings?

"You know you'll probably get expelled for your latest prank," he says with a smirk.

I freeze from the shock – he's talking to me? My pulse races, and I fight the urge to react to him. With a tremulous breath, I plaster on an expression of disbelief and raise my brows in challenge. "I haven't pulled any pranks lately," I manage, surprised at how strong my voice sounds despite the trembling in my chest.

The door to my father's office finally opens, only it's not my father who emerges first, it's Kara wearing a smug grin. She struts out of the office, leaving the door wide open and stands in front of Mac.

From my vantage point, I can see my father push himself out of his chair, the leather creaking in protest as he straightens to his full height. His face is a mask of barely restrained fury, and he enunciates my name with a sharpness that cuts through the air like a blade. His terse —"Nina"—is enough to convey every bit of anger he is trying to hold back. I want to stand up for myself, tell him to shove it and find out what Mac had said. But experience has warned me this isn't the best moment to do so; it's better to hear him out before his anger consumes him.

Of course, I never was very good at taking my own advice. "I did nothing wrong." I uncross my arms and try not to glare at him, trying to look less defiant and as innocent as possible.

My jaw is tight, and my eyes wide; but I'm not sure how convincing it looks—especially since I'm usually lying when this expression is directed his way. But no, this time I'm telling the truth. I had no part in causing trouble with Mac's girlfriend.

The Bitch, Kara Phillips is an unmistakeable figure in the school hallway with her bleached blonde hair, cheerleader uniform, and entourage of admirers. Everyone knows she's the head cheerleader and head of the debate team, but what most people don't know is that she isn't quite living up to her good girl image. She's often spotted at parties puffing away on cigarettes and sipping drinks while flirting shamelessly with guys, social media really doesn't allow for secrets.

My dad's voice hums in my ear like a drone as I study Kara. Her thin lips are pulled into a triumphant smirk and her sharp eyes glint menacingly. My mind races with possibilities. Why does she keep targeting me? I don't deserve this treatment. She cocks her hip, no doubt relishing in the power she believes she holds over me.

My father's voice fades into the background as I cross my arms, pushing my breasts up in indignation. Mac's eyes flicker from my breasts to the girl he's holding, but it's clear where his attention lies. My gaze narrows and the temperature in the room drops a few degrees. Kara whispers something into Mac's ear, but Mac's focus doesn't waver, he continues to stare directly at my chest, despite Kara hissing furiously into his ear. If my dad wasn't here right now, I'd wipe that lustful look off Mac's face with a single punch.

Kara grabs Mac's arm, her face a mask of impatience as her

fingers dig into his skin. He stumbles along behind her, tripping over himself to keep up. I watch them go with a raised eyebrow - why was Mac even here? Did he just come to watch Kara get me into trouble?

A sigh escapes me and I shake my head before turning away.

"I can't believe you would do something so cruel. I thought I raised you better than that." Whatever the bitch has accused me of must be really bad; dad's face has gone bright red. My dad's a good-looking man I guess, he's a lot like I am; dark auburn hair, his is close cropped where mine is past my shoulders. He has coffee-coloured eyes, where I have blue ones like my mother's. I wasn't lucky enough to inherit his height though; he's six feet, where I'm only five-seven.

"Seriously Nina, how could you?" I raise my brows in question. I still have no idea what I supposedly did this time. "Do you have any idea how dangerous that is? You could have hurt her really badly."

"I didn't do anything." My voice goes up an octave. I'm ready to shout and scream at him to just listen to me for once, but then he says the last thing I was expecting, "Oh, so you expect me to believe that her locker was just magically filled with smoke bombs?"

I burst out laughing, which does not help my case any, but come on - someone filled her locker with smoke bombs. That's classic and I really wish it had been me. I'd have loved to see the bitch's face when they went off.

"It's not funny Nina! I have to suspend you for two days."

My head snaps up to look at him. He can't be serious. "Two days? But it wasn't even me."

"Get your stuff and go home."

I growl curses under my breath as I pick up my bag. "This isn't fair. I always get blamed for shit I didn't do."

"Watch your language." Dad points his meaty finger in my face.

"Why? Is it going to do a party trick?" I cock my hip to the side and give him a shit-eating grin.

Dad's face is hilarious; he's redder than a tomato and you can see the veins on his temples throbbing, but I'm trying to do my best to hold in my laughter. If he catches me laughing again, it'll only make things worse. Besides, I really want to remain ungrounded. Derik Thane is throwing a party this weekend and his parties are epic.

"Don't get smart with me young lady."

"Isn't that the whole point of school? To get smart?" My voice cracks as a laugh escapes.

"Nina Joline Hart!" Ooh, I'm so scared now, he used my full name. Rolling my eyes to the ceiling again, I turn my back on my dad and walk out of the office. He calls after me, "And you're grounded for the next week." I don't want to be grounded, but I just don't give enough of a damn about him to bother acknowledging him.

I know I'm being a bitch, but I don't care. My dad deserves everything he gets. If it hadn't been for him, mum might still be alive. He was supposed to pick her up from her night classes and drive her to my play that night. He didn't because he was '*too busy at work*'. Which is a load of bullshit, I'm sure he was really holed up in a hotel somewhere banging his secretary.

Yeah, my dad's a cliché; sleeping with his employee. He swears it didn't start until after mum died but I don't believe him. You don't ask someone to marry you four months after your wife dies unless you're A- expecting a kid (which considering they've been engaged for two years now and still no kid, I think we can rule that out), or B- have been seeing the person for a hell of a lot longer than they're admitting. In a way I'm kind of glad they haven't tied the knot already.

Look I get it, people deal with their grief in different ways. Some move on right away, some mourn for years and some don't even wait for the body to go cold before jumping into bed with someone new. But seriously, why does it have to be his secretary? Why does it have to be Mac's mother?

Mac and I haven't gotten along in years. All because I sort of, maybe, kind of, destroyed his brand new Aston Martin Roadster....

Rain pounded the pavement and lightning lit up the sky as I made my way through the night. I heard thunder in the distance and tried to ignore the sinking feeling of dread inside me. My tires fought for traction on the slick roads as I rounded a sharp corner, but just then a streak of white light illuminated a car ahead of me that had crossed over into my lane. The sound of metal grinding against metal reverberated in my ears as my motorbike skidded wildly out of control, only to be slammed by an oncoming car moments later.

The crunch of metal filled the air as my bike collided with the car, sending me flying off and tumbling across the road. I heard the horrified shrieks of the woman in the passenger seat; her pale face framed by a curtain of blond hair was frozen in shock. Even through my helmet I could feel the impact of the crash, and, when the ambulance came, they had to cut me out of my leather jacket. The couple in the car, Mac and Kara, fared better; they only needed some stitches after my handlebars went through their window. Despite it all, no one was seriously injured or arrested, although I did lose my license for riding while under the influence of alcohol.

You see? Mac has a good reason to hate me.

But that's okay, the feeling is mutual. His bullying ruined my life after all.

I've been holed up in my room for two days, snacking on chips and gummy bears while playing the latest video game. Whenever I needed a break, I picked up one of the romance novels I bought last week and got lost in their worlds of forbidden love and longing. Dad thought he was punishing me by suspending and grounding me, but nope, he just gave me two days off with no homework and no one to annoy me.

Of course, he did take my motorbike keys and hide them in his home office, but they weren't that hard to find. I creep out the door, stifling a nervous giggle as I thought of outsmarting my dad. The keys to my beloved motorcycle jangling in my pocket.

It's been months since I was last able to ride it; if my father found out, there would be hell to pay. Father's been on a no motorbike kick for the last few months. You'd think he would've been that way after I crashed the old one, but no, he waited until I got a new motorbike and cracked down on me about riding it. Three months ago he punctured my tyre just to stop me from leaving. Took me this long to save up enough for a new tyre.

The wind whips through my hair as I ride across town towards the pet store, anticipation building with each twist of the handle. After buying what I needed, I made my way back home, knowing that this time, they really will be able to blame me for the prank.

The sun peeked out from the horizon and its rays lit up the sky in a hue of golden yellow. I hopped down the stairs heading towards the front door, practically skipping with joy. My house was built at the end of a cul-de-sac, with only three other houses. Mac and his mum, Dee lived next door, and Layla Forentes and her family were two doors away. At the end of the block was the Taylor's house where Elise and Grace Taylor lived with their two older twin brothers, Ranger and Hunter. The twins were Mac's best friends and were at university. The Taylor twins used to run with a wilder crowd at school before tragedy struck their family – four years ago their parents perished in an unexpected fire that destroyed their home across town. Since then, the girls had moved in with their brothers.

Opening my front door, I see Mac trudging down the driveway; his head bowed low and his shoulders slumped. I watch him from my doorway and a wave of concern sweeps over me. He hasn't noticed me yet, so I step out onto the porch and call out "Hey Mac." He stops in his tracks—I can tell he's surprised I'm talking to him.

"I'm not in the mood Nina." My jaw hits the ground. It's not like Mac to pass up an opportunity to torture me.

"Something wrong?" I ask.

"Yeah, our parents are engaged." His anger is palpable.

"I'm not happy about it either, you know." He just stands there, staring at me like he's seeing me for the first time. His sparkling green eyes hold curiosity now instead of the anger I saw before. My heart skips a beat as he changes direction and walks towards me.

"Want to walk together?" He asks as he leans on the fence separating our two properties.

A walk with Mac, that's a disaster in the making. A more optimistic part of me pipes up with, *or it could be good to get to know him a bit better. This might be our only chance before the stupid wedding.* It's not the first time Mac and I have spent time alone together; we've been forced to do family stuff together in the past, but it is the first time he's initiated anything. Normally at family events, he's polite, kind even, but the moment others are around, it's like a switch flips.

"Sure, I guess, but why are you walking? Where's your car?"

"My father took it away." Is all he says in response. I know better than to question things. The quickest way to piss Mac off is to mention his father. I found that out the hard way when we were forced to have dinner over the last lot of school holidays. He practically bit my head off just for asking if he was going to his dad's for the holidays.

The walk to school isn't a long one, but the silence that stretches between us makes it feel like it's taking forever. When we reach the gates, Mac goes left, and I go right. Neither of us giving any indication that we just walked to school together or that we know each other outside of school.

My classes are so boring that I spend most of my time playing with my phone. Dad messages me about halfway through my English class. I shake my head at the message on my screen.

Dad: Byron has his phone off, he needs to go back to Andersons Formal Attire. His measurements are off. Dee wants everything perfect for the big day. Could you pass along the message when you see him next?

I sit there playing games while trying to find a way to pass on the message without having to deal with the asshole version of Mac.

Mac walks passed the door of my classroom and my heart leaps in my chest. This is my chance. If I talk to him now, there won't be anyone else around. I hate how he acts like two different people. So nice and like a real person when we're alone but his normal asshole self when other people are around. With my mind made up, I stand up and grab my bag off the floor.

"Where do you think you're going Miss Hart?" Mr. Roles snaps his fingers like an idiot, trying to get a response out of me.

"Bathroom." I growl. I don't have time for his stupid argumentative ass right now.

"You can wait until after class."

"Yeah, no. I'm going." I gather my things, fully intending to not return to this class. Mr. Roles is such an asshole. All he cares about is getting his lessons out. He doesn't give a shit if anyone actually learns anything. When I take over this school, he'll be the first one of these asshole teachers to go.

"Miss Hart, get your ass back in this classroom right now!"

"God you're such a nestle-cock."

"What did you just call me?" Mr. Roles' face is bright red. He looks like one of those cartoon characters that have steam coming out of their ears. I can hear the class snickering at Mr. Roles' reaction and it only makes me smile.

"Go teach something or did you forget who actually pays your fucking cheques?" I wave my hand dismissively over my shoulder and hurry down the hall.

Mac is just coming out of the bathroom when I finally find him. "Mac, I have a message from my father." I pause, unsure if I should just give him the message or find out why he has his phone switched off.

"Well, you going to tell me or just stand there all day?"

Well, that solves that issue. Why should I care what his problems are if he's going to be like that? "Fuck you!"

"Was that the message, because I have to say, it's not very eloquent." This guy makes me want to punch him right in the mouth. My eyes go straight to said mouth, more precisely his puffy bottom lip that he's now chewing on. I've always been curious if kissing him would be good. If the feel of his thick lips would make the kiss more pleasurable or if they'd just make it feel weird.

Quit it Nina, just give him the stupid message and walk away. One fuck up this week is enough.

"God you're such an asshole." I huff trying to expel all thoughts of kissing, "Fine, whatever. Dad wanted me to tell you that you need to go back to the suit place, something about the fit being off or whatever." With my message delivered, I turn my back and start walking towards the cafeteria. "Oh, turn your fucking phone back on so I don't have to relay any more messages." I toss the words over my shoulder. Mac's hand landing heavily on my shoulder halts my steps. The warmth from his skin seeps into me. That heat pools in places I don't want to mention.

"Is this what it's going to be like from now on?"

My breath hitches as he whispers right in my ear. It'd be so easy, just a slight turn of my head. Those thick pillowy lips would be on mine in an instant. "I don't know what the fuck you're on about." I snap pulling away from his touch. I am such an idiot, getting turned on by a simple touch from an asshole like him.

"Nina." My stupid traitor eyes close of their own accord. Why does he have this effect on me?

The bell rings before he can say whatever it is that he was going to say. Students start filling the halls and the asshole returns to his former self.

Raising his voice, he pushes me away from him as he says, "Watch it Nina, people might start to believe you actually care about something other than yourself."

I don't bother responding, he's only being an asshole to impress everyone else. At least that's what I keep telling myself as I make my way to his girlfriend's locker. It takes me less than a second to open the mint container and push it through the holes of the locker. I can't help the snicker that leaves my mouth as I walk away.

Two Days Later

"Nina, get down here, we need to talk." Groaning, I throw off my covers and climb out of bed. Just to annoy dad for interrupting my sleep, I stomp heavily on the stairs.

"You sound like a herd of elephants."

My scream can be heard from miles away. I'm sure of it. Once my heart has stopped trying to beat its way out of my chest, I turn to face the asshole himself. "Parade."

"What?"

"It's a parade of elephants." *Urgh, why did I say that? Who cares what a group of elephants is called.*

"You're so weird."

My fingers curl into a fist. My mother's voice floats into my mind; *Use your words Nina, not your fists.* "Right back at ya, asshole."

The cocky asshole pushes me against the wall, leans right in and whispers, "One of these days, you'll learn to love me."

"Not fucking likely." I growl pushing him away from me.

"Nina! Watch your language." Dad growls as he comes into the hallway from the loungeroom.

"Can we just get this over with, I want to go back to bed."

"Not happening. We're going on a trip. All of us. Pack your suitcase with clothes suitable for tropical weather." Dad starts to turn away, "Oh, and Nina, no weapons."

"What? I would never." I bat my lashes at my dad, all while trying to figure out how I'm going to sneak my pocketknife onto the plane.

"Liar." Mac hisses. I narrow my gaze at him, wishing with all my heart that I could make him drop dead with a thought alone. "Can we bring a plus one Mr. Hart?"

"Suck up."

"At least I have friends."

"Yeah well, I hear money can buy you just about anything these days." I laugh as I walk away. I really don't want to admit it, but I'm starting to enjoy our little back and forth. He might be an asshole, but he's got wit.

Mac brought a plus one alright; he brought his stupid girlfriend. The first time I think anyone has seen them together outside of school and it just happens to be our "Family" trip to some island off the coast of Fiji. They've been sitting across the aisle from me the entire flight, Kara giggling like she's high and him looking so uncomfortable that I almost want to offer the seat beside me just so he can get a break from her incessant laughing.

"Ladies and Gentleman, if you'll please fasten your seatbelts, I'm afraid we've run into a storm and will be experiencing a bit of minor turbulence." The woman on the speaker sounds like she's ready to put on a parachute and jump. I grip the arm rest of my seat, turning my knuckles white as the plane is jostled.

"Are you okay Nina?" Mac asks, leaning across the aisle.

I shake my head, "Not really."

"I guess that means you don't like it rough huh?" The huge grin on Mac's face is full of mischief and brings out those dimples.

I groan. "Real fu-." I don't get to finish, thunder booms, drowning out all other sounds. A chilling creak sounds from my left. Everything feels like it's going topsy turvy as the plane dips nose down. My entire body is thrown forward as my seatbelt catches me. The raging of the storm outside is nothing compared to the smell now filling the cabin.

Smoke.

I smell smoke. I'm trapped in an airplane with no land in

sight and I smell smoke.

Rain batters the windows, making it impossible to see. The plane shudders then tilts too far to the left. Something splashes against the window on Mac's side or the plane. "That's not rain." I scream as straw-coloured liquid sprays onto the window.

Lightning flashes and is instantly followed by another boom before the fuel on the wing catches alight. My scream is lodged in my throat as the plane tips the other way.

My eyes meet green ones across the aisle as the plane flips over. All gravity is gone. It rights itself again and Mac unbuckles his belt while the hyena aka his girlfriend starts screaming. Staggering with the movement of the plane, Mac drops into the seat next to me. Quickly doing up the belt. A strong set of hands clamp down on mine, pulling me down between the seats. "Keep your head down Nina." He says something else but it's lost to the sound of my ears popping painfully. My stomach recoils from the fast plummet, threatening to bring up the little food I have in it.

The plane levels out again, giving me hope that despite the fire still raging on the wing and at the rear of the plane, we might just survive this. The orange oxygen masks drop from the ceiling, mine smacking me in the face.

A bright light and boom at the same time have my heart leaping out of my throat. I can't catch my breath. The belt digs into my stomach. A heavy weight covers my head and arms.

The last thing I hear before everything goes black is Mac's voice, "I've got you Nina."

~

I wake up to Mac hovering over me. His hands poised above my chest. "Breathe, just breathe." My hands are in water, my body propped up on the wing of the plane. Rain continues to pour down all around me. I cough, puking all over the metal beneath me.

"You're okay Nina. I've got you." Steal arms band around my middle, holding me tight enough to squeeze the precious air from my burning lungs. Nothing is okay. I want to laugh but my body can't even bring itself to do that. Mac sees the panic in my eyes the moment I'm able to move my numb limbs. "Where's the rest of the plane?" I sit up, rocking the wing and dislodging Mac's arms. Water splashes over me and I scream. "Where's everyone else?"

"Just stay still. Don't worry about everyone else right now. Just keep breathing. Please." The desperation in his voice is enough to stop the scream from leaving my lips. "I'm sure they're swimming to shore as we speak." He grabs my hand, holding tight. "Do you think you could swim?" It's not really a question. There's a steal undercurrent to his voice, like he's really saying, that even if I couldn't swim, I don't really have a choice. "I saw an island over there when we were falling." Mac points to his left, but all I see is more rain crashing down on the rough waves.

Rain falls steadily on my face as I glance around us, trying to figure out how I could make it far enough to reach land when I'm not the best swimmer. I never really went swimming very often. There's only one place to swim back home and I found the idea of swimming in a river with unknown creatures beneath the surface daunting to say the least. A silver case floats past and I grab onto it. "This floats; I think I can use it as a paddle board." I slide off the wing into the frigid water. Gripping the case with all my strength as the waves threaten to drag me under. I flinch when another lightning strike booms all around us.

"Stay close, okay?" Mac shouts over the storm. He grabs the strap on the silver case that's keeping me afloat and loops it around his arm. All I can do is nod numbly as he begins kicking and churning the chaotic waters with swimming strokes that pull us both in the direction he pointed earlier.

I've always thought the ocean was a beautiful beast. The way the waves crash and kiss the shore always put me in mind of those old poems about lovers playing in the game of push and pull before finding their ultimate rhythm together.

But as I feebly kick my legs through its churning waters, all I can think is how the poets got it wrong. The ocean isn't like a lover, it's more like a murderer. Selecting its victims with no reasoning. It's ebb and flow nothing more than unadulterated fury threatening to drag even the strongest of swimmers beneath its inky depths.

It feels like we're swimming across the entire world. No land in sight. My limbs feel heavy the longer we keep going. I have no idea how much time has passed since we started swimming as the sky is still a broiling mess of dark clouds interspersed with the occasional streak of lightning. The rain hasn't stopped for even a second while we've been swimming. I'm too tired to keep going. Too stubborn to stop moving my legs even though I don't think I'm gaining any distance through the choppy waters.

My foot hits something and for a moment I freak out. My heart pounds so hard, I swear it's louder than the crashing waves. Thoughts of sharks and other nasty animals swimming beneath me have my entire body freezing in place. I vaguely remember something from watching TV, if a shark comes near you, just stay still. Allow it to pass without touching it or bothering it. After a few seconds where nothing has touched my foot again, I kick out and my foot hits the hard surface. Slowly, with my heart in my throat, I reach my hand down.

Sand.

It's just sand. I let out a small chuckle at my own expense.

We've reached the shore. I could squeal right now if I wasn't so exhausted.

"Come on Nina, just a little further, then we can rest." Mac easily wades through the water, but I just don't have the strength to stand, I wait for the next wave and just float along with it, onto the cold wet sand. Crawling is easier without the box, but the damn thing saved my life, whatever it is, I'm not letting it go.

Debris covers the shoreline for miles in either direction. I tip my head back on the sand, squinting through the darkness. Behind me is a forest of what looks like tropical trees. Everything from coconut palms to... "Is that a banana tree?"

"I guess we won't be starving at least." Mac laughs sitting

up beside me. His hands clench the sand beneath us as though he too was worried that we'd never make it to shore.

"Yeah, cause being trapped on an island with you wasn't bad enough, let's add in diarrhea with no toilet in sight."

"Well, you could always use the toilet on the plane. It's probably still in one piece."

"I'll just take a swim every time I need to go then, shall I?" I shake my head as I climb to my feet. "Not sure the toilet paper would be much good being that its most likely over two-hundred feet below the water though." I state sarcastically. He's laughing, which is not helping my mood any. The asshole hasn't been an asshole for hours now and it just feels wrong. Why can't he just be an asshole, I don't want to see any other sides to him. It's all too much. I feel the warmth of my own tears mixing with the water dripping from my hair, but I keep the sobs locked down. No matter what happens, I won't let him see me as weak.

We wander up the beach a bit, getting further away from the water crashing onto the shore and I literally collapse beside the first tree I find. My eyelids droop as I lean back, watching as Mac drops down beside me.

I don't know how long we were asleep for but when my eyes open next, I have to pinch myself to make sure I'm not still dreaming.

The glow of the sun as it crests the waves is absolutely

breathtaking. The pristine white sands turn to every treasure hunter's golden dream as the sun begins to warm the grains. Streams of light pulse upon the waves making everything glow like an enchantment has been cast upon the world and shining just for me in this moment. It gives me hope even as the warmth from the light begins to settle my shivering body.

"If we're still here to see the sunrise, then perhaps my father and the others are as well. Wherever you are dad, I hope you're seeing this." I whisper as the birds begin to trill their morning songs.

Mac stirs and it's like a switch flips. One second, he's muttering something in his sleep, the next he's wide awake and climbing to his feet with all the energy of a toddler after eating far too much sugar.

As I watch, he stretches his arms above his head, bends down and touches his toes, then pulls his shirt off, dropping it onto the sand at his feet. His wet hair is plastered to his head, and hanging down onto his broad sun-kissed shoulders. The rain must not have let up at all throughout the night as both of us are still soaked through. I don't know how either of us managed to get any sleep, but I'm going to blame the exhaustion. The thought of hyperthermia invades my mind for a split second, but even my macabre thoughts can't drag my gaze away from Mac's shirtless body. He's so toned that his muscles bunch and contract as he wades back into the water and starts pulling bits of wreckage to the shore. I spy a tattoo running across his left shoulder, from here I can't see what it is, but it's weird seeing something so bad-boy on the goodie-two-shoes. He's also lost his glasses somewhere along the way which has me staring at his face almost as much as his body.

I'm usually a pretty laidback person, who doesn't let much bother me. Being stranded on an island, not knowing where my father is, or anyone else who was on the plane is my breaking point. It's been hours and there's still no sign of anyone else. "Should we have stayed with the wing? It was still floating when we left."

"What use would it have done us to stay there when it was being tossed about during the storm?"

"I don't know but the others might have been able to find us easier if we'd stayed."

"And we might have been too exhausted from trying to stay afloat to make it to shore if we had waited."

"You... urgh! You are the last person on Earth I'd want to be stranded with." My voice cracks as my throat burns from the bile clawing its way up. I'm heaving with both the effort of trying not to throw up and the fury burning through me.

"Trust me Princess, you wouldn't be my first choice either!" He shouts back.

For a moment we just stand here staring at each other, then he turns on his heel and walks off down the beach. With a low wordless growl, I turn and walk into the trees, keeping my back to him.

When I return, Mac's going through a pile of stuff he's collected from the ocean. I drop my armload of vines, branches and fronds. I drop to the sand beside him and tinker with the case for a while. No idea what it is inside though. The damn thing is locked up tight with some kind of combination lock. There aren't any numbers on it though so I can't figure it out.

Mac finally takes a break, sitting down beside me in the sand. "Any luck getting that thing open?"

"None. I don't recognise the symbols on the dials. Figuring out the pattern could take years without knowing what each symbol represents."

"Alright well, let's take stock of what we have." Mac starts going through the pile of stuff we've gathered so far.

"Not sure what this was but it might work to make a shelter." He says holding up an orange piece of rubbery plastic sheeting that looks kind of like a slide. "I'm not sure anything in here will be of any use, but it's a first aid kit, so...." He trails off as he pulls a long vine out of the pile. "What are we going to do with this?" He asks, shaking the vine.

"Rope." I grunt.

"It's not strong enough to be rope, look!" He pulls a section and it snaps off.

I give him a look, one that says you're dumber than an ox, "You're supposed to braid it together. That makes it stronger."

"Oh." Is all he mutters as he tosses it back onto the pile. "I found a few empty plastic bottles." He says, changing the subject. "If we find some fresh water we can fill them."

"I wouldn't drink water from the ground. We're in the tropics, you never known what bugs are in it."

"Well then, we'll collect some rain water. Will that appease you princess?"

"Don't be a dick!" I snap, climbing to my feet. "I don't care if you spend your nights crying in agony because you drank worms or bacteria, but I would rather avoid any potential problems."

"Great. Just fucking great! I'm stranded on an island in the middle of the fucking ocean with a germophobe."

"I'm not a germophobe. I'm just not stupid enough to add to our problems when there are better solutions."

"Alright Princess Know-it-all, how do we get fresh water?"

"We collect rainwater and boil it."

"And how do you propose we start a fire? I don't have any matches or a lighter, and I don't think we could just plug a kettle in anywhere around here."

"Yup, I'm done. Good luck." I grab the vines and bundle of fronds and turn my back on the asshole. My feet carry me a fair way down the beach before I realise that I left the silver case behind. I drop everything at my feet and stomp my way back, grabbing the case while growling under my breath about asshole males who think they should be in charge of everything. Mac doesn't say a word as I grab the case and once again, walk away from him.

I drop the case in a nice little area beneath some trees and go into the forest lining the shore. It's peaceful walking among the trees with no sounds of traffic or people. It doesn't take me more than a few hours to gather everything I'll need to build a shelter out of palm leaves, vines and sticks. As I stand back to look over my little shelter, I realise that I built it big enough for two. Not that Mac is welcome here. Okay so if he can't build his own hut, I might take pity on him and allow him to sleep in here tonight, but only if I must.

My stomach growls, reminding me that I haven't had anything to eat since the small packet of peanuts from the flight. I really don't want to be reduced to eating nothing but fruit, but I can't see any other options right now. With a sigh, I gather some low hanging bananas and grab a coconut that sounds like it has plenty of milk inside. It takes me a few tries to tear the husk off the coconut, but I manage just fine on my own. Opening it, however, is a different story. I throw it at a rock on the ground, but the stupid thing remains closed. After several minutes of angrily attacking it with a smaller rock, I give up and toss the coconut onto the ground.

I haven't seen Mac in hours and for some unknown reason, I begin to worry about him. Annoyed at myself for thinking about the annoying douche, I grab the case and fiddle with the symbols. First I try matching them, then I try putting them in sequence, but when that all fails, I just start randomly flipping them. The sudden click of the locks have me squealing.

"What happened? Was it a spider or a snake? Are you alright?"

"Where the hell did you come from?" I snap at Mac as he appears in the entrance of my hut.

After silently looking me over from head to toe, he says, "I wasn't far. Despite you being a royal bitch, I'm not about to let you wonder off on your own when we have no idea what dangers are lurking."

"Let me?" I growl.

"You just have to argue with me about everything, don't you?"

"You're the one who was acting like he's in charge of everything."

"Why did you scream?"

I ignore him as I flip the lid of the case open and peer inside. "Woah." I exclaim as I pull out a sheet of paper. "This thing has everything we'd need. Emergency blanket, canopy, flares, duct tape, knife, firesticks, rope, water purification tablets, fishing kit, first aid kit, fire extinguisher, oxygen bottle, micro megaphone, but what the fuck is a PSE?" I pull each item out until only one is left. A small black and yellow box. The writing on it is faded and unreadable, but there seems to be an on switch. "Do you think this is one of those emergency beacon things?"

"Turn it on, see if it works." Is all he says as he looks curiously at the odd device. Nothing happens when I press the power button. Even after five minutes of staring at it in silence, nothing happens. Rolling my eyes, I put it back into the metal case and grab the pack labelled canopy. Mac doesn't complain or question me as we work together to secure the canopy over the shelter using the thin rope to tie it down at the back and leaving the front section loose. Once it's in place, the inside of the hut begins to warm up to the point where it's almost uncomfortable. "Not sure this was a good idea." I mutter as seat beads on my forehead.

"We'll be grateful for it if it rains again."

"True." I look back at the case before pulling out the bag

labelled fire stick. It's an odd device with what looks like a rough metal rod and a flat silver disc attached to a key ring. Curious, I separate the two items and strike them together. Sparks flare to life making me giggle. "It's like a little sparkler." I say striking it again.

"I'll get some wood, maybe put that thing away for now so you don't set the place on fire."

He's gone for so long that I again begin to worry. Tossing everything back into the case, I close the lid, careful not to latch it before leaving the shelter. The sun beats down on me ferociously as I walk along the beach. I'm not sure what happened to my shoes, but the sand sure feels nice between my toes. After a while, I hear a grunting sound coming from the trees to my left. Curious I follow the sound, winding through the trees carefully. Mac is shirtless still, but its what he's doing that has my eyes glued to him in wonder. He's attached a sharp rock to the end of a thick length of wood and is using it like an axe. He seems stronger than I even imaged he could be. The way his muscles move as he swings it over and over is hypnotising. At least it is until his vine rope snaps and the sharp rock flies off the end landing in the trunk of a tree a few feet away.

"Just fucking great. Stranded on an island with *her*. The moons going to be full in three days and I can't even make a stupid axe to get firewood."

"What does the moon have to do with anything?" I ask, startling him enough that he throws his hands up and the makeshift handle goes over his shoulder.

"Everyone knows full moons bring out the crazies and monsters." He laughs, but I can tell he's hiding something.

"What's so bad about the full moon?" I repeat.

"Nothing, just go gather some sticks or something." He growls, turning his back on me. Leaving the moody bastard to his own devises, I head back the way I came, collecting firewood and sticks along the way. After a few trips back and forth, I manage to collect enough wood to last through the night with some to spare.

The sun begins to set and I start to worry about Mac not returning yet. I finally find him sitting on the beach not far from our camp site. He has his head in his hands, so I can't see his face but the way his shoulders shake tells me that he's really upset. Despite my dislike of him, I move closer, reaching out my hand to touch his shoulder.

"Do you think our parents survived?" His husky voice is barely above a whisper.

"I don't know. I have hope that my father and your mother made it. Hell I even hope that Kara made it to shore somewhere. There's no point in worrying about them when we're stranded here."

"That's true. They've got the better end of the deal. At least wherever they are, they're not stuck with you."

"Asshole." I growl before stomping back to the campsite.

Can't believe I was trying to be nice to that asshole. What was I thinking?

two

Restless

Night falls and Mac returns to the campsite, choosing to lie down on the sand at the front of the canopy instead of actually inside with me. I tell myself I don't care, but I'm lying. I don't want to be alone right now and having a strong, good looking guy to protect me seems like a far better idea than being alone. I pull the silver foil emergency blanket out and look over the instructions to distract myself. It says its for single use only, but it also says you can use it to line the inside of a tent or shelter to aid in keeping the area warm. It doesn't take me long to pin it up on the inside of the shelter. I lay back down, casting a glare at Mac as he shakes his head and rolls over, facing the dwindling fire.

As I lay there, shivering, I can feel the sand digging into my skin. I close my eyes and try to relax, but my mind is racing. I can hear the waves crashing on the shore and the sound of

Mac's breathing. He's asleep now, and I can't help but wonder what he's dreaming about.

Suddenly, I hear a rustling sound coming from the bushes nearby. My heart starts racing as I realize that there's someone or something out there. I sit up and try to make out what it is, but it's too dark to see anything.

"Mac," I whisper, nudging him gently. "Wake up."

He stirs, groggily opening his eyes. "What's wrong?" he mutters.

"I think there's something out there," I reply, pointing towards the back of the shelter.

Mac sits up, immediately alert. "Stay here," he says, grabbing a thick branch off the ground.

"No, I'm coming with you."

"Nina, stay here where it's safe."

"No!"

"For fucks sake Nina, just this once, do as I fucking say." Stunned into silence, I simply sit here watching him disappear into the darkness, feeling both frightened and grateful for his protection. My heart is beating so fast that I can hear it in my ears, and I hold my breath, waiting for something to happen.

Seconds pass, and then minutes. I start to wonder if it was just my imagination, but then I hear a low growling sound. My blood runs cold, and I realize that there really is something out there. I slip out from under the silver blanket, trying to be as quiet as possible, and follow the sound of Mac's footsteps. It feels like it takes forever to reach him, when I finally do, I find him crouched down behind a bush, staring at something near what looks like a stream. Kneeling down beside him, I whisper, "What is it?"

"A pig." My stomach rumbles at his words. "Exactly my thoughts." Mac smirks at my stomach's growling. Ignoring him making fun of my empty stomach, I ask, "How do we catch it?"

"Can pigs swim?"

"I guess we're about to find out. On the count of three, we jump out and chase it into the water." Mac hits three and we both leap out from either side of the bush. The pig squeals, heading right into the water then swims right across to the other side. "Guess that answers that question." Mac laughs while my stomach lets out another hungry growl. "Come on *Beasty*, we'd best get back to camp and feed you before you scare away the bananas and coconuts as well."

"Smartass." I grumble beneath my breath as we head back the way we came. We eat a few pieces of fruit each, then Mac lies back down on his side, this time inside the shelter, close to my side.

Once more I find myself lying restless watching Mac sleep like the dead. He doesn't seem to be bothered much that we're stranded on an island in the middle of nowhere. I, on the other hand am exhausted but unable to even shut my eyes. Every tiny sound in the darkness has me jumping.

An arm wraps around my waist pulling me in against a warm chest. I don't dare move for fear of him pulling away again. I needn't have worried.

Warmth floods me as Mac breathes against my neck. His hand slides from the innocent position of my ribs up to the underside of my boobs. Being that I took my only bra off to sleep and my shirt rode up during my tossing and turning he's now lingering on the verge of touching me in places only one person has gone before.

My heart beats faster the higher he goes until he's full on cupping my boob in his warm hand. "Tell me to stop." His whispered words should pull me from my daze but they have the opposite effect. I turn to face him, letting my hands roam over his toned body before he pushes my hands away. "I need you." Mac doesn't waste any more time on words, he lifts my shirt over my head, nipping his way down my body before stopping and looking up at me from between my thighs. "Last chance to tell me to stop."

"Please don't-." the rest of my words are drowned out by the moan escaping my lips as he pushes my knickers aside and presses a soft kiss to my tender flesh. His tongue does wicked things as he explores and tastes me. I almost scream in agony as he pulls away long enough to remove my knickers and dives right back in.

Grasping his thick hair in my fingers, I guide him to the perfect spot. The orgasm comes so fast I can only scream as he devours me to the point of insanity. I chant his name over and over until I can't take anymore. "Please, I need more." I beg.

Mac slides up my body, somehow managing to remove his pants as he does. He's completely naked and it's only now that I realise he wasn't wearing any underwear at all. His thick cock presses against my entrance, teasingly as he struggles to push his pants off his legs with his feet.

"We shouldn't...." He hesitates and for a split second, I agree, but then he sighs. "I can't. I want you so badly. Nina, I lo-." With one hard thrust he sheaves himself inside me. I'm incapable of words as he sets a rough, fast pace.

Wrapping my legs around him, I pull him in deeper, begging without words for him to give me more. Take me higher. I need to come undone and he doesn't disappoint. My second orgasm hits me like a freight train, screaming through me with such force I feel like I'm going to black out.

Mac doesn't give me even a second to recover, he keeps that punishing pace, kissing me, touching me everywhere and driving me towards another mind blowing orgasm in mere moments. His movements match mine so perfectly that f I were a romantic, I'd be convinced we were made for each other. I'm not a romantic though so I shut those thoughts down and just enjoy the moment. Enjoying the fact that the man who drives me crazy is finally driving me to insanity in the right kind of way.

I swear Mac is trying to set a world record. I've lost count of all the orgasms he destroys me with. Just when I think I can't keep going, his rhythm changes, slowing down until he's practically still and staring deeply into my eyes. "You've plagued my dreams, my nightmares and everything in between for years, but none of that compares to the real thing. I don't want to ever stop. When all this is over, I'll find a way to make it work. I promise."

I'm not sure what he's talking about, my blissed out mind is struggling to make sense of it all but when he starts to move again all thought flies right out of my head. My final orgasm sends Mac over the edge right alongside me.

I fall asleep encircled in Mac's arms, and completely exhausted and satisfied.

three

SURVIVAL

The morning sun rises over the island, casting a warm glow over everything in sight, including Mac, who's still sleeping soundly. I stretch and crawl out of the makeshift shelter, feeling the sand sticking to my skin. I shake it off, pull my clothes back on, then start to walk down the beach, looking for something to eat. Thankfully, there are plenty of coconuts and bananas to be found, and I collect as many as possible. I also find some wild berries and a few nuts, which I add to my collection. I head back to the campsite, where Mac is finally stirring out of his slumber.

"Morning," I greet him, holding out a coconut for him to drink from.

He takes it from me, drinking eagerly. No thanks or anything as he wipes his mouth on his arm. I'm not sure what I was expecting, but for him to act like last night never happened is not it.

"Any idea what we're going to do today?" I ask, sitting down on a nearby rock, trying to get him to talk.

"Survive," he replies, matter-of-factly. There's something off about the way he's acting this morning. Almost as though the truce we had up till now is suddenly over. He grabs the nuts and berries, sniffing them before tossing them into the ashes of the fire. "You trying to poison me Beasty?"

"No." I gasp, when he continues to glare at me, I finally snap, "What the fuck is your deal?"

"Just sick of looking at your dumb ass." He bites back before storming away.

I watch him go, mentally shaking myself free from the metaphorical whiplash he's giving me. I can feel tears pricking at the corners of my eyes, but I refuse to let them fall. He's not worth it, one night of epic orgasms doesn't make him perfect. I take a deep breath and start to gather some firewood, refusing to let him ruin my day.

As I work, I can feel his eyes on me, but I don't look up. I don't want to give him the satisfaction of seeing me upset. The rest of the day is spent in tense silence between us. I try to keep busy, building up the fire and sorting through the food I've gathered, but every time I glance in Mac's direction, he's glaring at me. It's like he's trying to pick a fight, but I don't understand why. We've made it this far, we should be working together, not against each other. I decide to confront him about it, as I can't take the tension anymore. I stand up and walk over to where he's sitting, staring off into the distance. The sky begins to darken above us.

"Mac, what's going on?" I ask, feeling desperate to mend this between us.

He turns his back on me again, "Nothing." He mumbles.

"You're acting like a complete asshole. I thought last night meant something."

"Yeah, well, it didn't. I'm sick of your shit." His words are emphasised by a clap of thunder.

"What shit?" I ask just as the sky opens and rain begins to fall all around us.

"You know what I mean. You're constantly relying on me to protect you, to feed you. You're like a helpless little girl."

"I am not helpless!" I practically shout.

A storm of anger fills his eyes. His forehead wrinkles, soft lips drawn into a tight line. Water dripping down his cheeks like tears of anger. I've never seen him so angry. It takes me a moment to realise his anger is not directed at me. This anger is directed at himself. I've never seen Mac so vulnerable, so real. Like he's hidden a part of himself away and is only just now letting it out.

Yet, I'm not scared. I know he'd never hurt me. Call it instinct, call it faith, whatever it is, I know in my heart that Mac could never, would never, hurt me on purpose. Something more is going on here and I'm determined to figure out what it is.

I crouch down in front of him, staring at him right in the eye, my gaze steadfast. His hands drop from his head, falling to land on my shoulders. In one frozen moment of time, I finally see him. The real Mac, sitting before me. Begging me with only his emerald eyes. Begging for me to understand. He opens his mouth, a sob escaping. "You have every right to hate me. My father killed your mother."

His words shatter me. Tear right through the remnants of my heart. My knees give out. A cry so hollow and devoid of emotion crawls out of my mouth and into the night. Echoing all around our lonely island.

"How long?" I don't want to know but a part of me asks anyway.

"What?" He sinks to his knees beside me, hand outstretched as though he's going to touch me.

"How long have you known?" My voice is filled with an emptiness that I don't feel. Inside I'm a maelstrom of pain, betrayal, anger.

"Since the night it happened." The moon shifts out from behind the clouds, illuminating the tears streaking down his cheeks. Even in the dim light I can see the red rimming his eyes. Suddenly his body begins to shake. Fur sprouting all over him as his nose elongates. A scream lodges in my throat but I'm too scared to let it free for fear the monster in front of me will tear me to shreds. Mac drops down to all fours, his body shifting into more animal than human. I've read about shifters. I've seen them in movies but nothing could have prepared me for the wolf now shaking his head in front of me.

The animal growls, slowly stalking closer. I want to run. I want to hide. My limbs refuse to respond. Freezing me in place. As the wolf approaches, its growls become softer, almost like a purr. It lowers its head and sniffs at my face before licking away tears that I hadn't even realised I was shedding. I realize that this is still Mac, just in a different form. He's still the person I've been surviving with, fighting with, and now, he's exposing a part of himself that he's clearly been holding back for far too long.

He shifts back into his human form and looks at me with such intensity, I can barely handle it. His eyes are filled with hurt, pain, and hope all at once. Hope that maybe, just maybe, I'll forgive him.

"I know I can never make it up to you," he says, his voice raw with emotion, "but I had to tell you. I couldn't keep it inside anymore." He's talking like he didn't just turn into a wolf right in front of me.

I'm frozen, unsure of what to say, unsure of how to even begin to process the information he's just told me or the fact that he just turned into a damn wolf.

"You're a...." Words fail me. I swallow thickly, trying to come up with something to say, eventually I just turn on my heel, ignoring Mac as he calls out to me. "Nina!"

"A fucking wolf. He turned into a fucking wolf." I mutter to myself as I continue to walk away. "Did I die on that plane? No, I must be in a coma, this is all a nightmare. A fever induced nightmare and I'm going to wake up at any moment." As I walk, I can feel his eyes on me, but I don't look back. I'm too angry, too hurt, and too confused. I don't know how to feel about Mac anymore. He's been keeping such a huge secret from me. A secret that has changed my life forever. I've been living with my mother's memory, trying to survive on this island, and all the while, Mac has known the truth. He's known that it was his father who killed her, and he's been keeping it from me. I don't know if I can forgive him for that.

My thoughts are interrupted by a rustling in the bushes. I tense up, my heart pounding in my chest. I don't know what to expect anymore. I don't know who or what is out there. I reach for the huge stick Mac dropped earlier near the campsite, ready to defend myself, but then I hear a voice.

"Nina, wait up." It's Mac.

I raise the stick higher, "Stay away from me."

"Nina, please, just let me explain?" Mac puts his hands up in surrender. "I'm not going to hurt you. I just want to talk."

I eye him warily. "What is there left to say?"

"I don't know. But we can't just keep avoiding each other like this. We need to figure out how to move forward, together."

"Move forward?" I scoff. "How can we move forward after what you just told me? How can I trust you? How do I know you're not going to turn into a wolf and attack me?"

Mac's face falls. "I understand if you don't trust me. But you have to believe that I would never hurt you, no matter what form I'm in. You're my mate."

I bite my lip, considering his words. It's true that I've never felt threatened by him, even when he turned into a wolf. But how can I trust him after keeping such a huge secret from me?

"I'm your what?" I screech as his words finally sink in.

"My mate," Mac repeats, his voice softened with an emotion I can't quite place. "We're...we're meant to be together, Nina. It's just...complicated."

I stare at him, my jaw slack. "Complicated? That's an understatement. You just told me that your father killed my mother, and now you're claiming we're mates?"

"I know, I know," Mac says, his hands clasped in front of him. "It sounds crazy, but it's true. I've known it since the day we met."

I shake my head, unable to wrap my mind around what he's saying. "I don't understand. Mates? Like, soulmates?"

Mac nods, a flicker of hope in his eyes. "Yes. That's exactly what it is. Wolves mate for life, Nina. And I...I've been waiting for you. For so long."

I take a step back, my mind reeling. "No. You've been dating Kara. You even brought her on this nightmare of a trip with you."

"I didn't have a choice. My father's been pushing me to reveal my mate and when I refused he set me up with Kara, I dated her for appearances only. Nina, if my father ever found out that my mate is human he'd kill us both."

"Why would your father kill us both?" I ask, my voice barely above a whisper.

"Because it's forbidden for wolves to mate with humans," Mac explains. "It's been that way for centuries. My father is a pure-blooded wolf, and he believes in keeping our bloodlines pure. He won't allow me to mate with a human."

"Then how can I be your *mate?* " I ask, looking at him incredulously.

Mac nods, his eyes intense. "I couldn't help it, Nina. From the moment I saw you, I knew you were the only one for me, but I also knew we could never be together. That's why I've done everything I can to stay away from you, until last night. The problem is my mother decided she was going to marry your father and I knew without a doubt I couldn't stay away any longer. Fate has a sick sense of humour, putting our parents together when we're fated to be together."

"You're blaming fate for our fucked-up situation?" I bark a disparaging laugh.

Mac looks at me, his eyes softening. "No, I'm not blaming fate. I'm just saying that we can't control who we're meant to be with. And I know it's not fair to you, to be thrown into this mess, to have your mother's killer be my own father. But I'm here to protect you, Nina. I'll do whatever it takes to keep you safe."

I shake my head, still trying to comprehend everything he's just told me. "I don't know if I can trust you, Mac. You've been lying to me this whole time."

"I'm sorry, Nina," Mac says, his voice heavy with regret. "But I had to keep the truth from you. For your own safety. If my father found out that you're my mate, he would stop at nothing to kill you. And I couldn't let that happen."

I take a deep breath, trying to calm my racing heart. "So what do expect from me? It's not like we're going to live out our lives in secret on this fucking island. We'll get rescued, go back to our normal lives and then what?"

Mac takes a step forward, his eyes locked on mine. "I don't know. But we'll figure it out. Together. We'll find a way to make this work, Nina. I promise you that."

I stare at him for a moment, my mind still reeling from everything he's just told me. But despite everything, I can't ignore the feeling inside me. The feeling that he's telling the truth. That he'll do anything to keep me safe. And that maybe, just maybe, we're meant to be together. As crazy as it sounds.

"Okay," I say, finally. "Let's figure this out together. But first, we need to get off this island."

Mac smiles at me, relief flooding his face. "Agreed. We'll work on a plan."

We walk back to the campsite together, and for the first time, I don't feel alone. I don't know what the future holds for us, but I have the strangest feeling that somehow everything will turn out alright.

four

I never expected things to turn out as they did. Mac and I were trudging up the hill, exhausted and dejected after our misadventure, when a small red boat appeared on the horizon. As it sailed closer I could make out my father's silhouette at the bow, his arms frantically waving in the air. We watched in disbelief as the boat pulled up to shore and my father leapt out of the boat, sprinting towards us with tears streaming down his face. Before I could move he had gathered me up in a long embrace, sobbing and repeating "Nina, I thought I'd lost you."

"Did...?" Mac's voice cracked and he stumbled over his words, unable to form a complete sentence. Tears pooled in my father's eyes as he reached out and squeezed Mac's shoulder. "I'm so sorry, Mac." A broken wail erupted from deep within Mac's chest and his body shook with grief. In that moment, my father had told him the worst news without actually having to say it; Mac's mother was gone. Mac crumples to the ground, his body wracked with grief. I move to his side, wrapping my arms around him as he sobs uncontrollably. I can feel the pain of his loss, the weight of it crushing him. My heart aches as I hold him, wishing there was something I could do to ease his pain.

After some time, Mac finally stops crying, his body shaking with exhaustion. We sit in silence, watching the waves crash against the shore. My father stays nearby, giving us space, but ready to provide comfort if needed.

Eventually, Mac speaks, his voice hoarse. "I always hoped that she was still alive," he says, his eyes filled with tears. "That maybe she made it to shore like we did. That she somehow survived." I squeeze his hand, wishing there was something more I could do to comfort him. "I'm sorry, Mac. I can't even imagine what you're going through."

Mac looks up at me, his eyes softening. "Thank you, Nina. It means a lot to know you're here for me."

I nod, not trusting myself to speak. In that moment, all I can think about is how much we've been through together. How much we've grown to care for each other, despite everything that's happened. And how, despite all the odds stacked against us, we've managed to find each other.

After a few more minutes, my father approaches us, a solemn expression on his face. "I'm sorry to interrupt, but we need to head back to the mainland. The authorities are waiting for us."

Mac nods, standing up slowly. "Right. I understand."

My father puts a hand on Mac's shoulder, his expression kind. "I know this is hard but you'll get through this."

five

HOME

Thankfully we took a boat back home. I don't think anyone wanted to fly after our ordeal. Turned out my father saved Kara. The moment we arrived on the mainland, she ran right into Mac's arms. He glanced once at me, a sad but determined look in his eyes, before he wrapped his arms around Kara and led her away.

My stomach twisted as I watched them, my father's eyes filled with hope and expectation that I had found something on the island to make me happy. But how could I answer his questions when all I wanted to do was scream out that I'd fallen for someone only to have him ripped away from me? My heart shattered a little more every time he asked what had happened, for this secret of mine was too dark and dangerous for anyone - especially my family - to know. The wolf shifter who said I was his mate was not an option for me because of our species differences and yet, here I am stuck between two impossible choices. I fell for a monster and that's not something I'll ever be able to tell anyone.

To be continued...

Monster's Treasure

S.D. Hegyes

one

T he Darkside Market buzzed with the noise of commerce and haggling. If any monster had asked Zeth a decade ago what he thought of the market that took place every Friday, he'd have told them it was a treasure that he'd never grow tired of. A lot had changed though, and he no longer found it as charming as before his punishment.

Not that the Darkside Market had changed. It still vibrated with the same energy it always had. Monsters of various looks and sizes milled about the busy cobbled streets, ready to haggle and deal with sleazy merchants.

Many paths carved through the Darkside. Each one lined with large boulders and lit with gemstones. It prevented any monster from slipping into the In-Between, the blackened expanse beyond the Darkside.

The Darkside Market took place on one of those many paths. Stalls lining both sides of the cobblestone street.

Merchants harking wares on one side while vendors selling treats and meals lined the other.

Most of the stalls were available for any monster who wanted to use them during the Darkside Market. There were a couple monsters who staked out a spot they frequented on a regular basis.

Zeth stifled a yawn, blinking lazily as he glanced over the market.

Aglozek was selling human charms, items that were of no use to monsters—at least in Zeth's opinion—but humans found them comforting. He had brought Aglozek a trinket or two over the years himself. Rabbits' feet mostly. A pair of loaded dice here or there. Whatever he found under a child's bed that he thought might bring in a killion or two.

Pushing away the memories, Zeth watched as a large blob monster, wiggling and jiggling like a lump of jello on a plate. They picked up a penny and held it up to the light. The gemstones that hung along the market stalls cast a low glow over the entire cobblestone street, but it wasn't enough to make the penny shine. No. Aglozek had polished the penny—with troll saliva, no doubt—to brighten its countenance.

Zeth flinched as the penny gleamed, casting a ray of light into his own eyes. He fought the urge to growl and lash out at the blob even as they put the penny down. He found the strength to remain where he was. He reminded himself that he chose that spot, and if it bothered him, he could move elsewhere.

Watching the market, as boring and predictable as it was,

had become Zeth's only form of entertainment. He ignored the itch to go somewhere and do something. He fought the irritation the blob's gleaming penny raged inside him.

Down the line of market stalls, he saw the rest of the monster merchants selling their wares. The merchants all lined on side of the street while the vendors lined the other.

Zeth took a deep breath through his nose. He could smell rats roasting on a spit somewhere down the line. Divl sent her younger sisters into the human plane to catch the rats and return with them fresh every evening before market. The cat-like monsters had grown quite good at catching the little beasts. Their business boomed, even before their first century in the market.

Pride blossomed in Zeth's chest for the cat-monster sisters. They'd worked hard to find their place in the Darkside Market, and it showed. They were excellent at their craft. They made it better over the years, drawing in new customers every day. All while making sure their current ones remained loyal.

Still further down the line, a squid-like monster with more tentacles and barbs than Zeth could count sold sealife in jars as well as on the grill. Igran once told Zeth even humans kept some sealife as pets while eating others, and they exploited that amongst the monsters.

Zeth wasn't a fan of the sealife Igran caught and sold. They fished in the In-Between. The ones in the jars available for sale as pets were the weirdest creatures he'd ever seen or smelled. He avoided Ingran's stall as much as possible.

Shaking his head, Zeth settled back on the boulder

bordering the edge of the Darkside Market. It lay out of the glow of the gemstones above, perfect for resting when he grew bored of the market. A spot between his shoulder blades itched and he rubbed his back against the boulder to take care of it.

That was how Malgrumek found him.

"What bringsss you to the market today, Kilvazzzeth?" The snake-like monster was taller and wider than Zeth. He bore a single appendage that sprouted from his body, seven long blades curling from the nubbed end like a hand. Bright greens and purples decorated the snake's hood. The venom that dripped down from his fangs were of the same mottled colors.

Zeth didn't even spare the other monster a glance. "Just looking around." Even if he hadn't been bored, he wouldn't have let Malgrumek know otherwise. Malgrumek lived for instilling fear in others: monster or human.

"You're jussst looking around?" Malgrumek didn't seem convinced. Not that Zeth blamed him. If their roles were reversed, he wouldn't have believed him either.

"Sssome sssay you've grown sssoft, Kilvazzzeth."

Zeth knew Malgrumek only said it to get a rise from him, and it might have worked if he hadn't already heard the same rumors.

"Maybe I have," he told the monster.

"You ssspend too much time with the girl."

Not true, but no point in correcting him. The truth was, everything came down to *her*. And that single night. Zeth hadn't seen her since she'd been a child, begging for help from whoever could hear her.

Helping the children they'd been assigned to scare was forbidden, but Zeth hadn't been able to stop himself. His decision got him cast out and branded. The Host carved her name painfully into his skin. Deep gouges spelled out each letter in their monstrous language. They ran down the length of his body on his left side from his temple to his ankle. When his emotions ran high, the pale indentions produced an eerie red light that glowed almost as bright as the gemstones in the market.

As if he could forget her.

Once upon a time, Zeth had been one of the most feared monsters in the Darkside, both worshipped and hated by lesser monsters. He'd had his pick of jobs and could choose to scare any child he wished, when he wished.

All of that was before she appeared in his life.

A child who scared all other monsters away. Zeth hadn't known how back then. He might not have believed it true if he hadn't watched multiple monsters leave the dark, cracked shard of her portal in tears, blubbering nonsense and vowing never to return. None would explain why she terrified them.

A mixture of curiosity and the notion that he might be one of the last available to sign on as her monster led him to volunteer. Surely he, one of the best among his kind, could scare the child so many failed to.

It had been both the best and worst decision of his life.

He didn't regret saving her. Quite the contrary. He'd been the first monster to return through her portal filled with righteous anger rather than sorrow. No one should have to live through what she did, and yet none of the previous monsters assigned to her had ever done anything about it.

Zeth was the first to put a stop to the bad events in her life, and he brandished her name upon his skin because of it.

A heavy sigh rang through him. He only minded his punishment, unable to take on another child, when he was bored. Like then. Most of the time, he didn't mind. It brought him great pleasure to be her monster, to be marked as hers and only hers.

He fought not to reach across and touch the object that adorned his wrist. If Malgrumek saw it, he would remain nearby and continue pestering Zeth until he got what he wanted. That was never a good idea with the snake monster.

His tail started thrashing around. The gesture could be interpreted a number of ways. He hoped Malgrumek saw it as one of irritation rather than pleasure.

"What do you want?" Zeth asked, still not looking at Malgrumek.

The snake monster chuckled, his forked tongue coming out to run along Zeth's marked arm. "Jussst wondering what you're going to do with your child when ssshe's an adult. Before you were banisssshed, that wasssn't a problem. You could move on to another child. But what will you do when this one growsss up? You can't take on another one."

Pretending Malgrumek's words didn't influence him was hard. Really hard. Especially when it was something he'd been thinking about off and on for a bit himself.

He'd never admit it to Malgrumek though. Not in a million years, if he lived that long.

The truth was that no other monster before Zeth had broken the unspoken laws about monsters and their children. No other monster was marked the way Zeth was. No other monster had to worry what would happen when their child grew up.

No other monster in the Darkside was bound to a child the way Zeth was to his.

"That's none of your concern." Zeth was careful to keep any worry or frustration from his voice, keeping the same neutral tone that indicated his boredom. Maybe it would be enough to convince Malgrumek to go away and leave him be.

The snake monster snorted. "You ssshould think about that, Kilvazzzeth. Children grow up."

Zeth didn't look at him, but he felt the snake's tail brush against his thigh as he slid away. He fought the urge to shiver. He refused to show how much the conversation with Malgrumek had affected him. The snake monster wasn't wrong.

Peyton Thorne. Frustration flickered through him every time he thought about her. He'd saved her life once long ago, and now he was stuck with her as his only child, and he hated that Malgrumek was right. He needed to figure out what to do when Peyton grew up. He was a monster. He was meant to scare children, and he couldn't do that if he was stuck with a child who wasn't a child anymore.

But the question was: what could he do about it?

With Malgrumek gone, he lifted his right hand and fingered

the beads wrapped around his left wrist. Several different colors separated the white letter beads that spelled P-E-Y-T-O-N.

Several times over the years, he'd thought about pulling the bracelet off and throwing it. Let the darkest shadows and the creatures that waited In-Between have it. He'd always held back though. He'd made a choice, and he didn't regret it. Plus, she had given him the bracelet. It had been her way to thank him, and the small gesture pleased him to no end.

He couldn't bear to part with it. The black paint had worn off the letters of the beads, leaving behind a ghost of what they said. He knew the word by heart though, having it carved upon his side as well. Peyton. Peyton Thorne.

Zeth sighed and closed his eyes, rubbing a hand over his face with a groan. What was he going to do once she grew up?

No answers came to him as he sat upon the boulder and watched the Darkside Market through half-lidded eyes. Even as the market wound down for the evening and the glowing gemstones dimmed, Zeth did not move from his position.

His eyelids remained closed for longer bouts of time between blinks. Finally, a small sigh escaped between his lips, and he found himself on the brink of sleep.

Thud.

Zeth jerked upright, wrenching his shoulders. He twisted his mouth in annoyed pain. He stared around him until his eyes landed on the large rat near his left hand, steam still rising from the fur. If he'd scooted his hand a little farther from himself, it would have landed on the steaming carcass.

He blinked at it. Then he lifted his gaze up and found

himself looking into brilliant orbs of amber and emerald. The dark thin slits in the center grew into large round pupils and then back again.

"Divl," he greeted the large cat. She was too big to be considered a normal house cat, no matter how much she looked like one. Her fur was tan, marred only with the sable points of what Zeth knew humans called a Siamese. When he stood before her, her head reached his waist. Sitting on the boulder, his gaze was level with hers.

She dipped her head his direction before she opened her mouth in a wide yawn. He'd seen cats yawn before, but hers wasn't like that of a cat. Her mouth widened into gaping jaws capable of snapping off his head, minus his horns, with a single snap. Cats, he knew, had a single row of teeth, but Divl had dozens of rows of serrated teeth, made for ripping and shredding. Her tongue was long and thin, split into two at the back of her throat.

There were few monsters who had multiple forms, but Zeth knew Divl was one of them. She possessed this form and a more anthropomorphic cat-human hybrid form. He'd never understood the purpose of having two forms, but he wasn't dumb enough to ask either.

When she finished her yawn, her eyes looked meaningfully from the steaming rat to Zeth.

"This is for me?" he asked her.

Her ear twitched, but she said nothing.

He started to reach for it and then hesitated, looking back at her. "Why?" he asked.

Both her ears flicked backward. He didn't think she meant it in irritation at him, but it was clear something irritated her. He pondered that for a moment. "Malgrumek?"

Divl opened her mouth and hissed, standing and arching her back, her fur rising into the air, as if the mere mention of the monster's name might bring him to them.

Zeth shrugged one shoulder and grabbed the rat, biting off its head and chewing before he spoke again. "Thanks," he told her and was rewarded when she sat back on her haunches again with a polite nod of her head. "He doesn't bother me."

It was a lie, and from the way her ear twitched again, he knew she understood it for what it was. Still, she said nothing, which was more disturbing for he knew she could.

"Why won't you speak?" he asked her.

"What would you have me say?" she asked, her mouth not moving even as her head cocked to the side with another twitch of her ear.

"Why are you helping me?"

"Maybe I pity you, Kilvazeth."

"Do you?" he retorted.

"Do I what?"

"Pity me."

She considered him for a long moment, studying him. "No."

He scoffed, but it wasn't because he didn't believe her. Divl had no reason to lie.

"I envy you," she told him finally.

That surprised him. He jerked his attention from the rat and met her gaze again. "What?"

She nodded. "You've laid claim to a human child, and she to you. Do you even know what that means?"

Zeth did not stop himself from reaching for the bracelet on his wrist. She watched him smooth one hand over the faded beads spelling out Peyton's name, but she said nothing.

"What does it mean?" How could she know? She wasn't bound to a single child. She still had the freedom to travel between the Darkside and the human realm without hinderance.

"She is *yours*." There was something about the cat's words that spoke more than Zeth could understand. He didn't get a chance to question it though.

Divl inclined her head once more and then stood. In the blink of an eye, she seemed to fade in and out before his eyes, like static on an old TV he'd once seen in the human realm. Then she was gone, as if she'd never been there before. The only hint he hadn't been imagining the interaction were the strange questions swirling in his mind and the cooked rat in his hand.

two

T here was always darkness somewhere in the human realm. The opposite of the Darkside, which was always bathed in darkness. Unless there were gemstones lit up. Some monsters, like Divl, were able to see in the dark.

Zeth wasn't one of those lucky ones. As the lights dimmed in the Darkside Market, only those with night vision, remained behind. Zeth wanted to join the ranks of those leaving the market, but he had nowhere to go. Some returned to whatever caves and fissures they'd carved out for themselves. Others would go to the human realm and sleep under the beds or in the closets of their assigned children. Zeth usually stretched out on a boulder to sleep, as he'd been when Divl found him.

The Darkside never wavered in temperature. It was as if the land of monsters was frozen in time and space, never changing and always the same. Maybe that was why Zeth found it so monotonous now that he couldn't go anywhere else. Part of him felt a sense of jealousy rage through him aimed at those who would visit the human realm.

Long ago, he'd scared children as he crawled his way from under their bed through one of the Darkside's many portals. He felt a restlessness he knew he needed to handle before he could even think about sleeping. Curiosity gnawed at his bones and curled his tail.

It had been a while since he visited the human realm.

At first, it was because he'd been angry he'd involved himself in Peyton Thorne's life. He was angry he'd sacrificed so much of himself to save her, that he'd disobeyed the one rule of monsters for her sake.

After he'd returned from the human realm and gained his punishment from saving her, he'd stayed away to heal.

Once healed though, he hadn't an excuse. He simply hadn't wanted to see her, the only mortal child he was allowed to visit after his trial.

When Zeth had been able to terrorize children, he'd frightened anywhere from five to twenty in a single evening. Their screams of horror had always filled him with such pleasure.

He couldn't remember the last time he'd set foot near one of the portals.

No one, at least no one Zeth had ever spoken to, knew how the portals between the Darkside and the human realm worked. He wasn't even certain the Host knew.

All he understood was that when a monster came to the Darkside, the Host assigned them a time zone. When a monster stepped through a portal, they ended up under the bed or in the closet of a mortal child.

Whatever magic that allowed a monster to step through a portal was different for Zeth. If he stepped through any of the portals, in any of the time zones now, he'd only ever arrive under Peyton Thorne's bed.

His fingers grazed the bracelet on his wrist once more, and his tail thrashed behind him. He knew he shouldn't let Malgrumek get to him. Between the snake-monster's taunts and Divl's envy, he couldn't help but think about the child he'd once saved and then never seen again.

What would happen when Peyton Thorne grew up? Would he be stuck in the Darkside forever? Would he be assigned a new child then, his punishment over as she was no longer able to be scared?

He wasn't certain, and the question rolled over and over in his mind, keeping him awake when he'd rather sleep. He hadn't ever met a monster who'd blatantly disregarded their one rule the way he had. As far as he knew, he was the only one.

Curiosity ate at him, and he knew he needed to go see her for himself. He had to find out exactly how long he had before Peyton Thorne was grown.

A shudder ran through him. Maybe that was why he'd remained in the Darkside. He knew, with her name carved upon his flesh, she was the only human child he was allowed to scare, and even now, he felt no desire to do so. He'd protected her once, and he would do so again.

She hadn't been scared of him then. Would she now? A

monster was meant to scare children. If his child wasn't afraid of him, was he still a monster? He didn't think so.

Zeth rolled over, off the rock, dropping down into the soft patch of dirt surrounding it. He straightened and brushed the dirt and dust from his chest and back. He shook for good measure, like a dog he'd seen once in the human realm. Then he strode up the center of the market, now empty, toward the portals on the far side of the Darkside.

In some ways, it was easy to find one's way in the Darkside, depending on where one started. There were paths leading to various homes everywhere one turned one's head, but they were all labeled. It was a tradition the monsters stole from the humans, labeling the streets with names to make it easier to find them. There was The Dreary Witch, The Ancient Gnoll, Weblich, and The Vicious Hunting Lynx.

Zeth didn't know what monster named the streets, but they were nothing like the human street names. Although, he remembered enough about the human world to know they gave some streets weird names too.

He ignored the streets though, for they were home to the different caverns where monsters lived. Instead, he diverted from the main unnamed road for those with the portals to the human realm.

Like the neighborhoods where monsters lived, the portal roads had names too, but they were simply that of the time zones they belonged to. Greenwich Mean Time. Eastern Standard Time. Central African Time.

Each road curved through the shadows of the Darkside and

disappeared before Zeth could see the portal associated with it. He imagined all the portals looked alike though. He'd never felt any need to explore and find out.

Maybe one day he would, but he continued along the center path, heading for the Central Time Zone path that he'd been down so many times in the past.

He found it easy enough and soon found himself facing the portal that would take him to Peyton Thorne's room. The portal warbled in front of him like a crack in space and time. Inky black shadows trailed from it like smoky tendrils threatening to curl around Zeth and pull him through. He stopped out of their reach. The edges of the portal glowed with a violet aura, as if that was all that kept the portal from overtaking the Darkside.

Looking at the portal, Zeth cocked his head to one side and considered it. No one disturbed him for several moments even as Malgrumek's and Divl's words—one of mockery and the other of envy—echoed throughout his head.

Then, the portal seemed to grow impatient with his indecision for soft whispers started echoing from the portal, all calling his full name. *Kilvazeth*. It made goose bumps rise along his skin and sent an odd tingling sensation through him. The longer he stood there, the louder and more insistent those whispers became.

Then, with a final glance behind him to see if anyone saw him, Zeth stepped forward, through the portal, eyes closed.

It went the way it always did. There was no shift in feeling, no weird sensation. It was as if he'd walked through a doorway except the room on the other side looked different than he might have imagined based on the one prior.

He stepped through the shadow and found himself lying on the floor under a bed. This time, instead of carpet, there was pale oak hardwood or something similar to it. He blinked in surprise. Had Peyton Thorne moved?

Lifting his head, he glanced about, wondering what toys she might have lying around her room. What did she play with now versus when he'd last seen her?

The last time he'd seen her room, it had been dark. He remembered the gleam from the doorway that had allowed him to see of a couple toys back then.

There were no toys though. On one side of the room, he clearly saw what had to be a dresser and a bin, for clothing he supposed, but no toys. On the other side of the room, the floor was clean from the edge of the bed to the wall.

Weird. This didn't look like Peyton Thorne's room. He frowned. It looked like a parent's room. Had he somehow found himself in the room of Peyton Thorne's stepfather?

A low growl rumbled through him at the thought. It was her and her stepfather that had put him in the predicament he was in now. He knew if he saw her father now, he'd kill him.

Already, he felt his talons gouge holes in the hardwood floor as he curled his fingers with another fierce growl. His mouth curled into a sneer, and he felt his canines pierce his lower lip.

He hoped, for the sake of her stepfather, that he wasn't in Peyton Thorne's parents' room.

He cocked his head to the side, listening. Voices. Voices

drifted down the hall towards him, coming closer and closer. He remembered what Peyton Thorne's stepfather sounded like, and this man didn't sound like him. Who was it?

"You need to get back out there and clean up the mess you made! " the man shouted.

The woman, walking before him—Zeth saw their feet as they entered the room—only said, in a small voice, "I'm getting a pair of shoes, Oscar. It's broken glass. I'm not going to risk cutting myself cleaning it up."

"You should. It's your fault the damn thing broke after all."

The woman sighed, as if this was an argument they'd had multiple times on various occasions.

What the hell? It took everything in Zeth not to growl again. He restrained himself from slashing the man's throat to make him shut up.

He took a deep breath in through his nose and released it out through his mouth. His temper with humans was what got him in trouble in the first place. It was why he'd been branded with the runes now glowing red against his skin.

Zeth placed his hands flat against the hardwood floor and pulled himself forward, determined to see the faces of those fighting.

He remembered Peyton Thorne's stepfather well. The sound of his raised voice, the weight of his wrist clasped in his hand, the look of rage and then terror on his face. The man in the room did not sound like the same man. He needed to know.

When he looked out from under the bed, careful to stick to

the shadows, he blinked in surprise. The man who yelled at the woman was not Peyton Thorne's stepfather.

Peyton Thorne's stepfather had been tall and largely built with a trim waist. This man was thick and heavy everywhere. Her stepfather'd had dark hair that framed his face and dark eyes that looked black in the darkness. This man had short pale hair and eyes that would have turned Zeth's blood to ice if they were aimed his direction.

Where was he? Why was he here? Where was Peyton Thorne?

He turned his attention to the woman the man yelled at. He didn't care for the man who looked more and more like a tomato with every word that escaped his mouth.

She remained calm and silent, but she winced at his words. Her mouth turned down as a frown crossed her face. However, when she faced the man again, her expression turned neutral. She seemed to shut down her emotions as she faced him. This wasn't the first time something like this happened, Zeth knew.

Zeth studied the woman, curious despite his desire to leave the pair to their shouting match and find Peyton Thorne. He supposed this could be her mother and the man shouting at her a different man than the one he'd met before. He couldn't recall if he'd ever seen the child's mother, but something told him this woman was too young to be her anyway. Who's bed had he found himself under?

The woman had long blond hair. Two braids curved around her head along the right side of her scalp, ending at her nape where the end joined the loose hair.

There was something familiar about her, but he couldn't place her for the life of him. Could she be related to Peyton Thorne? A cousin, perhaps? Was that why she was in Peyton's room?

The man continued yelling at the woman while she pulled on her socks and shoes. He raised his hands and waved them about. Zeth couldn't tell what he was saying anymore. The sounds came out of his mouth with no consequence or rhythm as the woman climbed to her feet.

She stole his complete attention. He felt the urge to repeat history and rise from his hiding spot to terrorize the man yelling at her. He fought the urge to threaten him never to return or speak to another woman the way he just had.

The more Zeth watched her, saw her face alternate between terror and shutting down, the more he wanted to curl himself around her. He wanted to protect her from the barrage of hate aimed at her. He wanted to enclose her in his arms, shield her from the outside world.

Whoever she was, he felt drawn to her in a way he couldn't explain. His chest tightened and need filled him. He felt a hunger for her he hadn't experienced before. His talons scraped against the floor as images flooded his mind. They told him to grab her, pull her into the Darkside and take her for his own, fill her with him, claim her with his bite.

He blinked, surprised, as his thoughts turned a darker corner. He'd never felt such a raw emotion for anyone, much less a human woman who he didn't know. He knew other monsters coupled with one another, but he'd never wanted to do so himself. He'd never felt the need or desire to wrap himself in another the way he wanted to with this woman.

Zeth shook his head. Familiar or not, there was no way he was going to sit around and listen to this man put her down and tear her apart.

He could see the faint glow of his runes from the corner of his eye. He didn't have to look down at his arm to know they blazed with his growing anger and desire. The two emotions warred with one another inside him, his righteous fury winning.

The yelling man raised his hand, as if to slap the woman, and Zeth knew he couldn't stay silent and remain hidden anymore.

His growl echoed throughout the room, low and rumbling, even as smoke billowed out from under the bed, covering the floor in a thick blanket.

Even though the curtains were open and the sun shone through, the room suddenly fell into inky darkness. The smoke remained on the lower half of the floor. It only rose as high as the underside of the bed. Something blotted out the light in the room, like a hand raised to ward off the sun, and left the room in shadow.

When he spoke, he could feel the voices of the Darkside echoing in his words. He reveled in the power that he still held despite his outcast station.

A sharp hiss punctuated each word as he said, "You will not touch her."

three

Z eth's full attention was on the man, but he didn't miss the way the woman straightened, her mouth dropping open with a silent, "Oh!" even as she glanced around the room.

Interesting. Zeth did not have a moment to be curious about her reaction.

"W. . . Who's there?" the man stuttered. He stared at the smoke on the floor, and Zeth knew there was no way he could miss where it came from.

The woman's brows furrowed as her attention turned toward the bed as well. It was as if she was remembering something she'd long forgotten.

He needed to forget about her for the moment. There'd be more time to learn all the woman's intricacies later, he decided. Once the man was gone. Once they were alone.

The sooner the man left, the better. He pondered how to best answer his question. Did he give him his name? No.

"Your worst nightmare," came his echoing response, and then he released a dark chuckle.

"Show yourself!" the man snarled.

"As you wish," came the response.

Zeth took his time crawling out from under the bed. He used the smoke that billowed from the Darkside to shield him, making sure his talons scraped and scratched as he crawled out. He could almost see the pinpricks of fear as they rushed up and down the man's spine. A trickle of cold sweat dripped down his brow.

He rose slowly, the smoke pillowing over him and creating a blanket he shed as he rose to his full height. He stood taller than the man who shrank in on himself and cowered against the wall as if to try to escape Zeth's fury.

The runes along his left side burned and glowed bright red in the darkness that surrounded them.

He wondered what the man saw before him.

Did he only see the glow of the runes that ran the length of his form? Did he see the sharp canines, bright white against his dark skin? Did he see both sets of horns that protruded from the top of his head? Did he see his tail whipping behind him and making small popping noises as it cracked in the air?

He heard the man whimper in fear and realized it didn't matter what the man saw. He drank in the man's terror, swallowing it like a man dying of thirst. How long since he'd fed on another's fear?

Children's fear was sweet and intoxicating. This man's

tasted bitter and filled with spice, but that didn't matter. It had been so long since he'd fed on the emotion that he found himself gorging on it now. He remembered now, adult fear was so much more satisfying.

"Ah!" he said with a heavy sigh of satisfaction as he swallowed another lungful of horror from the man staring up at him. He spread his hands out, talons sharp and clicking together. "This is what I've missed all this time! Your fear tastes so," he pondered his next words, relishing in the way the man's panic rose as he waited for the outcome of Zeth's sentence, "delicious." The word came out as a purr as Zeth bent down near the man, a taunting smile on his face. "What's your name, human?"

The man whimpered, visibly trembling in fear, but didn't answer.

"He's Oscar," the woman said.

Zeth turned his attention to her and felt another wave of desire ripple through him. The smoke shifted around him as he took a step toward her. "Oscar?" he repeated.

For a brief moment, she glanced at the man cowering against the wall and shrank in on herself. When her gaze returned to Zeth though, she tightened her jaw and steeled her gaze. She nodded at him.

Oh. How interesting. The man terrified her, but she wasn't afraid of the monster under the bed? Another wave of lust threatened to overtake Zeth. He struggled against the urge to grab her and yank her down into the shadows with him.

Another petrified whimper from the man reminded him they weren't alone.

Besides, he was there for Peyton Thorne, not this woman. No matter how attracted to her he found himself.

Still, his nostrils flared as he took in her scent. He couldn't help himself. She smelled of something flowery he didn't recognize, and underneath it all was her scent. His eyes widened as she licked her lips.

She wanted him as much as he wanted her. Oh, this was definitely interesting. Maybe he could spare her a chat before he found Peyton Thorne. Once he disposed of the man, Oscar, that was.

He turned his attention to the pest still in the room. He wanted Oscar gone. He wanted to grab the woman and pin her against the wall, bury himself in her scent, her hair, her body, bite her and claim her as his own. Then he could get her out of his system and check on Peyton Thorne. Either way, Oscar needed to go first.

"What the hell are you?" Oscar asked, the words meek.

A chuckled escaped Zeth's throat, filled with more threat than mirth. "Haven't you realized yet? I'm the monster from under the bed."

From the corner of his eye, he saw the woman jolt as if his words had sparked a memory in her. She shifted her gaze to the bed, her eyes glazing over with haunted memories for a moment. A shudder passed over her and she took a step back, away from him and Oscar, as if he were her enemy as well as Oscar.

He fought the whimper that caught in his throat, wished her to move closer to him, not away. Still, he could comfort her as soon as he was through with Oscar. The man still hadn't left. Why? What sense of false bravado kept him in the room?

Zeth growled at Oscar, his tail thrashing in the air behind him. "You will leave this house," he snarled. "You will leave, and you won't return."

Oscar straightened, anger seeming to make him mad enough to counter the monster before him. "You can't make me leave my own home!"

"I can, and I will," Zeth told him. "Or I will kill you." He raised one talon and pointed it at Oscar. The smoke around his feet swirled as he took a step closer to the man. "My talons are sharp, so it could be quick and painless, but the longer you defy me, the more I'd like to make it slow and torturous." He gave the man a devilish grin. "Your death, I mean."

He shrugged and tilted his head to the side. "Or I could just feed you to those who will kill you over the course of a thousand years."

As if to emphasize his words, the portal to the Darkside opened under the bed once more. Hundreds of whispering voices climbed over one another from the In-Between.

"Join us!"

"Feed us!"

"Live with us forever!"

Even Zeth shuddered at the sound. He didn't know what made those noises. He'd heard them inside the portals hundreds of times, used the fear they elicited to scare kids often.

He knew monsters and humans alike could get caught In-Between. It didn't happen often, but he'd heard of it. Either way, the voices were creepy enough to make even his skin crawl, and they were *always* hungry.

Oscar took a step toward him, but he trembled with the effort and his bravery was failing him. Trepidation slathered across his face like a sheen of cold sweat. "You will not threaten me in my own home!"

"Such a brave little human," Zeth cooed, mockingly. "Standing up to the big, bad monster when, only a moment ago, he was about to beat on a poor, weak human."

"I wasn't..." Oscar's eyes widened, as his eyes flickered to the woman.

She flinched at his gaze but said nothing. He stared at her, as if waiting for her to deny his words, but she didn't speak. They all knew he was correct. Sure, Zeth was a monster, but was he really? He'd never hurt a woman. He never even hurt the children he scared. It was one thing to scare someone. Another entirely to touch them, to hurt them.

But oh, how he wanted to hurt Oscar. He wanted to wrap his hands around the man's throat and squeeze until he stopped breath. Preferably forever. He wanted to run his talons down the man's arm, ever-so-lightly, and watch the scarlet trickle from his veins. He wanted to swallow the man's panic and hysteria, listen to him scream in terror for hours, days, weeks, months. He wanted all of that and more. He wanted to kill Oscar for daring to touch his woman.

The thought shocked him, and he took half a step back. He

recovered quickly, raising his hand as if to bring it down upon Oscar the way the man had threatened to do to the woman. A hallow and menacing laugh escaped his throat.

"Leave," he told Oscar when he flinched. "Or would you rather my beasts feed upon your flesh?"

As if to emphasize his words, growls and snarls rippled from the portal under the bed. It sounded like a pack of wild dogs held back in the shadows.

Oscar paled. Then he glared at the woman, as if this was all her fault. She quailed beneath his glare and shrank in on herself.

His attention returned to Zeth as his lip curled. "I'm going," he snapped and raised a hand to point at him. "Mark my words, I'll be back though, and you and this bitch better be out of my house when I do."

Zeth saw the woman bristle at the words—he wasn't certain which ones—but her jaw tightened and she said nothing. He got the impression she was biting her tongue to not start a fight though.

"Get. Out." The voices from the portal In-Between backed Zeth's words. They whispered dark seductions to lure one to their doom.

The man paled, flinching at the sound of so many voices surrounding him. Then he spun on his heel and left the room. A few moments later, Zeth heard the front door slam shut and then the roar of a car as it tore out the drive and down the road.

He waited a few moments more before releasing the energy he'd held. The smoke throughout the room billowed back through the portal as it shrank. The portal under the bed closed. The voices from In-Between fell silent.

The darkness that enveloped the room seeped away as if it had never been. Zeth stood alone in the room with the woman. No sound except for the tension-filled breaths leaving their chests entered his ears.

He rolled his head in a full circle and working the tension from his shoulders before facing the woman.

She stared up at him, blue eyes wide and her mouth gaping a little. He growled low in his throat as he stared at her lips. He wanted to take them in his mouth and bite, taste her blood even as he devoured her. She closed her mouth and swallowed hard, but her expression didn't otherwise change.

"Thank you," she said in a small voice. Then her expression hardened and her voice grew louder, more confident, and did he hear a hint of sarcasm in her tone? "At least, I guess I should be thanking you. I'm not certain yet."

He cocked his head to the side, considering her. "Maybe. Depends."

"On what?" Her eyes flashed, and he grinned. He liked her fire, the same fire that hadn't flared around the man—Oscar—until right there at the end. He was glad to see she wasn't as meek as she'd seemed.

He shrugged though. He wasn't certain what he'd even meant saying that. His thoughts ran ragged through his mind. All he wanted to do was pin her to the wall. He wanted to drag his lips over her skin, sink his teeth into her shoulder, claim her

for his own. He wanted to bring her back to the Darkside
with him.

Zeth wouldn't do that, couldn't do that. He'd yet to meet a
human who could survive the Darkside. Perhaps humans who'd
tried to cross were the ones between in a realm even Zeth
couldn't visit. Still, the sudden primal need to make her his
filled his mind, threatening to drown any other sensibilities
from his mind. He shook his head, as if to clear it, but that only
helped a little.

Why was he even there? What was he doing? Why had he
come to the human realm? To protect this woman? Scare off
her abusive. . . Whatever he was? Partner?

Thoughts of tangling in the sheets on the bed with this
woman coursed through his mind. Where were these thoughts
coming from? Why were they consuming him? He needed to
taste her, to run his talons over her flesh, sink his fingers into her
hair.

"Who—or what?—are you?" the woman asked, pulling
him from his lust-filled thoughts.

That helped. Her talking to him helped. He needed to keep
her talking. At least until he could figure out why he was in the
human realm.

"My name is Kilvazeth."

"Kilvazeth?" she repeated.

He nodded, not trusting himself to speak or move closer to
her. He needed her to keep talking.

"And," she said, dragging out the word as she waved one

hand in a circle, "What are you exactly?" She gave him a once-over and he wondered what she saw when she looked at him.

It wasn't the same as when he'd questioned what Oscar saw. He'd been shrouded in darkness then, and he knew the man could only see him based on the glow from his runes.

The room was bathed in light now. There were no shadows for Zeth to hide in. The woman could see all of him. Every inch of his dark skin, purplish gray in the low light, the leather pants that hung low on his hips to allow his tail to swing free behind him. The two pairs of horns that protruded from his skull, the razor-sharp teeth he'd snapped at Oscar and wanted to sink into her neck. The burning red eyes and knife-like talons.

Nothing about him was hidden in the shadows as he might have liked. When was the last time he'd been seen in the light of day? When was the last time a human looked upon him at all?

Not even Peyton Thorne had really seen him the night he protected her.

Peyton Thorne.

He was in the human realm to see her.

The realization that he'd forgotten in his lust-driven state punched him in the gut. How could he forget he'd come to see his child, the one whose name had been burned into his skin one letter at a time?

"Are..." She hesitated, reaching out with one hand, as if to touch him, but then thought better of it and pulled away, crossing her arms over her chest. "Are you OK?"

He nodded, but his breath came out in heavy pants. He reached down and stroked the bracelet on his wrist. As usual, he found comfort in the faded letters. It took a few moments, but he got his breathing under control. "I'm fine."

"I can see that." A frown crossed her face, and then her eyes drifted down to his hands, saw that he rubbed his wrist. "What are you doing?"

"Nothing," he said, fighting the urge to hide the bracelet from her the way he might've Malgrumek or even Divl. He did cover it with his hand when she stepped toward him, a curious expression he couldn't interpret on her face. She grabbed his hand, and he released his wrist more from the shock of her actions than her touch.

She'd touched him, and she hadn't recoiled in horror. She didn't find him disgusting or horrific.

She pulled his wrist toward her, her eyes only for the bracelet on his wrist. Her breath sucked in hard between her teeth, and her eyes flicked up to meet his for a moment before dropping back to the bracelet once more.

Featherlight fingers brushed over the worn beads where the letters P-E-Y-T-O-N had once been black. He'd touched them over and over again over time until they'd faded.

"Where did you get this?" she asked, her voice so low he barely heard her.

That was an odd thing to ask and certainly not a question he'd been expecting. "It was given to me," he answered honestly, not knowing if it might be better to lie to her or tell her the truth. He didn't see the harm in telling her though. Maybe she knew where he could find Peyton Thorne anyway.

He decided to risk it and ask. The worst she could say was

that she didn't know who he was talking about. He knew it was her bed he'd crawled out from. He bore her name because she was now his only charge, and her bed was the only one he could come out from under.

When she looked up at him, a mixture of wonder and fear in her eyes, part of him wanted to ask her what was wrong. Why did she seem afraid and excited all at once?

He didn't even know her name, and she had him swirling on a dangerous precipice of desire. He wondered if this had ever happened to any other monsters.

His mind swirled around that thought before he cleared it with a quick shake of his head. He had other, more important matters to attend to.

He needed to find his child before he took care of her, before he did any of the dark and naughty things twisting his mind in knots whenever he looked at her.

"Where can I find Peyton Thorne?"

She blinked up at him for several moments, swaying on her feet as if she couldn't figure out how to hold herself up. There was something wrong with her, he knew. What though? She had to know Peyton Thorne. Why else would she look so...

He couldn't explain the expression on her face, didn't have any experience with it. She stared at him, taking in all his features.

His desire ebbed away as he worried whether she'd suffered any injuries he didn't know about and couldn't see. She didn't move except for the slight sway of her body every few moments.

When he reached out to steady her, she straightened herself. She held out her hand in a gesture he knew meant not to touch her.

So he took a step back from her instead and watched her, wondering what she was thinking. Her mouth opened and closed several times. Many emotions crossed her face before she met his gaze and told him, "I'm Peyton Thorne."

four

With an involuntary step backwards, Zeth lifted his taloned hands as if to ward her off. She didn't move toward him. His eyes roamed over her from head to toe. His brows knit together as he pondered her words and tried to make sense of them.

The woman wasn't his child. Sure, she looked familiar, but he felt an undeniable attraction to her, and he wouldn't be attracted to his child. Would he? She couldn't be Peyton Thorne.

He told her as much. "You can't be," he said. "She's a child. She's *my* child."

The moment he said the words, he wished he could take them back because that would lead to explaining things he didn't wish.

He'd have to tell her she was his child because there were no others left to assign to her. Every monster who'd visited her begged not to return. None had ever explained why, and so Zeth went himself. He'd wanted to see what the fuss was about.

Zeth had been cocky enough to think he could scare the child where others had failed. If he'd known then what he knew now, would he have changed his mind about visiting the child?

Yes? No? Possibly? He wasn't certain.

She didn't remark on that though. Instead, she put her hands on her hips and said, "Well, last time I checked my birth certificate, it said Peyton Thorne. I haven't gotten married or changed my name so it should still say that."

The runes down his left side blazed scarlet for a moment. Her eyes drifted along the markings before they roamed back over him and met his again. He studied her once more, trying to find the features he remembered on his Peyton Thorne's face.

It had been too long though. He'd only met her the one time, only seen her in the dark. He didn't have any night vision capabilities some of the other monsters, like Divl, had. He hadn't been gone from the human realm that long, had he?

Time worked different in the Darkside than in the human realm, he knew. In the past, he'd gone back and forth without incident, without more than days passing. But he hadn't visited the human realm since he'd protected Peyton Thorne.

He remembered arriving in the human realm the same way then as he had now. He remembered how he'd heard the child on the bed suck in a breath of air. Almost like she'd known he was there...

The darkness was silent, as if holding its breath. His skin prickled, as if he anticipated something horrible, but he had a job to do.

Zeth reached out a taloned hand to touch the girl, but her voice made him hesitate.

"I'm not afraid of you, monster." The steel in her voice, the fearlessness, aroused his curiosity.

Somewhere else in the house, a door slammed and voices rose. Zeth turned his head toward the girl's bedroom door. It was closed. Locked. Why would a child's door be locked?

He hadn't had much time to ponder that as something—or someone—prodded his side.

"Move. Let me under."

He met the child's face, saw blue eyes brighter than anything he'd ever known before. He'd heard humans describe blue eyes to match the sky or the ocean, but he hadn't seen the first in ages and he'd never seen the second.

Stomping boots. Heading for the door.

"Move. Over." She punctuated every word with a hiss even as she shoved him over. He half turned, facing her, too shocked to do anything else. The girl's voice was small and demanding, but full of terror. Not at him. Not at the monster under the bed. Someone else.

The child crawled under the bed with a whimper of fear. Zeth registered the clomp of work boots on hardwood, heading their direction. A tear slid down the child's cheek and she sniffed hard through her nose.

"Peyton," a voice called out, the sound full of dark lullabies. "Come out, come out. Wherever you are."

The hair at the base of Zeth's neck prickled, and he bit back a growl.

Instinct took over, and he pulled the child toward him, settling over and around her. She stifled a sob with her fist in her mouth and curled into a fetal position under him, trembling.

Zeth realized his emotions for the woman now were as high and unexplainable as the child back then. He hadn't thought. He'd acted. He told himself over and over that he wouldn't change the outcome. Even if he'd known everything beforehand, but it wasn't that he wouldn't. He couldn't.

Something drew him to her, even back then. When she'd been a child, she'd needed a guardian, someone to protect her from the unwelcome advances of her stepfather.

He took a deep breath, breathing through his nose. He knew how to tell if the woman before him was Peyton Thorne, the child he'd once protected from her stepfather.

Reaching out, Zeth took one of her hands. He pulled it from its crossed position, pulling it toward him without taking a step closer to her. She resisted only a moment before he saw her curiosity win out. He held her wrist in his hand with care, talons barely pressing into her flesh.

He bent over her hand, pressing his nose deep into her wrist and taking in a deep breath. When he exhaled, his hot breath hit her flesh, making goosebumps rise along her arm. He followed the trail up her arm, pausing at the crease in her arm to inhale once more. Then again at her shoulder and lastly where her neck and shoulders met.

"What are you doing?" she asked, her voice breathy. He could hear her need in her tone, but he ignored it, concentrating on her scent.

He breathed out once more, watching her skin prickle. "What do you think I'm doing?" he asked, unsurprised to hear the low, husky desire in his own voice. His talons pressed into her flesh, ever-so-slightly, running along her bare skin and rising up over the path his nose had traveled.

When he got to her neck, he wrapped his hand around her throat, pressing one talon into the skin under her chin. He didn't press hard enough to cut off her air, but he heard her sharp intake of breath as she tilted her head back to allow him access. Her breath came out in short gasps now. Her chest rose and fell, pressing against him as he continued his ministrations. It threatened to drive him mad.

A loud moan rippled from her mouth as he tilted his head and dipped down to inhale at the hallow of her throat. He released her with a frustrated sigh, stepping back before he forgot himself completely and sank himself into her.

"You smell like my child," he admitted, "but you are not my child."

"I am not," she said, and he watched her fight the urge to grin. "And what do you mean—" She held up her hands to make quotations. "—'your child'?"

He shrugged. "I am the monster under the bed. I've been assigned the same child for years." No reason to tell her everything, but it couldn't hurt to tell her some.

She gave him a hard look, as if she knew he wasn't telling her everything. Her eyes skimmed over his runes, as if she could find the answers in the pale gray markings. He reached up one hand to brush his fingers over the markings, as if to check if they still glowed, even though he knew they didn't.

"That doesn't explain what you mean," she told him.

He blinked at her as his hand fell away from his arm. "What do you mean?"

"I mean that children grow up, and if you've been assigned to the same child for years, you should know that this one—" She gestured to herself. "—did."

He frowned. No way she knew the reason he'd come to the human realm was to check that out. No one else knew he was there yet, and he'd yet to meet a monster who could turn back time anyway.

His eyes roamed over her once more, drinking in her presence. She squirmed under his attention, biting on her lower lip even as she tried to rub her thighs together. He undressed her with his gaze, stripped her bare. He wasn't trying to look at her body though. He wanted to reach down inside her and see her soul. He wondered if she found any of the heat in his expression he saw in hers.

He inhaled once more, wondering if he could smell her desire or if he needed to be closer to that source before he could.

"You are Peyton Thorne?" he asked, as if she hadn't just said she was.

"Yes." He could tell his questioning it again annoyed her, but not enough to turn her off. Her eyes scorched his skin, and she shifted once more, as if she couldn't comfortably stand. When her thighs rubbed together again, a small moan escaped her throat. Her eyes widened and she bit her lip, her cheeks coloring with embarrassment.

He looked her over once more. "You're sure?"

"Where did you get that bracelet?" she asked in retaliation, gesturing to the one on his wrist.

Zeth held up his wrist and looked at it. "It was a present."

"From who?" Her frown returned.

"If you're Peyton Thorne—"

"I think we've established that, yes," she said, cutting him off.

"—then you," he finished as if she hadn't spoken. He growled low in his throat, watching her shiver. It wasn't with fear though. The scent of her desire flooded his senses and nearly blinded him with his own need to have her in return.

"You're not scared anymore."

"Of what?"

"Me." Not that she'd been scared of him then. He wondered if she'd remember.

"I was scared of you?" Her brows pinched. "I've never seen you before in my life."

He grinned at her. "If you are indeed my Peyton Thorne, my child, yes, you have."

"When?"

"The last time?" He reached up and scratched behind one of his horns, thinking. "It was before I had these." He gestured to the runes. He watched her fingers twitch and wondered if she wanted to touch him, touch the mark of her name upon his skin. "You would have been eight or nine. If that."

She sucked in a sharp breath and her eyes widened. Something about her expression made him realize he didn't doubt her anymore. She was who she said. Somehow, he hadn't been gone days or months. He'd been gone years.

Was that why both Malgrumek and Divl had shown such interest in him? The latter didn't bother him. Something about this woman version of his child intriguing the snake-monster sent a cold chill down his spine.

"Monsters are supposed to scare children, but none of my monsters could do so. Most came back in tears. Others were silent and stared off into the space. They all recovered in time, but none wanted to come back to you. So I did. I was determined to scare you." He sighed. "It didn't work that way. I ended up saving you instead from—"

"Stop." The words were only a whisper, but she held up her hand and covered his mouth, as if to silence him.

His eyes widened, his gaze darting down to her hand and back up to meet hers. Tears streamed down her face.

"Please," she pleaded. "Don't speak of that night."

Even if he didn't speak of it, he couldn't help but remember it.

The sing-song voice of the drunk man penetrated his skull. He growled, standing with the woman claiming to be his child. He lost himself in the memory of what had happened that night, when he'd earned every rune etched into his skin.

Somehow, the drunken man got into the room. He probably had a key. When her stepfather reached under the bed, searching for Peyton, he'd said, "You can't hide from me, girl. I'll always find you."

The meaning in his words had sickened Zeth then, and thinking about it now still made his stomach churn. He'd made a split decision, was already halfway through the action before his mind caught up and he'd realized what he meant to do.

The man grabbed Zeth's wrist and yanked. The monster under the bed allowed the man to pull him out. He rose to his feet before the man. Satisfaction filled him as the man's eyes widened in terror and his mouth dropped open in a silent scream.

"What the hell?" The man released Zeth so fast, the monster barely registered the action.

He let his arm drop to his side, and a dark chuckle rippled from his mouth. "What?" he asked. "Not as brave now when faced with the likes of me?" His forked tongue slipped between his teeth and licked his lips as he towered over the man. He stretched out his hand, talons itching to scratch and rip the man to shreds. He held himself back for the moment.

On the wall behind him, his shadow stretched out even larger than himself. It seemed to laugh in delight at the man's distress, soaking up the fear that rippled from him in a tidal wave of emotion.

Zeth sighed his pleasure as he fed upon each undulation of terror. It filled him faster and more than when he scared children. Why didn't they scare adults more often? Was it because children were easier to scare, more susceptible to the idea that monsters were real?

It didn't matter. Zeth knew the man before him, Peyton's

stepfather, was terrified of him, and he loved it. The man had
used and abused his child. He wasn't certain how he knew, only
that he did.

Even as Zeth drank in the man's fear and horror upon seeing
Zeth in his glory, he felt his fury rise within him. He reached out
a clawed hand and wrapped it around the man's wrist, yanking
him forward. He flinched as Zeth's breath washed over his face.
"If you ever harm my child again, I will return and eat you
myself."

His words were low, too low for the child hiding under the bed
to hear, full of dark menacing promises.

The scent of urine hit his nostrils and he wrinkled his nose in
disgust.

"Get out of my child's room, and never return," he snarled at
the man, shoving him toward the door.

Peyton's stepfather didn't hesitate. He ran from the room, a
terrified scream caught in his throat. Zeth remained where he
was until he was certain the man wouldn't return. Then he
walked over to the door, his tail lashing the air behind him, shut
and locked it again.

Only then did he turn toward the bed where the child
remained hidden. He crouched on his hands and knees and
looked at her. She was as he'd left her, curled in a ball, trembling
and whimpering in fear.

"He's gone," he said simply.

It was several moments before the child looked at him. When
she finally moved, she blinked at him, eyes wide and wet with
silent tears. "He's... gone?"

Zeth nodded. "You can come out if you'd like." He held out a hand, aware of what he was, what he was supposed to do with her, but he couldn't bring himself to scare her. Not then. Not ever.

She hesitated for a brief second, staring at his hand as if she expected he'd grab her and yank her out from under the bed. He suspected her stepfather would have.

Despite the pain that rippled through him from the uncomfortable position, he waited as the child made her decision. He could wait. He had time.

When she took his hand, her small hand drowning in his, he felt as if his world had both ended and begun at once. He'd known he'd broken every law among his kind that he knew about, but he couldn't bring himself to regret it even the tiniest bit.

Holding Peyton Thorne's hand felt like damnation and salvation all at once. The child trusted him, and it made his heart swell with pride and glee. She was his child, and no one would ever touch her again. He was sure of that.

He heard Peyton step up beside him, felt her hand as she grasped his arm. Her thumb ran over one of the gray indentations in his skin. Her fingers dipped lower until she traced her hands over the bracelet at his wrist. She hesitated then, her brows sliding as she lifted his hand and eyed the bracelet. Her gaze flickered up to his before looking back at the bracelet once more.

He still felt the need to protect her, but she was a grown woman now, and his devotion to her was so much more. He wanted her in ways he would never want a child, could never want a child. His lip curled as he remembered what he'd prevented her stepfather from doing.

Zeth was glad the man he'd scared off hadn't been him.

He twisted his hand around, palm up, as he had so long ago. "He's gone," he told her, repeating the same words he'd said then.

She met his gaze again, and he knew she understood what he wasn't saying. There was a shorter wait time than the last. She placed her hand in his grasp, just as she had back then. Her hand was still small, although larger than it had once been.

He'd known back then the man was Peyton's stepfather and that he'd been the source of many of her troubles over the years. Zeth realized he should have realized the woman standing beside him was Peyton, his child. His.

He felt it deep in the marrow of his bones, and that feeling only got stronger as he looked down at her, studied her as she sighed and glanced up at him. It had been so long since he'd seen her so he hadn't realized the change.

This was Peyton Thorne after all, his Peyton, and she belonged to *him*.

five

"I gave you that bracelet," Peyton said after a short while.

It wasn't a question, so Zeth didn't say anything. What could he say?

"You kept it?" She reached for it with her free hand and ran her fingers over the faded lettering that had once been her name.

He glanced down at her hand upon the bracelet. He wanted her to touch him the way she did it. "Of course. It was your greatest treasure."

When Peyton accepted his hand and crawled out from under the bed, she'd stared up at him for several long moments with a mixture of gratitude and wonder. Then she'd closed the distance between them with a single leap and wrapped her arms around his waist.

Her head snuggled his abdomen before he felt the press of her smile against his stomach. "Thank you," she whispered in a low voice.

Pride rippled through him, settling in his stomach, warm

and inviting. His tail lashed the air behind him, much like a cat's when it's pleased with itself.

She pulled away from him and aimed that sweet, innocent smile at him. "Thank you!" she said again, louder and more enthusiastically this time. Then she pulled away from him and stepped back. She looked down at her hand and he watched as she pulled something from her wrist and slipped it on his left hand.

"Keep this safe," she told him, patting it before pushing his hand away from her. "It's my greatest treasure." Another smile, and then she said, "Will you stay until I fall asleep?"

He nodded. What else could he do? She commanded him mind, body and soul. He'd do anything she asked if she but asked it of him. He'd never been so wrapped up in a human child, and something told him he never would again. Not just because his transactions this night would get him punished for sure, but because he belonged to her, his child.

"I will stay," he told her and jerked his head toward the bed. "Go to sleep, Peyton Thorne."

She crawled into bed and he helped cover her. As she closed her eyes, she grasped his hand, held it in hers, and released a happy, content sigh. "Thank you for saving me," she whispered.

A few moments later, her breathing evened out, and Zeth knew she was asleep. He stood, that warm feeling of pride rumbling through him with a purr. "Sweet dreams, Peyton Thorne," he whispered as he bent over her and pressed his mouth to her forehead in a quick kiss.

He started to crawl back under the bed to return to the Darkside, but her hand was still curled in his.

He looked down at their joined hands in wonder. Hers was so small compared to his. He studied her digits, fascinated with the differences between them.

How long he stared at their conjoined hands, he wasn't certain. After some time, the small girl gave a contented sigh and released him, rolling over to her other side, away from him.

With one last smile at the girl, Zeth crawled under the bed and returned to the Darkside. His fingers brushed over the object Peyton Thorne had slid over his wrist even though he couldn't see it.

He'd arrived back in time for the Darkside Market. He walked to a secluded corner where he could look down at his child's gift under one of the gemstone lights.

A bracelet. Crudely and simply made. Plastic beads on a string of elastic. Still, it was a gift from her, and he would always treasure it as he did her. He raised it closer to his face. A rainbow of colorful beads spaced the letters that made up her name: P-E-Y-T-O-N.

He was still smiling at it when Malgrumek found him. He lowered his wrist to his side and schooled his expression into one of neutrality, as he'd always done with the snake-monster.

"You've done it now, Kilvazzzeth," the snake-monster said in greeting. A wide grin revealed all the sharp points of his needle teeth. His fangs glistened in the low gemstone light.

"What have I done?" Zeth asked, angry that the other monster had ruined his mood.

"The Host wants to see you about your actions tonight."

Already? He'd thought he'd have more time. Still, he'd known

*it would happen. Better for him to have his punishment sooner
rather than later.*

Peyton pulled him from his thoughts and memories as she
ran her fingers over the etchings in his side. His skin tingled at
her touch. He wanted her to touch him in other places, felt the
heat in his belly roar into an inferno of need and desire. He
wanted those hot little hands everywhere.

He refused to move, in case that might scare her off and
make her remove her hands from him.

Her eyes darted to the markings running down the length
of him before she noticed his gaze. "What are these?" she
asked in a low voice, almost as if she were afraid to know the
answer.

Should he tell her?

No. He couldn't give her that guilt. He'd never regretted his
decision, even if he did hate that they'd occurred in the first
place, that they'd been necessary.

"They're my brand," he told her simply.

Now that the man was gone and he knew this woman was,
in fact, his child all grown up, he didn't know what to do. He
still wanted her with a desire that frightened him. He still
wanted to curl his talons in her long hair and pull her head
back. He still wanted to expose her throat and leave his claim on
her in the form of his bite mark.

He forced himself to relax. Maybe she wasn't scared of him,
but he wasn't about to frighten her away with the intensity of
his lust.

"Your brand?" She moved closer to study the markings as

she ran her fingers over them. He felt her warm breath on them. "Does it say something?"

He winced and pulled away. He didn't want to tell her that her name ran down the length of his body in a language she'd never be able to understand. Even if he spent the rest of her lifetime teaching her.

She wouldn't be deterred though. She stepped close to him again. This time, when she brushed her fingers over one of the runes, her lips followed. She pressed small kisses against the mark she'd touched.

His blood sang, and the runes glowed dimly. Her eyes widened and she looked up at him. "Did I do that?"

"Yes," he told her and it surprised him how heavy the truth sounded upon his lips. His talons twitched with the desire to touch her. How easy he could hurt her if he wished, he knew.

She stepped toward him again, staring at the markings in wonder. "Did you have these last time?"

"No." Again, the truth. He wanted to lie to her and hide that her name was carved into his flesh, but he couldn't bring himself to do that.

She met his gaze, as if she could sense his hesitation. Fearless. That's what she was. Maybe not with Oscar, but with him, there was no question about it.

He loved it. He hated it. It would be better if she feared him, better if she wanted to run from him and hide. Better for her. Better for him. He'd paid the price for his actions, and he didn't mind it, but there was no reason for her to know about it either.

"Tell me."

He couldn't deny her, no matter how much he wanted to. He groaned deep in his throat, wishing she'd asked him anything else.

"It happened after I stopped him, your stepfather. It was my punishment for protecting a child rather than scaring one."

She seemed to know he didn't want to talk about it, but he also saw she would not be swayed to another conversation or topic. "What does it say?"

He only hesitated for a short time, gnawing at his lip with his sharp teeth. It had no effect on her. "Peyton Thorne."

She started at the realization, and her eyes moved back to the runes on his skin. "You had my name branded upon you?"

"Not by choice." Now that he'd started telling her the truth, he couldn't very well lie about that.

"You were punished?" Her words were low and soft. "For saving me rather than scaring me?"

He nodded.

She contemplated his words. Then she leaned toward him again and pressed her mouth to the runes, one at a time. Her lips were a soothing balm, as if she could take away every pain he'd suffered upon their infliction.

The Host had been kind in their punishment in some ways, he supposed. They could have sent him to the In-Between, he realized, to be like those hands and voices. Always hungry.

Instead, Malgrumek had held him while one of the Host carved every rune until they could see his blood shine through.

Every monster's blood was as different as the monster, and Zeth's was red.

He'd screamed in pain with every mark they'd inflicted upon him, but he hadn't tried to fight or get away. He knew he'd deserved the punishment and while it had hurt like hell, he didn't regret it. Not in the long run. It was a physical reminder what he'd done, a reminder that he'd been assigned a single child.

One he'd abandoned for years it seemed. As Peyton bent and kissed another glowing rune, he cupped her chin in his hand and tilted it up. She met his gaze, her eyes watery with unshed tears. "Why are you crying?"

"It's my fault," she whispered, and it was all it took to break the dam inside her it seemed. She blinked and the tears streamed down her face.

Zeth shook his head. "No, my treasure. It wasn't your fault. I made a choice. We always have choices."

She started to shake her head, but he clasped her chin firmly in his hand.

"This was *my* choice," he told her, hoping she'd believe him. "And I'd make it over and over and over again if I had to."

Before he could question what he was doing or why, he bent his head and captured her lips. She gasped in shock and he groaned into the cavern of her mouth, his tongue diving inside to explore.

The hand at her chin smoothed out until he cupped her face, and his other hand slid into her hair, turning her head at another angle for a better kiss.

Her hands slid up his chest and then around to his back. Her short nails dug into his shoulder blades and he grunted and deepened the kiss further.

She tasted of sunshine and spice and heat. So much heat. He felt like his entire being was on fire around her, and only from a kiss.

Her response to him was more than he ever could have hoped for. She stood on the tips of her toes and moaned into his mouth, her tongue dancing with his. Her hands were everywhere, and when she slid them down over the curve of his back, sliding them over his tail, he shuddered.

No one had ever touched his tail, stroked it like. . .

He broke off the kiss and stared down at her. The fire inside him threatened to light the entire room ablaze. He wasn't certain how much longer he could control himself around her. He wanted to claim her, to brand her with his bite the way he'd been branded with her name.

None of it made sense to him. He'd never heard of monsters claiming anyone or anything, but the notion in his mind felt as much a part of him as her name. Instinct drove him to bend his head to her neck and smell the same scent he'd used to recognize her. Saliva dripped from his mouth and onto her skin. He licked the spot, delighted when shivers worked their way up and down her spine.

"Peyton," he breathed her name, saying it without her last name for the first time.

She panted, her chest rising and falling. He could see the fire of desire burning in her eyes, and her mouth tantalized him once more, but he didn't kiss her again. He pressed his thumb to her lips, tracing them with a slight press of one claw. Her breath hitched and her eyes blazed with need.

"Why. . ." She started to speak, but then cleared her throat and licked her lips. "You're a monster."

"Yes," he admitted, his voice a purr.

"Why do I feel this way about a monster?"

He grinned. He knew from her reaction to him she wanted him as much as he wanted her, but it still felt good to hear her say it. He wanted to hear more about how she felt about him, but that could wait for the moment.

The runes along his side burned as he took her in his arms and kissed her once again. She moaned and arched her body into him, her nails digging into his back and scratching him.

When he pulled away, they both panted for air, hunger burning deep in their eyes as they gazed at one another. He could almost see the glow of the runes on his face from the corner of his eyes.

"Because you are mine," he told her. The fierceness of his words surprised him, but he didn't question it. He gestured to the runes running up the length of his body. "And I belong to you as well. If you'll accept me, that is."

She smiled at him, and it felt like sunshine to have it warm his skin the way it did. She stroked his cheek with the back of her hand, running over the runes on that side of his face. "You've saved me, not once," she said in a low voice, "but twice. I think I can see where this takes us."

He gave her a curt nod of his head. "Good. Because I wasn't about to give you up."

Zeth didn't know what he was supposed to do now that his child was grown up. He'd been in the Darkside for a long time missing out on his child's life as she became a young woman. He didn't mind spending some time in the human realm learning more about her. Kissing her and building a relationship with her seemed as good a place as any to start on his way to figuring that out.

Everything else could wait until after he'd shown his woman how much he treasured her.

love Conquers Fury

Artemed Sullivan

one

M odern dance hits pump through the radio as I drum my fingers on the steering wheel. The wind whips through my hair as I drive along the back roads with not a care in the world. My name is Alecto. I'm on my way to a town called Santa Cambri for a little vacation. After all, a woman has to rest sometime.

Oh, one more thing about me: I'm a demon.

Since we're on Earth, Tess, my hellhound, has taken her favorite earthly inspired form, that of a cherry red Tesla convertible. Tess is a huge fan of the Tesla car and of the book Christine. She has always wanted to read an updated version of the book where Christine is now a Tesla. She likes the thought of instead of the victims hearing the throaty roar of a V-8 engine, they'd hear the whine of an electric motor sneaking up on them. Tess has a unique sense of humor.

I try to get away at least once a year, more if time permits. It's hard for me to sometimes get away since I do have a business empire to run. You may know me as one of The Furies from Greek mythology. As the years went along, I started to realize that I needed to branch out and diversify myself. Sure, there were plenty of things I could busy myself with in the underworld.

But I started to recognize my skillset could be of use to so many more people on Earth—I am known for unending anger, after all. Without my influence, countries waged war less. Neighbors were getting along more. Businesses weren't as cutthroat. In short, Earth needed more of me. So, a little nudge here and big shove there when needed. Now, in the modern age, you can find my work done as a behind the scenes ferocious consultant. My job is to find failing businesses, buy them, gut them, and sell what's left for a profit on behalf of my clients. I am a profiteer.

Inhaling deeply, I taste traces of sea salt in the air signaling that I'm getting closer to my destination as I pass farmland. Santa Cambri is a small coastal town in southern California about thirty minutes north of Oxnard. What makes Santa Cambri special and a desirable vacation spot for the supernational and celestial alike is it's considered neutral ground. Neither side is allowed to fight within the town or around a ten-mile radius of it. No one can harm or kill any of the townspeople either.

To do any of the previous would violate a pact that has been in place for thousands of years. Even though Santa Cambri has only been around for a few hundred years, this area has been used as a spot for respite far longer than that. A violation means death to whomever violated the pact and possible war to the race of the offending party.

In case of trouble each side has selected their own version of a lawperson of sorts. My side has Red, that to most looks like your average red-headed man with a beard who happens to own one of the local bars, Red's Pub. Said bar caters to non-humans, but humans are welcome if they know what they're getting into. The non-humans just need to remember to play nice at times. What most of the humans don't know is that Red is also a shapeshifter who transforms into a red wolf.

For the angelic side they have Angelica, she's an angel who looks like a normal human that owns Santa Cambri Inn that also caters to our kind, but again, humans are welcome to stay if they're friends of our kind. The most that Red or Angelica have ever had to do is quiet the non-humans down every so often.

Most the town is unaware that they live in a vacation hot spot for non-humans. Some of them are aware and welcome us. Others choose to ignore us and pretend that we don't exist. What they all like is the year round money they make off us. So what if they might think they saw a ghost out of the corner of their eye. That was a trick of the light. Or heard something howling in the middle of the night. Just a pack of dogs. Maybe that woman's canines were just abnormally long. Yeah that's it. And that angry woman didn't just morph into something with black eyes with slithering snakes as hair for a split second. None of those things could be real? Could they?

After a while I see the welcome to Santa Cambri sign. I sigh in blissful anticipation of what's to come. Me under a beach umbrella with my toes in the sand with the latest angsty spy thriller on my e-reader with a cold drink nearby. Getting caught up with friends over drinks as we retell wars stories from thousands of years ago.

I see the sign for Santa Cambri Inn and turn into the side parking lot and park. In reality, I actually didn't even need to drive; I could have just appeared here or even had Tess drive us, but I enjoy driving.

Tess turns herself off, and I step out, shutting the door behind me and heading toward the front door. I'll let Tess decide if she wants to stay a Tesla or transform into another form and hangout. Her other favorite earthly form is that of an American golden retriever. A hellhound as the top, all-American breed. The humor is not lost on me; neither is it lost on her.

Heading to the front desk, I'm immediately greeted by Angelica.

"Hi, Alecto, how was your trip over? Did you travel or transport yourself?"

"Hey, Angelica, I like the route, so Tess and I drove up. How's business been?"

"Great as always. I was just..."

Just then I hear the inn door open, and I turn and see an angel stride through the door. She holds the door open for Tess, who is now in her American golden retriever form, and allows her to enter.

"Thanks Dina," Tess says in her deep throaty, growly sounding voice.

"Anytime, Tess," Dina says melodically.

I instantly groan inwardly.

Great, just great, it's Dina.

I'd had many dealings with her through the years. Eons ago, it was direct war with angels against demons on the battlefield. I'd faced off against her, sword against sword. Later on, my job was to fuel anger in places like the crusades, the inquisition, and even the Salem witch trials. Hers was to defuse the situation and save lives. Now, she has her own angel investment business that tries to swoop in and save failing businesses and get them back on their feet and make a profit. Today, we compete on who can get to a failing business first.

"Hi, Dina, I'll be with you in just a moment," Angelica says.

"Sure, no problem, Angelica," Dina says. Then, she nods in my direction and adds, "Alecto."

"Dina," I say with a nod back.

"Hey, Tess, how goes it?" Angelica smiles at Tess.

"Rather well, Angelica," Tess says.

"Where was I?" Angelica smiles. "Ah, yes! Alecto your room is all set, room six is yours. As always, it's warded so only you, Tess, Red, and I have access. Let me know if you need anything and have a pleasant stay!"

I step to the side of the check-in desk and start to head toward the steps leading upstairs to where the rooms are, Tess in tow. I catch the beginning of the conversation between Angelica and Dina as I walk upstairs.

"Dina, it's always a pleasure to have you here," Angelica says. "From the rumors I've been hearing, business for you is booming."

"I get so much joy in helping others," I hear Dina's annoyingly chipper voice chime.

Angelica lets out a happy sigh. "It really is about helping others, isn't it?"

"It really is," Dina responds.

I tune them out. *Angels.* Man, I think I'm going to be sick. Don't get me wrong, they're all not bad. Angelica for instance isn't that bad. Dina though, she's a whole other level of do good'er. Whatever. I'm here to relax, not think about my competition. I reach the top of the first flight of stairs. I turn and walk down the hallway until I find room six which is on the left. I stand in front of the door and just as I'm about to place my hand against the door I hear a very familiar voice from behind me.

"I guess we're neighbors," Dina says.

Turning slowly, I see that Dina is looking at me while standing directly across from me at the door for room seven. She gives me a little wave. I squint my eyes and look at her closely. Until now, I never noticed that her blue eyes are actually a steel blue. Or that her dark, wavey hair has curls to it as well, and that it also has auburn highlights. Wait! Stop! What the heck am I doing? This *thing* is my direct competition. I snap myself out of whatever just happened.

"Looks that way," I reply gruffly.

"Now, Alecto, play nice. We're both here on vacation."

"Dina, this is me being nice."

"Tsk, tsk. Tess sounds like your demon needs a nap."

Tess laughs.

I glare down at Tess, who just continues to laugh.

Slapping my hand against the door, I hear it unlock. I turn the knob and enter with Tess right behind me.

I look at Tess again. "I should just leave you out there, you traitor," I say to her.

"Hey what can I say, it was funny," she says to me.

"Just get in the fucking room," I huff to her.

Once the two of us are in I shut the door.

I hear a laughing, "Bye" from Dina through the door and then a door opening and shutting.

Fuck my life.

Flopping down on the bed I throw my right forearm across my eyes.

Why does she always get to me? *Always*. She's constantly goading me on. *Grr*.

"Because you let her," Tess answers.

"Stop reading my thoughts," I snap back.

"I'm *your* hellhound. Part of *my* job is to look out for *you*," she says coolly.

Jumping up without any real thought, my feet start quickly pacing back and forth across the worn wooden floor of the room. Stopping suddenly in the middle of the room.

"I need to get out of here," I mutter to myself.

Since I'm a demon there's no real need for me to have a suitcase with me for clothing. I just think myself out of my jeans and ankle boots and into knee length shorts and sandals. Leaving the *Star Wars* Kylo Ren T-shirt that that I already have on—the one that reads "Be the Kylo"—because well, we all could use a little of The Kylo in our lives.

Leaving the room, I head downstairs and outside toward the beach. After a short walk, I find what I'm looking for. There's an outdoor bar right on the beach called Surf's Up; it's owned by a demon that goes by the name Patch. Patch lost his left eye long ago in one of the many angels versus demons skirmishes. Now he wears an eye patch when in human form and looks just like any other average man. About ten years ago, he decided to retire Earthside and open this place. Besides serving great drinks, Surf's Up also has a tasty food menu as well. Since it's lunchtime the place fits the bill for what I want.

Walking right up to the bar I take a seat in one of the highbacked bar chairs, with Tess hopping up on the seat next to mine. Right away Patch spots us and walks over to us and sets down two menus in front of us.

"What can I get you two ladies?" Patch asks.

I quickly glance at the drink section. "I'll take an el diablo." Flipping over to the food area of the menu. "With a burger and onion rings," I finish.

"And I'll go with a devil's margarita, a cheeseburger, and an order of fries," Tess says.

"Coming right up!" Patch says as he takes the menus back from us.

With everything ordered I pull out my e-reader from the small crossbody sling bag that I have with me.

"Tess, do you want your e-reader?"

"Sure, a little reading would be nice right now."

I hand Tess hers and close my bag.

"What are you reading right now?" I ask her.

Tess turns to look at me, "Honestly, I'm not quite sure. It's not the typical romance that I'd normally read. It's this really weird age gap romance. The premise is that this professional softball player goes to her estranged daughter's engagement party. Where it turns out that the daughter's bride-to-be was a long weekend vacation hookup from years ago. The whole thing is just this horribly written trainwreck that I can't stop reading." A look of confusion crosses her face.

"Huh? I can't even follow that," I say with a look of puzzlement.

"Neither can I really. So, what are you reading?" she asks.

"This SEAL is given drugs as an experiment while out on a mission without his knowledge to make them some sort of super soldiers. Then his team is all killed to cover it up. He survives and is on the run. It's pretty good so far," I say.

"Sounds way better than what I'm reading," Tess says.

Our conversation is interrupted by Patch coming back and placing our orders down in front of us.

"I think I'm going to adjust my form a little bit to make it easier for me to read and eat," Tess decides.

Tess transforms herself into more of half golden retriever, half human form, like a shifter would. She does this so she can sit upright and use her front paws more like hands to eat and drink more comfortably. Now what would happen if an average unbelieving human saw her you might ask? Tess has used a spell on herself. So, unless you knew what she was, you'd just see a golden retriever there lapping at a glass and eating off a plate like any normal dog would using their mouth.

After eating and reading for a bit, Tess is the first to break our silence.

"This is a great burger, I'm glad we came here," she says between bites.

"I really like the food and the fact it's right on the beach so you can see and hear everything going on from here," I say.

She gestures toward my e-reader. "How's your book going?"

I finish the last of my drink and food. "It's still a fun read. How's you trainwreck doing?"

"Still a trainwreck. Hey, what do you want to do after this?" Tess asks as she pops the last of her burger in her mouth.

"How do you feel about grabbing a bucket of Devil's Brew from Patch and renting an umbrella on the beach?" I ask as I set a credit card down on the bar.

"Sure, it'd be nice to relax down there," she says as she returns to her full golden retriever form.

"Will that be all for you ladies?" Patch asks.

"I'd like to tack on a bucket of Devil's Brew longnecks with limes and a bowl for Tess. We're gonna go hangout on the beach," I reply.

"Sure thing," Patch says.

In about a minute, he comes back with our bucket and bowl.

"Just sign here," he says.

A quick signature and then Tess and I are a quick walk over to the umbrella rental place. From there we find a clear spot on the beach away from people and we pitch our newly rented umbrella. I think of a couple of beach blankets, and they appear on the sand beneath the umbrella. I pour a beer into the bowl for Tess and grab one for myself. I think a pillow for under my head and lay back, closing my eyes.

This is just what the doctor ordered. A little fresh air, the sun shining, and the sound of the surf lightly crashing against the shore. I take a sip of my beer and feel myself starting to relax. I lay there just enjoying the sounds of the waves and the scent of the salt spray as I drink my beer. The warmth from the sand under blanket starts to relax me even more. Before long I feel myself being lulled into a light nap.

"They'll let just anyone on this beach, won't they?"

I immediately recognize the singsong voice. My eyes snap open and upon looking to my right I'm greeted by Dina sitting under her own umbrella. She gives me a wink and a salute with her wineglass before taking a sip from it.

"You, again," I growl.

"Hi, Dina. Oh, hey, Peggy," Tess says.

I look a little past Dina and see her war steed, Peggy. I've never had a beef with Peggy. She's currently transformed into the form of an English golden retriever. In her normal form she's a Pegasus.

What is the difference between an English and an American golden retriever you may ask? Well, they're both considered golden retrievers, but an American has more of the typical, as-seen-on-TV golden coat. Meanwhile, an English golden retriever dons a cream coat, much lighter than the American, and the snout tends to appear a little more defined and proper. While English golden retrievers tend to be on the calmer side (tend being the key word here), American golden retrievers are typically more on the hyper side, especially in their younger years.

"Peggy," I say with a nod.

"It's always nice to see both of you," Peggy replies.

"It's such splendid weather for a day at the beach, isn't it?" Dina says with a clap of her hands as she rubs them together.

"Was," I grumble in reply.

"Was? Oh, Alecto don't be *that* way. You're always just so... *moody*," Dina says as both retrievers snicker and nod.

"I am not," I grit out through clinched teeth. "Look right here." I gesture around me. "If I were moody?" I use my two first fingers from each hand to make air quotes. "Would I be out on a beach in the sun enjoying the sounds of the surf with one of my closest friends and having some drinks?" I counter. "I am not moody." I take a long sip from my beer.

"Okay, you're not moody," Dina replies and picks up the book that's sitting in her lap.

We all sit in silence for a while and for whatever reason I start to feel like I should say something.

"What are you reading?" I ask, voice low and not much more than a grumble.

"Hmm, what was that?" Dina asks, nose still buried in the book she's reading.

"I asked, what are you reading?" I reply, a little louder this time but still using a monotone.

"Oh, it's about angels who use swords made of light to fight evil across the universe. The angels do all of this with prayers they call The Force. They fight these demons that I've never heard of called the Sith. It's really fascinating," she says with complete seriousness in her voice.

"Gimme that," I say as I reach over to her and snatch the paperback from her hands. I flip it over to quickly read the cover. Looking over to her I say, "This is a *Star Wars* novel."

Dina starts to laugh. "Gotcha," she says while giggling, and I suddenly realize I've been played.

I toss the book back over to her as she deftly catches in her hands while still laughing. "I have the high ground," she continues.

"You're killing trees by reading traditionally printed books," I say.

"I like the feel of a book in my hands. There are tree farms specifically for paper. Besides this book is used, so there," she replies.

I sigh and take another sip of my drink. She got me yet

again. Smiling slightly to myself I have to admit that was a good one that time. I walked right into it.

"That's the latest one, right?" I ask.

"Yes, it is," she answers and takes a drink from her glass.

"How is it so far?" I ask.

"It's a page turner for sure. I can tell from your T-shirt that you're a fan, so I don't want to give anything away," she says.

"I'd call that a definite recommendation, so I'll have to grab it then. Dina, I never knew you were into *Star Wars*," I say to her.

Dina sighs. "Alecto, there are a lot of things you don't know about me," she says wistfully as she turns her head and looks me directly in the eye. Her gaze is so intense and penetrating that I find myself instantly wet. I swallow and look away out into the surf.

"Are there now?" The words tumble out before I can stop them. I hear someone clearing their throat. It might be Peggy, but I'm not sure though.

"Tess, wanna go for a walk with me?" Peggy asks.

"Sure!" Tess says much too quickly.

And just like that, I'm alone with Dina.

Dina appears right beside me. She slowly laps at the whole edge of my left ear and then whispers into it, "Yes, Alecto, there is."

She runs her bottom lip from the base of my neck to my chin where she gives my lips the most devilishly deep kiss that I've ever received. Who knew angels could kiss like this. I lean into the kiss without thinking and run my fingers through the base of her hair. Eyes closed I lose myself in the moment. Then it hits me. This is Dina. An angel. My competition, no less.

I start to get up and gently push her away. "I can't do this," I say.

"Why not?" Dina asks.

"I just can't," I reply.

And with that I transport myself back to the door of my room at the inn and enter it.

two

I t had been a few hours since I just left Dina there on the beach. Tess went back to the room about twenty minutes ago.

Now, I'm getting my ass handed to me as I'm pacing back and forth with Tess sitting on the bed looking at me like I have two heads.

"So let me see if I'm understanding you correctly. You just left Dina right there sitting all alone on the beach?" Tess asks.

"Yes, you heard me right. I did just that," I grumble back.

"What is wrong with you?" Tess says.

"Nothing is wrong with *me*. Why are you questioning me? What does it matter to you?" I snap back. My birthright as one of the three furies is showing right now.

"*What does it matter*? Just because we're demons doesn't mean we have to be assholes. Dina is a nice person and I for one like her. You shouldn't have just left her like that."

"I panicked, okay. I just panicked. She scared me," I shoot back.

"The big, bad, demon was afraid of an *angel*," Tess mocks.

"It's true," I plea.

"Yeah, right," she says.

"I mean it, I'm not lying," I say. Then, I mumble, "She makes me so nervous."

"What did you say?" Tess asks.

"It doesn't matter."

"You need to fix this."

"How?

"*How?* By apologizing, *that's how!*" Tess snarls back, she then points at our closed door. "You need to go across the hall to her room. Knock on that damn door and talk to her."

"Fine, I'll go over and talk to her," I whisper dejectedly as I stop pacing and turn toward and head toward the door.

"Alecto, you better make this right," Tess calls out to me.

I pause with my hand on the doorknob and turn my head to her. "I'll try, Tess, but you know how I am with interpersonal skills."

"Try harder this time," she says.

I tun back toward the door, opening it and walking out into the hallway. Squaring my shoulders, I take a deep breath, walk across the hall, and stop in front of Dina's door. What am I supposed to say to her? I'm never any good with of this type of stuff. Lost in thought, I startle back when the door opens.

"Well, look what the cat dragged in," Dina casually says as she leans against the door jam, arms crossed.

My mouth just hangs open and all I can say is, "Umm."

"Cat got your tongue? Is that it?" she asks.

"Well..." I start.

She stands there watching me intently with a slight smirk on her face.

I take another deep breath. "I'd like to apologize. I'm so sorry I handled things the way I did. What I did back there at the beach was wrong."

I take another deep breath. Her sudden appearance has rattled my nerves, so I'm at a loss for words, a demon shaking from jitters. What the hell do I even say? I had planned to have another minute or two to process, but now I'm at a loss. For the next moment, I stutter, until only words I did not know were even inside of me come tumbling out.

"To make up for it I'd like to take you out to dinner tonight..." I say, the words spilling out, regret consuming me the second I ask. What? What has possessed me to ask this?

She quickly moves away from the doorway and into the hallway, shutting the door. Grabbing my arm, she threads hers through it.

"I—" I start to say.

Dina cuts me off. "I know just the place."

Next thing I know, we're walking arm and arm toward the stairs.

I'm guided down the stairs and out the door where we make a left on the sidewalk.

Dina leans into me, "There's a relatively new restaurant that I've been meaning to try but haven't gotten a chance. It's just delightful from what I've been told."

"Sounds goods," I say.

After a short walk of a few blocks, we stop outside a building that says Sal's Steakhouse. Holding the door for her, I gesture for her to enter, "Ladies first."

A quick glance around and I get an old school rat pack feel from the place. In fact, I hear Sinatra playing in the background. A hostess quickly grabs menus and seats us at a small round table opposite of each other.

The hostess quickly returns to fill our water glasses and then promptly leaves.

Dina moves her chair closer to be more beside mine.

"It'll be easier for us to talk this way," she says and gives my forearm a gentle pat and leaves her hand there.

I cover my awkwardness with a sip of water and then I turn my focus to the menu in front on me.

"How do you feel about figuring out what we want to order and getting that out of the way and then we could talk uninterrupted. Does that sound okay with you?" I turn to Dina and ask.

"Sounds find to me," she says as she picks up her own menu and begins to look at it.

"Any recommendations?" I ask.

"I've heard the roasted chicken with thyme is good. Along with the prime rib, and the lamb as well. Honestly, I haven't heard a bad thing about this place," she replies.

"Wow, that's some glowing reviews there. I guess I'll go with the roasted lamb then. How about you?" I ask.

"You know what, I'll do the same. How do you feel about a couple of glasses of port as well?" she asks.

"Sure, I like port," I say.

Just as we close our menus a waiter comes over and takes our order. He comes back a couple of minutes later with two glasses of a thirty-year tawny port.

Clearing my throat, I look Dina directly in the eyes. I feel my mouth going dry. Butterflies start to form in my stomach. I notice her hair and must fight the urge to not play with a loose curl of it.

"Dina," I begin. "I might be good in a boardroom situation. But if it isn't already obvious, I'm absolutely terrible when it comes to talking to people in social settings."

"I would have never guessed," Dina deadpans, then she nudges me with her shoulder.

"I'm being serious here."

"Okay, okay I'll stop and let you finish what you have to say."

She looks at me with playful eyes with a hint of seriousness to them.

"Thanks, I'll just spit it out. I'm sorry I left you on the beach like that and ghosted you. I apologize for doing that to you. That was very childish of me."

"I accept your apology," she says as she slowly runs a finger up and down my forearm while running a tongue over her lips.

I feel my pulse in my ears and I lick my own lips.

"Now, why on Earth did you leave?" she asks.

"Because..." I start and then stop. "Because..." I start again. "You make me so nervous." I blurt out just as the waiter shows up with our meals right at that very moment. My face changes to a look of embarrassment. All I want to do is crawl under the table and return to hell at once. The waiter quickly sets our plates down and scurries away.

"Well, that's one way to start a meal. Let's eat," she says with a smile.

We unfurl our napkins into our laps and begin to eat. In between bites, we start to talk again.

Dina points down at her plate with her fork. "This lamb is just divine."

"And it is delicious, I agree." I take a sip from my wine glass.

"Why do I make you nervous?" she asks abruptly.

"I don't know why. You just do."

"I won't bite, you know. Or at least when I do, I don't bite hard," she says with a small chuckle.

I feel a blush starting from the base of my neck and running up my face.

"Now you're messing with me."

"Alecto, I'm always messing with you."

"And why is that?"

"Why? Alecto, do I have to drop breadcrumbs?" Dina says while she gentle places a hand on my thigh. Which causes me to start slightly in surprise.

We're both looking at each other now, like really looking at each other like it's the very first time we've truly seen one another.

"Alecto, we could have killed each other time and time again on the battlefield eons ago. We both know it; we've just never spoken about it. There were plenty of chances by both of us.

Yet neither of us did. One of us would conveniently just land a glancing blow or would miss by a millimeter. In the times where we were able to land a killing when the other was prone on the ground, we'd pretend we didn't see the opening. If we saw the other fighting another and the odds didn't look good, we'd somehow interfere and save the other."

Dina was right, there's always been something there between us. I'd never had the heart to ever kill her or even Peggy for that matter. There was something about Dina that I was always drawn to through the years. And yes, there was an unspoken rule about it. Even Tess and Peggy knew about it. I'd seen Tess run across a battlefield countless times to get to Dina if I couldn't. Same for Peggy, who saved my bacon on several occasions. I'd been under Dina's sword many times, and she'd never killed me. The four of us had a bond.

Still, fear tugs at me from the deepest of places.

"I... I..." I stutter, unsure of how to finish. Running a hand through my hair, and staring deep into her eyes, I shake my head. "I'm a fury! I don't get scared. And here I am with you, like this; you make me *shiver*."

Dina places an introspective finger to her bottom lip, a devilish grin crossing that mouth I want to taste.

"I know why," she says.

"Why?" I dare ask.

"You're scared of getting hurt," she says. "Afraid of what it might look like if you let yourself care about someone else other than your hellhound."

She's probably right, but I'll never admit it to her.

"So, what if I am?" I ask.

"Eventually you're going to have to let someone in," she replies.

She knows she has me and that I'm just being stubborn.

"What if I don't want to?" I ask.

I'm just painting myself into a corner and I realize it.

Before she can reply, I say, "Don't answer that." With a heavy sigh, I continue.

"Dina, we both recognize there's always been chemistry between us. But what do we do about it? I'm a demon and you're an angel," I finish.

"Alecto, we take a chance, that's what we do," she says matter-of-factly.

"And what does that mean exactly?" I ask.

"It means we spend time getting to know each other. If we click, we can figure out the angel and demon thing later," she says and then grabs my face with her two hands and kisses me deeply on the mouth.

My eyes go wide in startlement at the suddenness of the kiss. Next thing I know, I'm reciprocating when my own mouth moves in response to her kiss. There are years of unsaid emotions in our kiss from both sides. When we finally break apart, I'm left breathless.

"I guess that was the getting to know each other part?" I shakily ask.

"That was part of it, yes," Dina says as she reaches for my hand. "Would you like to get out of here and go somewhere else to talk?"

I'm not positive about what I actually want but Dina's right, we need to start somewhere. Talking is no doubt the best next step. I'm still confused about things, but I have nothing to lose.

"Sure, I'd like that," I hear myself say, while placing my other hand on the table, covertly materializing cash onto the table. Payment handled, I stand and help Dina to her feet with the hand I'm still holding.

We walk through the restaurant, only slowing so I can hold the door for her to exit. Once we get to the street I turn to Dina and ask, "Where to next?"

She looks back at me, "I was thinking Red's, does that work for you?"

"Red's is a nice choice." I realize I've been looking at her for a bit too long and that it's turned into staring. "Shall we?"

"We shall." Dina smiles grasps my hand in hers as we begin to walk over to Red's.

The walk over to Red's is a short walk. Along the way, each of us point out different things we see in windows or places we've either been or want to go to.

In no time we're there. Red's is your average bar, leaning more toward the dive side. Sometimes there's a live band, if not there's a jukebox in the corner and TVs over the bar itself. It holds about fifty people, more if it's packed body to body. Red's is half full when we walk in and head up to the bar. Red himself walks from the other side of the bar counter to take our orders.

"Hi, ladies, what'll be tonight?" he asks.

"I'll take whatever pilsner you have on draft," Dina says.

"And you, Alecto?" Red asks.

"I'll take the same," I reply.

"Coming right up," Red says and walks off to grab our orders.

"I'm sure there's a joke about this somewhere. An angel and a demon walk into a bar," Dina says with a smile.

"I'm sure there is too," I say with a shy smile back.

Red comes back and places our drinks on the bar in front of us. With a thanks from both of us we decide on a table off in a corner so we can talk. Our table is round and has two seats, so I move my chair to be closer on Dina's right hand to make is easier for us to talk.

Looking down at my beer and at a loss for words and not knowing where to begin, I run my thumb against the condensation on the glass.

Dina breaks the silence with, "I know this is hard for you." She places a reassuring hand upon mine.

Slowing raising my head to make eye contact, I say, "I've never been great at relating to others. So, to say this is hard is an understatement. To wage war is easy. To drive others to anger or enact justice. Those things are a piece of cake." I wave my hand between us. "But this, I don't know how to do *this*. Dina, *this* scares me."

"This isn't easy, Alecto, it *is* scary. It requires putting yourself out there with the possibility of getting your heart broken. But with it is the opportunity of so much joy for yourself and the person you're with." Dina says with a deep heartfelt smile. "Now enough of us being so serious. We both like *Star Wars*, right?" she asks.

"We do," I answer.

"Now who are your favorite characters and why?" she asks.

"Anakin Skywalker slash Darth Vader and Kylo Ren aka Ben Solo, both because they're misunderstood and manipulated by Palpatine. Who are yours?" I ask in return.

"Padmé, Leia, and Rey, because they all fought against the dark side and Palpatine," she answers without missing a beat.

"Do you see yourself as fighting against the dark, Dina?"

"I do. Do you see yourself as misunderstood?"

"I do. I guess we see ourselves in our *Star Wars* favorites then as well."

Dina bites her bottom lip in the most adorable way while she ponders this before answering. "I guess we do."

I take a deep drink of my beer to help steady my nerves. I look up and see Dina looking me in the eyes just as the jukebox in the corner starts playing a tune I recognize immediately. It's "Angel Eyes" by The Jeff Healey Band. It sounds so cliché, in fact, so I start to chuckle to myself.

"Something funny?"

"You, me, and this song," I say while pointing up toward the ceiling.

"Oh," Dina says while chucking back. "I get it now. Angel. Angel eyes. It *is* a good song though. I've always liked it."

"Me too, I've always liked The Jeff Healey Band's music. I like a lot of blues type music."

I realize I've been humming the song under my breath and stop. Dina just gives me a knowing smile.

"I never knew that about you," she says. "I like blues, too. Country as well."

"I can picture you with a cowboy hat and boots. It suits your personality."

"Oh, with just those things on?" she says with a wink of an eye.

Sighing, I roll my eyes as I feel my face flush. "Dina, play nice."

"Relax, dear, I was only having a little fun. An angel has to live a little, ya know, and you should too," she says while giving my forearm a reassuring squeeze.

Chuckling to myself, I take another sip of beer.

"I know, I know." I smile. "I'm trying."

"Yes. You. Are," Dina says while swooping in and kissing me gently on the lips. "Did that help a little?" She breaks our kiss. "To live a little that is."

"I believe it did, but I need to be sure," I hear myself say, butterflies still fluttering nervously inside of me.

Mustering up the courage for what *is* the unthinkable for me.

Looking into her eyes, I capture her lips with mine. At first, it's just a gentle kiss, a return of the kiss Dina gave to me, but then I feel myself deepening the kiss. Our tongues twirl around each other in a slow dance. I hear a low moan escape from Dina as I cup the nape of her neck. I slowly break away from the kiss and rest my forehead against hers, both of us slightly panting.

"Wow," Dina whispers. "Are you sure now?"

"I think so, but I may need to check periodically. If that's okay with you?"

"Oh, it's *more* than okay with me, Alecto," Dina says my name with a purr to it.

Instantly, I feel myself throbbing from it.

"Good to know," I huskily reply as I try to keep my composure. "Is it me or is it hot in here?"

"It's warm in here but it's *you* that's sizzling, Alecto," Dina playfully says as she breaks our touch with a kiss of my nose.

Feeling myself blush from what Dina's just said, I sigh happily. I feel the words fall from my lips before I can stop them, "Want to get out of here?"

"Sure, where to?" Dina asks.

"Honestly, I don't know," I surprise myself with my candid answer.

"My place?" Dina asks with a quirk of a brow.

"Sure, seems neutral to me," I deadpan as my lip slightly quivers with a quirked brow back as I try to hold back a giggle.

"*Alecto*, I'm deeply hurt." Dina feigns with a clutch of her heart.

We both get up and walk toward the door, giving Red a wave.

"Night ladies," Red says with a wave.

Once outside I continue our conversation.

"I'm just looking out for my virtue," I innocently reply.

"Your virtue?" Dina sly questions.

"Yes, I know how you warrior angels can be, I've heard the stories." I continue with my schtick.

"I'll show you stories," Dina says with a smirk while taking my hand and hauling me down the dark alley of Red's. Pulling me into an embrace she passionately kisses me as I feel her unfurling her opalescent white wings which then envelope me. I immediately lose all coherent thought, my joking cast aside as I'm lost in the kiss. A sigh of contentment breaks free from my lips as I ease more into the kiss. My mouth demanding more from Dina, which she freely gives.

After a few moments, Dina steps back and asks, "How's your virtue now, Alecto?"

"Much better now," I answer, a bit dazed sounding.

"Still wanna hang out at my place?" Dina asks.

"Of course I do!" I answer.

three

We hold hands on our short walk back to the inn. Once upstairs, Dina places her hand against her door, unlocking it. With a twist of the knob, she opens the door and gestures for me to enter with her trailing behind. I know upon walking in that Peggy won't be there and that she'll be with Tess either over at my room or off doing something. The room is the same layout as mine. A loveseat with a coffee table in front of a fireplace with a TV mounted above. The next part of the room has a bed with a bathroom off to the side. Suddenly I see something scurry across the room. It's fast and blurry but it looks like the shaft of a dick.

"Is that..."

"A weird looking tiny penis with four legs running across the floor?'

I nod.

"Why yes."

"What the fuck, Dina."

"It's Peggy's pet Girt. Back in the battle days a demon kept whipping out its itty bity pee-pee on the battlefield. Peggy got tired of it being waved around and cut it off with her sword. Well, it sprouted four legs and started running around. She felt bad and scooped it up to save it from being trampled and made it her pet. Girt, go find Peggy."

I watch as Girt runs out the door. Dina takes a seat on the loveseat, following suit I do the same.

"How about some port?" she asks.

"Sounds great," I say.

Dina thinks a bottle and glasses into existence for us and hands me a glass and pours one for herself.

Lightly clinking glasses, I take a sip.

"This is a great vintage," I comment and take another.

"It's a forty year," she replies with a small smile. "I'm glad you like it. I had you in mind when I chose it." Setting her glass down she slowly moves closer to me and continues to speak at a soft whisper. "It's deep, sweet and, very complex, but well worth the wait."

I feel Dina's lips as they capture mine in a deep kiss. Instantly wrapping my arms around her, I stroke my hands up and down her back beneath her shirt, subconsciously straddling her. Releasing all of my fears. Knowing what I've known for years: Dina is home. Dina is *my home.*

I wait for that thought to scare me—because it *should.* It normally *would.*

Except somehow... it doesn't.

For once, I start to accept what would have been the unacceptable for me.

I sense Dina getting to her feet. I tighten my grip around her waist with my legs, running my hands through her hair as she walks across the room. Tearing my mouth from Dina's with a soft low growl, I grasp the hem of her purple blouse and lift it over her head, tossing it aside. I hear a hiss of an intake of breath as I slowly lap at the top of her breasts with my tongue over the top of her bra.

"Lover, it's my turn now," I hear Dina huskily whisper into my ear as she lifts me up and sets me down in front of the foot of the bed. There's hunger in her eyes as she removes my T-shirt, with my bra quickly following behind. Biting my bottom lip to stifle a cry as she takes one of my nipples into her mouth, I feel the swift strokes of her tongue before I hear and feel the pop of her lips as my nipple is released.

"I needed to make a quick stop before heading to my destination," she says as she once again purrs my name out, "Alecto."

Her lips graze from right below my breasts until they end at the top of my shorts with a slow kiss and Dina on her knees.

"Now, these are in my way." The words flow sensually from her mouth, eyes looking up at me with a sly grin. Dina carefully tugs my shorts down and unbuckles my sandals. I step out of the pile gathered at my feet, kicking it out and returning to right where I was standing.

Dina kisses me right above my bikini panties "What to do about these?" she asks before grasping the waistband of them with her teeth and releasing them with a snap.

Unable to take this slow burn anymore, I pant out through

gritted teeth "Dina, I'm throbbing so hard it hurts."

"Hang on Alecto, I'm almost there," she gently whispers as she peels the last piece of clothing from my body. "There, my darling, is this better?"

She slides a hand between my legs and lightly rubs. I dig my nails slightly into my palms as a moan escapes my mouth.

Watching as Dina removes her hand, I plead, "Please don't stop."

"Oh, I'm not stopping, I'm just slightly pausing. Now, may I have your left leg?"

She rests a hand on my left calf. I just nod vigorously, unable to answer. Shifting my weight over to my right leg, I see Dina draping my left leg over her shoulder. I balance myself with a hand on her other shoulder and the other running through her hair. Dina's hands grip the sides of my hips.

"Alecto, my love, you are a beauty to be hold, inside and out. I've always loved you. I've longed for you. You are the other half of my soul, and I intend to show you how much you mean to me."

Her tongue slowly enters my core, concentrating around my G-spot. A moan leaves my lips as my legs start to quiver.

"Lover," Dina says in a loving, yet commanding tone that only makes me wetter, "you will stand. I've only just begun."

I feel her taking on more of my weight with her hands to support me. Sensations of kisses on my inner thighs greet me as she returns to her position at my core with swirls that transition to gradual full, flat swipes up through my slit pausing at my pearl where I'm lavished with deep sucking kisses.

My knees buckle from the intensity of the building orgasm. Through the rushing of blood through my ears, I hear and feel a subtle growl from Dina as she adjusts her grip on me and switches to grasping my ass cheeks. The vibration from her growl on my pearl pushes me over to edge to my release. Dina rushes to her feet and steals my cry with her mouth as she cradles me into an embrace as I come down from my climax.

Leaning my forehead against hers, I catch my breath as I look into her eyes. In those eyes I see so much. I see passion and love.

I see all the things previously lingering beneath my own surface that I ignored and pushed away.

I really have loved her for a long time—and it only took this encounter for me to understand the gravity of my feelings. A fury in love. What a concept. But it's the truth, nonetheless.

A truth I can no longer run from.

Our kiss reignites and becomes heated again, and I break it for a moment. "Dina, I've never felt anything like this before. What's happening between us goes beyond words, but I think you've described it best: you're the other half of my soul. As a fury, I probably shouldn't be saying this, but you've showed me that heaven is right here with you. I can't wait any longer and need to show you how I feel about you."

Reaching behind her, I unclasp her bra and slide it free from her body. Cupping a breast in each hand I give both nipples a quick lick followed by a nip.

Dina throws her head back with a hiss of enjoyment "Alecto, I didn't know you had it in you."

"There are many things you don't know about me," I reply with a wink, echoing our words from earlier. Then, I lift her up and place her gently in the center of the bed. Getting right to work, I remove her sandals and cover her bare legs with generous kisses until I reach the bottom of her shorts.

Tenderly, I remove her shorts along with her panties and drop them over the side of the bed. Stopping, I admire Dina's beautiful body before sliding up to straddle her at her waist. Leaning forward, I can't resist giving her eyelids and nose feathery kisses. Moving down to her luscious lips, I take them with my own as I move my weight to one forearm. My passion on fire and overflowing with every deep kiss we have.

Pulling my mouth away, I'm met with pleading in Dina's eyes as she opens her mouth to speak.

I lovingly silence her with a "Shh" and a gentle finger on her bottom lip. Closing my eyes for a second to compose my thoughts. Willing myself to find the correct words I open them.

"Dina, I have something I need to tell you..." Taking a deep breath, I continue. "I love you, and I can't live without you. I'm sorry it's taken me this long to realize it and to tell you. Deep down I've always known this if I'm being honest with myself."

"Alecto, my heart, I feel the exact same way."

Seeing the need and love in her eyes, my lips cover hers in soft gentle kisses. Working my way down her neck and collarbone, I feel Dina starting to grind against me.

"I need you to take the edge off, my love," Dina pants out.

"I've got you," I say, giving her lips a quick kiss before moving my knee between her legs to gently rub against her as I stroke around the edges of her nipples with my thumbs. "Almost there, lover." I finish with a swirling lick and a kiss.

"Alecto, I can't wait another longer," Dina moans. Moving back to straddle her, I softly rub her rock-hard clit with my thumb.

"Lover, you are absolutely drenched. It's making me throb so hard. Pleasuring you gets me off." I hear myself panting out to her as I enter her and start stroking her G-spot while still rubbing her clit.

"Better?" I ask as I lean in and plant a generous kiss against her neck.

"Much, but I need more, Alecto. Love me." There's warmth in her eyes.

"I can do that, my heart."

Dina's hand reaches up and pulls my head down to bring my mouth to hers as I pick up the pace with my fingers down south. A moan leaves her mouth as she starts thrusting into my fingers. I feel her core pulse around my fingers.

"I'm so close," she says. My own climax is building. We both cry out each other's names in unison as we ride the crest of our joint release together. Leaning our foreheads against one another as our heartrates slow. Moving to my side, I wrap an arm around her while laying my head upon her shoulder.

"I've never felt anything like this," I say. "Thiis connection that we have. You've always been there all along right in front of me. I was just too dense to realize it. To acknowledge it."

I feel Dina stroking my hair as she kisses my forehead.

"Lover, you're not dense. We're fine," she says. "It's hard to let go and open your heart and trust. I completely understand that. We can go as slow as you want with our relationship."

Her words soothe me, making this even easier. I know now in my heart she's what I want—but she's also given me the option to take things at my own pace, which further helps my resolve to move forward with this.

It's probably from this where I draw my next strength to admit the full truth to her.

"I didn't notice how empty my life was before you," I admit. "I was thinking about this earlier, Dina. You're my home. You make me feel safe. No one has ever made me feel any of those things, except for you. I want to spend forever with you, if you'll have me?"

"My Alecto, I've been waiting for so very long for you to finally see me. To *really* see me. I've been right here in front of you this whole time, my love."

"Dina, I have something important to tell you," I say.

"What is it?"

Swallowing, I take a second to compose my thoughts, thinking of the bond that can be shared between the dark and the light.

"An angel and a demon can fall in love," I muster the courage to say.

"Yes, my love, they can."

THE END

don't know WHERE, don't know WHEN

Katie Commons

don't know where, don't know when

The forest had gone completely silent.

Nikolai spent a better part of the morning locating his snares and checking for any catches. Most of the snares he'd found had been empty, and it was hard to see in the dark, dense fog. At least one had snagged something that had tried to wriggle free. Something else beat the old hunter to it, though.

Nikolai worked to recover the pitiful remains of his prey. It struck him odd as he untwisted the snare from what looked like a leg and pelvis that a predator would leave any remains behind at all. The days were growing longer and colder. Resources were becoming scarce as game hid away or migrated before the heavy snows.

He finally freed his catch from the mangled snare wire, and it was then that he finally noticed the absence of ambient noise all around him. Nikolai tensed, then stood slowly from where he was crouched over the tree hollow. His bad hip shot pain down his leg and across his back. He winced and bit down on the inside of his cheek.

It was hard to see in the small light of the moon, but there was no need to peer too hard into the gloom. He could *feel* what was coming.

Nikolai quickly doused his lantern, pressed his back into the colossal tree before him, and waited. And waited.

Something large and ancient was coming. It crept slowly through the stillness of the forest like a final, dying breath. Only the soft crush of late autumn frost and rot gave away its movement. Nikolai knew he was in its path, but his instincts locked him into place like an anchor around his shoulders.

A gentle crunch of earth suddenly deafened his right ear, and Nikolai clamped a hand across his mouth to stifle any sound that may attract its attention. He held his breath and tried to ignore the ringing in his ears. He didn't dare look.

The looming creature stopped behind his tree and Nik's heart nearly leapt from his chest. He heard a rustle, then a snap. After a pause, a stomach-churning crunch made Nikolai flinch and scrape his neck on the bark. The monster then continued its sedate pace into the maze of

trees beyond him, its aura dragging behind like a cloak of velvet.

Nikolai waited until the forest resumed its heartbeat. He exhaled roughly and pushed himself off the trunk of his shelter. Pain was radiating across his pelvis and down his thigh, his whole leg now stiff. Using the tree to steady him, Nikolai limped out from his hiding spot to collect the scraps of his catch.

He was not surprised to find only the broken snare and a few chips of bone along a path of rotting grass. Nikolai had heard of this phenomenon, but had never seen it himself. It was unique to spirits of death that roamed the forests. He swallowed a lump in his throat. A passing god had stolen his dinner.

This forest in the mountains had always been full of strange creatures, ghosts and beasts of varying size and limb-count, most of which Nikolai himself had seen. There were primordial forces that lurked here too, however.

He'd heard stories from his mam and old hunters about the ancient gods his people had lived alongside for generations. His village mostly ignored them now, only occasionally offering tribute, praying the gods would ignore them too. Nikolai's meager hunt seemed to be an acceptable sacrifice.

He decided to take advantage of his luck and cut his losses. Scavenging what remained of his snare and tucking the bone chips away in his pack, he hefted it onto his back, ignoring the angry protest from his hip. The hunter then relit his lantern, and began hiking the fastest route through the trees.

He walked carefully over sprawling roots and stone, and heard a small creature skitter off long before he approached. Ambient forest spirits flitted through branches and peeked at him through hollows in the trees as he passed. These were harmless, just as much part of nature as he was. He'd spotted ghosts occasionally in the past, some animals, some of them human. None had ever given him the foreboding feeling the god-creature had. Nikolai felt weighed down with trapping supplies and his old rifle that hung across his shoulder. He still felt shaky from his encounter with the death spirit. *What would it have made of me instead of what was in that trap?* The thought made him shudder.

Hunger and anxiety churned his stomach, and he focused on the steady beat of his footsteps. *It won't be good if I can't catch anything before Winter.*

The trek through the dark fog would be slow even without his walking stick, and fewer of the glowing mushrooms and lichen that normally lit his way grew along this route. Despite the lack of light off the main path, his lantern held a steady circle a few feet wide around him. It swung gently from his good hip, clinking against the charms that warded off the more nuisance spirits that may trouble him.

After about an hour of walking, Nikolai emerged from the forest to a section of the town's lightning wall, a ways off from the nearest entrance. He followed along the humming structure, noting where parts of the cobbled sheet metal had begun to curl. Some had exposed wire that he was mindful to avoid brushing against. When he finally reached the entrance gate, he was greeted by a long sniping rifle covered in dark foliage. One of the sentries along the top of the wall trained their muzzle on him. Nikolai pulled back his hood to reveal his face. "Easy there!" he called up, "It's me."

The gun lowered immediately. "Sorry, Nik." The man

raised his arm to signal across the wall, then disappeared beyond Nikolai's sight. There was a popping sound as the electricity stopped along the large double doors.

Nik pulled on the handles, fighting his instinct to flinch in case the lightning current might still be running through the metal. He wasn't shocked though, and the gate groaned open enough for him to squeeze through.

"Frightened of an old man?" Nik called up as he limped through.

The sentry snorted, cradling his rifle in the crook of one arm. The indigo light from the lightning wall cast his face in sharp shadow. "It was a long night, Nik. Can't be too careful. Many freaks are out and about."

He could see the sentries on the wall better now from the other side. They were stationed high on the wall's edge to spot anything emerging from the surrounding mountain forest. All of them wore rubber boots and cloaks and walked on a dirt path laid on the walkways to minimize electrocution. Working the wall was a dangerous job, a fact Nikolai knew better than most. His bad hip sent another shooting pain down his leg.

"Keep up the good work." Nikolai said, and went into town.

The village of Zievon was small, maybe no larger than a few hundred people. Many of the houses that filled the village outskirts were now empty. Some people had moved to the larger cities on the coast; some had never come home from war. Nikolai spotted some of the village's women seated around a small fire, mending and chatting. He hoped they wouldn't notice him as he passed.

One of the women did spot him, however, and waved him over. Nikolai paused, then reluctantly diverted toward her, trying his best to conceal his gait. When he reached her, he smiled and dipped his head politely. "*Bore da*, Mona,"

Mona was dressed in thick clothing to keep warm. While beautiful in design, they were old and faded, not unlike their wearer. She smiled kindly at Nikolai, the firelight warming her features, "How are you, Niki? We haven't seen you in a while,"

"I'm good, Auntie. Just trying to stay warm,"

She clicked her tongue, "You're not getting too lonely all alone out there, are you?" "No, Auntie,"

"And your leg?"

"Fine," The words came out sharper than he meant.

Mona looked at him with soft, sympathetic eyes. She then asked a little more about his hunting. Nik hesitated, but told her about the entity he encountered and how his pillaged game allowed him to escape unnoticed. The circle of women before him gasped as he told his story.

"Niki! You are lucky to be alive!" Mona touched a talisman at her neck, "If the gods are waking, we must prepare for the change they bring."

"We'll be ready for winter, Mona." At least he hoped they'd be, though his hunting today was a poor sign. But Nikolai had a feeling she meant more than the changing of the seasons. Mona and the other women gave him a blessing of protection before sending him on his way. Nikolai thanked them and bid them goodbye. He trudged along the frosty dirt road toward the village center, a square clearing where people would gather to shop and exchange gossip. It was about midday by the time Nik made it to the pub on the far end of the square, though it was hard to tell without a sun moving through the sky. Hours were measured by name, determined by the moon's brightness and position. Or, if one were lucky, a rudimentary watch. The pub, affectionately named after the owner's ex-wife, was open and emitting a welcoming glow through small windows. Some of Nikolai's weariness lifted instantly from the warmth of the hearth and glowing lamps inside. He eased himself down on one of the worn pub stools at the bar, his groan of discomfort leaving as a long, slow breath. He tilted on his good hip, settling in the stool, and hoped the whole process wasn't so obvious. Patrons were gathered there already, some huddled around tables near the fire, others scattered about nursing drinks. Nikolai was greeted by two such men further down the bar. One had a close-cropped beard and was dressed like one of the wall-sentries. The man beside him was another hunter with a beard that Nikolai was almost certain had mushrooms growing in it. "Oy, Nik, been a while!" The sentry raised his glass.

The older hunter raised a thick brow, "How's your leg there, Nikolai?"

"About as well as your shooting, I'm guessing," Nikolai leaned his elbows on the bar and looked pointedly down at the man's empty game sack.

The sentryman laughed as the older hunter scoffed, "Aye, I don't see *you* bringing in the meat either. Must be hard without that lad of yours to show you how to aim," Nikolai's expression darkened. He turned his face away just as the sentryman elbowed the hunter roughly in the side.

"This is why he ain't shown his face, because of knobs like you!" the sentryman hissed at him. He hunched apologetically and offered Nikolai a weak smile, "He means nothing by, Nik, just the cold gettin' to 'im."

Before Nikolai could reply, the owner of the pub, a woman with a smooth face and rough hands named Hestia, stopped before him behind the bar.

"*Bore da*, Nik."

"What are you so chipper about?"

A ghost of a smile crossed Hestia's face, "What can I get you?"

He hesitated, then pulled some meager cash from his pack. They both eyed the small coins. Nikolai looked up at her, "Any leftovers from yesterday?"

There was a pause as Hestia considered, but the gruff hunter at the end of the bar chose that moment to loudly clear his throat. He placed some coin and what looked to be about a quarter pound of foraged vegetation on the bartop. The older hunter met their stares and simply said, "For soup."

Hestia calmly placed a glass out and poured Nikolai a beer. She swept both men's money and the older hunter's offering up. "Soup it is." She was sure to refill the older man's pint before she disappeared into the kitchen.

Nik inclined his head in thanks. The older hunter shrugged and they returned to companionable silence, but the grinning sentryman beside them could resist making conversation.

"So Nik," he started good-naturedly, "has it been rough on your side of the woods?"

Nik took a sip of his beer. "Not much out. The Creeper stole my only snare catch. So I suspect I won't catch too much more it'll be getting colder soon,"

The sentryman nearly spit his drink. Even the older hunter looked at him with wide eyes. "Did you look?" The sentryman leaned further over the bar toward him.

"He would be mad." The hunter pushed his younger friend back into his seat. "Of course not," Nik scoffed. "Nearly scared the shit out of me, though,"

They shared a laugh, two amused and one bewildered, and soon Hestia had appeared again bringing food for all of them.

The soup was almost gone and Nikolai considered asking for seconds when the door to the pub swung open. A young man in well-kept traveling clothes entered carefully, rubbing his arms against the chill. Nikolai recognized him instantly, though it'd been a very long time since he'd seen his face in Zievon.

The young man met his eyes and smiled. "Nik!"

"Arman–" He was cut off by the younger man hugging him warmly.

"It's been so long!" Arman pulled away and sat down between Nikolai and the two other men at the bar. He was still grinning as he looked around, but then faltered as he took in the atmosphere.

The older hunter was completely ignoring his presence, and

even the sentryman kept his eyes warily down on his soup, not offering even his sheepish smile toward the newcomer. Arman floundered for a moment, and was about to attempt a greeting when Hestia appeared to rescue him.

When asked what he'd like to order, he asked for a plate of meat and veg, with a cup of wine. "Anything you've got," Arman was saying, "nothing fancy."

"No meat," Hestia replied lightly, "no wine." The silence in the pub was like someone dropped a plate of dishes. Everyone seemed to be listening, but no one looked their way.

Arman had the decency to look a bit ashamed, his cheeks coloring. "Whatever they're having, then. Please," He waved his hand toward Nikolai and deposited some cash as payment. When Hestia left again, the awkward air settled heavier around them. Even the other patrons seemed to be leaning away from the newcomer.

"It's a surprise to see you, Arman," Nikolai said finally, "What brings you here from greater civilization?"

The sarcasm wasn't lost on the kid. He winced a little. "I'd heard things were bad..." The young man considered before continuing, "I just wanted to come home to check up on everyone."

"S'not so bad," Nikolai said. There was a snort from further down the bar. More silence. Arman tapped his fingers on the bartop. "I don't remember it being so cold this time of year," he started saying. "In the city–"

"Shut your damn trap already!" The older hunter snapped

at him. "I don't want t'hear smalltalk about that Imperial shithole,"

"Lloyd–" Nikolai warned, leaning around Arman to eye him hard.

"He can't get on his knees for Korvos then crawl back here like he's one of us," the hunter continued to rant, not stopping even when the sentryman placed a hand on his shoulder and urged him to relax.

"Talking to him like you're old friends!" Lloyd spat at him, "You're a *traitor!*" Hestia suddenly placed a bowl down hard in front of Arman, the sound cutting off the older hunter's abuse, "You're disturbing my customers." Her gaze cut into Lloyd like a butcher knife.

"Like it or not, he's from Faragara," she continued, jerking her chin at Arman, who seemed to be trying to disappear into the bartop. "The kid left after the war ended years ago, Lloyd. His money's good here."

Her words bore the weight of finality. Lloyd stared her down for a minute, then stood roughly and left the pub while still pulling his coat on, not sparing a glance back toward any of them.

The sentryman seemed torn, glancing between the rest of his meal and the way his friend had gone. He quickly picked up his bowl and slurped back the rest of his soup, then helped himself to the rest of the old hunter's abandoned bowl as well. After stacking and sliding them toward Hestia, he politely thanked her, nodded to Nikolas, and hurried out the door into the afternoon gloom.

Hestia looked after him for a moment before sliding a wrapped package toward Nikolai. She nodded at him, then Arman, and left to tend her other customers.

Nikolai unwrapped the bundle and found Hestia had given him some leftovers. He wrapped them back up with a huff of amusement, putting it away in his pack, and looked at Arman again.

The younger man was staring glumly down at his food. Nikolai patted him a bit on the back, "Try not to let him bother you, hm?"

Arman nodded. He watched Nikolai as he awkwardly braced himself on the counter to stand. "It was good to see you, Nik,"

"You too. Take care, Arman."

ikolai was soon back out in the cold. His hip felt stiff from sitting, worse now that he was shivering after being in the warm pub. It was a long trek back to his cabin outside of town and he could feel the wind picking up.

He hadn't made it far down the road when he heard someone calling his name. The hunter turned and saw Arman running after him. He couldn't help but feel a pang of envy watching the younger man catch up to him so quickly.

"Nik!" Arman stopped to catch his breath, "Here, please,

take this. For your leg," He handed Nikolai a packet. "I got it in the city. I think it could help you."

Nikolai opened one end of the packet. Inside was a shimmery powder, and it took a moment for him to work out what it was. He looked up at Arman and tried to hand it back to him, "I can't take this."

Arman gently pushed his hand away, "Please Nik, I owe you. It's my fault you're... you saved me. This is just me saying thank you."

N
ikolai arrived home in the early evening. He checked the hanging wards outside his small cabin. The bits of animal bones and chipped jewels clinked gently as he ran his hands over them. Since he didn't live within the lightning barrier, he used more homeopathic means of warding off ghosts and antagonistic spirits.

Once he was finally inside, he dropped his pack and gear by the door then limped to the fireplace. His hip throbbed from the activity of the day, and he groaned audibly as he bent down to light a log in the hearth. When the flames were licking up the sides of the wood, Nikolai eased himself down into his well-worn chair to prop up his leg.

He sighed, trying to let the tension leave his body. The ache from walking only seemed to weigh heavier in his joints. Closing his eyes for a while, he tried to concentrate on his

352

breathing, but he could only see the incident at the pub replay over and over again.

The pain in his hip didn't subside, and after a while Nikolai opened his eyes. They went straight to the mantle where an unfinished, formless carving sat, untouched for many years. The man who'd started it had left it there for NIkolai to look after until he returned.

Nikolai stared at it for a long time. He then leaned back and stretched out to reach his rifle by the door, dragging it closer and onto his lap. He began the process of unloading it and cleaning it, the kit he used to do so stored in a chest by his chair. Once it was clean, he put the rifle back together slowly and precisely, then loaded a single bullet into the chamber.

Nikolai leaned forward, resting his chin on the narrow opening of the muzzle. He let the butt of the rifle balance on the floor, his fingers holding it lightly in place. He sat for what felt like hours, the only mark of time passing were moonbeams traveling across the worn floor of his cabin.

An eternity later, he looked again at the unfinished carving with unfocused eyes, the dusty beams of his ceiling, the wood in the fireplace. All the while, his hip throbbed steadily in time with his heart.

Another eternity after that, Nikolai pulled the rifle away and unloaded the bullet. Without inspecting it, he dropped it into a tin bucket with all the others.

It was only a moment more before he was limping across the room to his discarded coat and searching through the pockets. He nearly fumbled the packet Arman had given him.

Nikolai dug through another old box for his pipe, wrapped neatly so as not to damage the wood while stored away. He hobbled to the fireplace to recover a discarded match.

His bad hip seemed to throb more intensely with each movement, a presence in his mind urging him on, knowing relief would be coming soon. Nikolai carefully shook some of the powder into the pipe. He held it to his lips, hesitated for only a moment, and lit it.

Nikolai inhaled deeply then immediately began coughing and wheezing. He briefly lost his balance and stumbled into the table, scattering the pipe out of his hands and sending a plate crashing to the floor. The sound rattled in his head, adding to the overwhelming cacophony as he struggled to catch his breath.

He coughed a few more times before his hip finally gave out and he fell hard on the floor, wheezing and staring at the underside of the ancient cabin roof. Nikolai's vision refocused after a while, then seemed to soften and grow hazy around the edges. His heartbeat felt slow, the noise in his mind quieted.

Soon Nikolai was closing his eyes and then there was nothing at all.

When awareness floated back to him, Nikolai felt both inside and out of his body. His vision has a soft, dreamlike quality, blurred at the edges like a vignette. Never before had the ancient wood rafters looked so beautiful, bathed in the yellow and orange light thrown by the crackling fire nearby. Something solid and warm gently pressed against his neck. He would have jumped had it not felt like a heavy blanket settling over him. He closed his eyes and hummed, leaning into the feeling. The warm spot then caressed upward and thumbed affectionately at his ear.

What a strange dream. His thoughts were floating past him when he realized he was sitting in his chair again. He didn't remember getting up, and it was then he noticed he felt no pain from his hip, or anywhere else in his body. In fact, he felt comforted and at peace, more than he'd felt in many years, not since...

"Jack," he sighed. He felt the warmth travel across his throat. It stroked his jaw. "I'm here," the murmured reply seemed clear in his ear. Nikolai's eyes fluttered and he felt he was watching himself from far away. He naturally imagined this scenario many times, and had dreamed it more often than not. But this time, the voice sounded so much clearer than his memory.

"Kolya."

Nik's eyes suddenly opened, wide and unseeing. He felt stiff as a brief lance of anxiety broke through his haze. Surely if he turned his head he would see what he always saw at the end of these dreams: a decaying, rotten corpse, his face frozen in an expression of terror or betrayal. Worse still, the illusion could disappear completely, slipping away before Nikolai could get a good look and leave him aching tenfold.

But then the fingers on his jaw moved again, spreading

warmth from his chin to the back of his ear, before resting firmly on his neck. Gentle fingers pressed into his skin, bidding him to turn his head and look. Nikolai did.

He was there.

Jack didn't look any different from when Nikolai last saw him. His brown-blonde hair, finger-combed to the side, glowed like a halo in the firelight. The soft brown eyes staring into his own shone with warm nostalgia and something else Nikolai's aging heart couldn't bear.

Nikolai had to touch him then. His hand jerked forward almost without thinking, placing his fingertips to the bone below Jack's eye, then cupped his cheek in his hand. "You're real," he wheezed, still sounding far away in his mind. "You *feel* real," His hand then slid to rest on the back of Jack's neck.

Jack's eyes shone brighter. "*Kolya,*" he said again.

Nikolai drew him down sharply and wound his arm tightly around his shoulders, his other hand fisting in the back of Jack's hunting jacket. The angle was awkward from where Nikolai was sitting, but it didn't stop the returning force of Jack's arms worming around him.

After a long moment half-bent over, Jack shifted back as if to let go. Nikolai leapt to stand, pushing them forward and tightening his grip on the other man. He ignored the distant, dull pang that raced through his hip and down his leg. Jack followed his momentum, stepping back to catch their weight and rocked forward again. Jack steadied them and readjusted his grip to fit more closely against Nikolai, crushing him against his chest until it was nearly painful. They stood locked together for several minutes.

Nikolai cataloged everything he felt: Jack's warmth, Jack's heart beating into his own chest, Jack's fingers digging into the older man's waist. His nose and lips were crushed against Jack's neck, and Nikolai wondered dimly how he could still possibly smell the same.

Jack's hands were moving. They ran up and down Nikolai's back, gripped his shoulders and squeezed, then clutched at his hair. He tugged firmly until Nikolai pulled his head back so he could see his face. He rushed forward to press their lips together, a desperate sound leaving him as his other hand came up to cup Nikolai's jaw.

Something close to relief overcame Nikolai then. A similar cry bubbled up in his chest. His fists, still planted on Jack, tightened until his knuckles ached. He swayed and would have nearly fallen if not for the younger man's hold on him.

That seemed to catch Jack's attention. He pulled back just enough to gasp, "Your hip! Kolya–"

"M'fine," he chased his lips, dragging him back in for another kiss. He missed as Jack was trying to look down at his leg and caught him awkwardly on the corner of his mouth. Jack tried to pull away again but Nikolai held him fast. "You're crazy if you think I'm letting you go," he growled into his ear.

The younger man sighed and Nikolai could almost hear his eyes rolling. "I'm not going anywhere," Jack assured him. "Can you walk?"

"No," Nikolai kissed the spot behind Jack's ear.

Jack sighed again. He began to shuffle backward in the direction of Nikolai's bed, pulling him slowly along. Nikolai nuzzled at the collar of Jack's sweater and breathed softly into the fine hair at the nape of his neck. He let his body relax, allowing Jack to support his weight. "You're not limping," Jack said with wonder.

"You're not dead," He felt drunk. *It was only a dream.*

"Kolya–"

"Shut up," Nikolai saw they were at the edge of his bed. He pushed Jack down, falling with him, their combined weight making the old wood frame creak in protest. Nikolai curled one arm protectively around Jack's head and leaned down to brush their lips together. "Just shut up"

Their next kiss was slow and deliberate. Nikolai felt Jack melt under him with every soft press of his lips. His free hand roamed across Jack's barrel chest, nails catching on the knit of his sweater. The younger man gasped when Nikolai slipped cold fingers under his shirt, and he took the opportunity to slide his tongue into Jack's mouth.

He stroked Jack's tongue, exploring and teasing, before pulling back to bite gently at his lower lip and drawing out his breathy moan. His fingers trailed across the waistband of Jack's trousers and couldn't help smirking in victory.

Nikolai briefly pulled away, taking a moment to shift on his arm and relieve pressure off his bad side. Jack saw the opening. He grabbed the older man and flipped them so Nikolai landed flat on his back. A hard breath punched through his lungs as he landed. He glared up at Jack's grinning face, a ray of light in the dark room.

"Showoff."

The younger man wasn't yet satisfied. He gripped Nikolai's waist, mindful of his bad hip, and with a threatening knee levered between his thighs Jack shuffled them up the mattress so he could comfortably stretch out his leg.

Jack then settled himself across the older man's thighs. "Much better."

Nikolai's hands drifted to rest on Jack's hips as if they were always meant to be there. "You haven't changed at all."

"Oh?"

"Never said much," Nikolai palmed his ass, "but always cheeky."

Jack leaned over him then, slowly pressing his hips down into Nikolai's and giving him a languid kiss. Nikolai moaned into his mouth, stuttering slightly when they opened their mouths at the same time. Jack drew away to mouth a line of kisses across his throat, never stopping the slow grind between them.

Nikolai's cock was stirring now, and he couldn't resist rocking himself up into Jack. A sudden shock of pain surprised him and he jerked without thinking, couldn't stop the breath hissing out from between his teeth.

Jack froze, pulling back to look him over. Nikolai's gut twisted as he felt him about to lift his body away, so he seized Jack's face in his hands and dug his fingers hard into his jaw. "Don't," Nikolai kissed his chin, the corner of his mouth, and couldn't help the note of desperation in his voice. "Don't. Please."

Jack's expression softened. He reached up to cover one of Nikolai's hands with his own and stroked down until his fingers encircled his wrist. Jack rubbed his thumb against his pulse point until Nikolai relaxed his grip. The younger man then leaned over him, resting one arm above his head and kissed him gently.

Jack waited until Nikolai relaxed, kissing him over and over until the heat started to build again between them. Jack distracted the older man by licking into his mouth, allowing his free hand to roam and reveling in the little sounds Nikolai was trying to bury in his skin.

His fingers skated lower and lower until he was palming Nikolai's hard length through the rough fabric of his pants. Jack laughed softly at the strangled noise that followed. He then started to pick at the button at Nikolai's waistband, scraping his teeth hungrily against his windpipe.

Nikolai breathing turned harsh as Jack slipped his fingers under layers of clothing until they met hard, hot flesh. A calloused finger gently stroked along the head of Nikolai's cock and dipped briefly into the bead of moisture gathered there. The older man squirmed and squeezed his eyes shut. *How long had it been since he felt like this?*

Jack drew his hand back just long enough to spit into his palm. He watches the growing pleasure on Nikolai's face, memorizing every detail both familiar and new. Nikolai's hips rise slightly to meet his hand. He whimpers, and Jack strokes the hair from his face.

"Relax," Jack told him gently. He squeezed his cock and the handful of hair he'd gripped before letting both slide through his fingers.

"I'm–*nng-!*" Nikolai panted. *"Relaxed."*

The younger man grinned. He leaned down to press his face into the exposed curve of Nikolai's neck, nipping and sucking at the skin there as his hand continued the steady strokes. Nikolai could feel the pressure rising in his gut, pooling like molten steel at the base of spine. He scrambled to get a hold on Jack, his hand searching blindly down the other man's front until he brushed against the straining bulge of Jack's cock. He was still trying to find the waistband when Jack suddenly seized his wrist.

"No. Let me." Jack met Nikolai's eyes. His look was fierce and soft all at once, and it made Nikolai's chest ache. He fisted his hand in the front of Jack's sweater instead. "Jackie," Nikolai wheezed, "I–"

"You're beautiful," Jack spoke softly, his hand picking up speed. His voice was full of emotion that matched the ache in Nikolai's chest. "I missed you so much." Nikolai surged up to meet Jack's lips in a searing kiss. With a final twist of Jack's hand, Nikolai stiffened, spilling over his fist. He groaned with almost a sob, pleasure sparking behind his eyes turning his bones to liquid. Jack kissed him over and over until he remembered how to breathe.

Jack eventually freed himself from Nikolai's pants, seizing a loose shirt from the pile of laundry on the end of the mattress. He clucked his tongue and shook his head while he cleaned up their mess.

Nikolai didn't have the energy to quip at him. He slowly uncurled his fingers from Jack's clothing. A wave of exhaustion crashed over him then, and he lay still reverently watching Jack's face.

The younger man was looking back at him. He kissed Nikolai's brow, then his cheek. "You're real," Jack said quietly, almost to himself. He sounded like he wasn't sure if he believed it or not.

"Mm." Nikolai hummed. His body felt light and he was so, so warm.

"Kolya..." Jack's voice sounded far away. He stroked the aging lines on Nikolai's face he didn't recall seeing before he left. "Nikolai, I don't think I'm dreaming."

"M'tired, Jackie," was the murmured reply. Sleep was coming fast now. Nikolai tried to hold on but he couldn't fight it for much longer.

"Old man," Jack quipped softly. "Rest. I'll see you when you wake up."

The last thing Nikolai felt as he slipped into the dark ether of his dream was Jack's warm weight beside him.

When Nikolai woke up, he felt disoriented, and wasn't sure if days or hours or years had passed. He rolled over with a groan, body stiff with cold. He was still fully dressed and the layers of his blankets appeared to be kicked and twisted by his feet. He noticed dimly that across the room the fire had gone out. The bed frame creaked in harmony with his joints as he rolled onto his back.

He laid still for another moment before realization hit him. Nikolai quickly sat up, his eyes immediately going to the spot on the floor where he remembered passing out. He spotted his pipe next, neatly arranged on the table with the sealed packet Arman gave him sitting innocently next to it.

The older man gripped his bad leg and swung himself so he's sitting upright on the edge of the mattress. The motion makes him dizzy, and he leans dangerously forward, fighting the urge to vomit.

The pain finally registers while he's hunched over his lap. The muscles in his hip and thigh were strung tight like bowstrings. A sharp, persistent pain stabbed into his joint with the slightest movement. Nikolai groaned and hissed, rubbing his palm over his leg to relieve the sting.

Images from his dream came to him in pieces. He remembered most vividly the sight of Jack, the feel of rough hands gliding over his skin. The scent of army-ration soap mixed with Jack's natural woodsy smell lingered in his nose. Another pain bloomed in his chest and his eyes stung. *It felt so real. Was it just a dream?*

Nikolai sat hunched over until the pain dulled to a manageable throb. He forced himself to stand, grasping for furniture and the wall as he moved. He dragged himself to check the cracked timepiece on the mantel.

It was well into the following day, he'd lost too many hours to do any valuable hunting. The state of his leg put the idea off completely.

Nikolai sighed, leaning his hands on the mantle and stretching out. He turned his head to look at the old wooden carving that lived there for ages. It took several minutes of staring for him to understand what he was seeing.

It had been moved. Not only moved but worked on. *Whittled.* Nikolai's whole body went cold. He had hardly been able to look at the small hunk of wood, much less touch it in years. It sat there, no longer formless but taking shape into some four-legged animal. A carving knife was neatly placed beside it.

Nikolai's eyes flicked downward to see the shavings in the fireplace.

His mind grasped at logic first, considering he must have done these things in his stupor. His gut answered with the truth.

It was real.

Nikolai limped to the window and looked out at the wards around the cabin. They appeared intact. He looked over his shoulder at the carving again.

He then decided to shake off the dream by going into the town, telling himself he was wasting moonlight standing and staring at the walls. He dressed quickly and was out the door before his thoughts could catch up with him.

The morning was cold, the chill cutting through his layers of clothing and straight to the skin. Winter was probably less than a week away. It would bring more than endless snow. The thought made him shudder and pull his coat more firmly around himself. It would be unlikely he'd be traveling to town too often then. Nikolai progressed slowly along the main route from his home to Zievon. Lanterns were nailed periodically along the path, lit from within by bushels of glowing lichen that grew through and dripped off the metal. The old hunter still carried his own lantern, lit with its own wild growth of bioluminescent fauna. He kept a small and precious supply of oil and a flintstone just in case.

When he finally made it to town, the air was quiet and thick with tension. The sentrymen on the wall barely spoke to him as he passed through the lightning barrier. They seemed on edge, pacing, some looking inward into Zievon.

On the ground a little farther in, Nikolai spotted two of them hunched over a third while she worked on some sparking cables pouring from a section of the wall.

He headed toward the general goods store, which was more or less just a man's house where goods were displayed in the front room. Nikolai had forgotten to stop through the day before and needed to stock up any supplies he could. The old hunter was considering if he could afford to hire someone to help haul things home when the shopkeeper appeared from the back room.

Nikolai greeted him, and they exchanged amicable complaints about the weather and aching joints. He still felt the prickly unease that had settled over the town when he asked, "What's going on?"

"Some beasties made it through the wall last night," The shopkeep told him. Nik's eyes widened in surprise. "Little things, mind you, but they screamed for *hours*, knocking against people's doors and frightening the lot of us."

Nikolai cursed quietly. The lightning barrier was meant to keep the more terrorizing ghosts and large beasts at bay. Very few could slip past, and often they were small, ambient spirits. Harmless.

Until now.

There was an awkward pause as Nikolai digested this information. Finally, he shifted off his hip and gestured to the large cupboards along one wall. "What have you got?" Not much, it seemed. Nikolai left with a small parcel of dried meat (so long past when it should be eaten, it was practically leather), as many vegetables as he could carry, and a few sacks of grain that he hauled on a sled across the icy ground.

He decided to stop by the pub and get at least one hot meal before the long trek back home. When he arrived, he left his goods at the door and made his way inside the bright warm space to shake off the chill. The tables were crowded with what looked like to be the bulk of the town. Nikolai scanned the crowd. He spotted Mona, and she waved to him to join her and several others on a bench by the hearth. As he made his way to her, he passed Lloyd and his sentryman, huddled together with a few other hunters. Their expressions were dark.

Mona pulled him down and squeezed him between herself and another woman he'd met the previous morning. "Oh, Niki, it was awful!" she began, and it was hard to hear her over the din. "It's never been this bad before, and so *early,*"

To think it would get even more cold and dark, even with the absence of a sun. Winter approaching meant the cold and darkness would come with even more sinister spirits. "It will only get worse as the season settles in," one of the men across from them echoed Nikolai's thoughts.

"Hardly got any sleep," complained another further down the bench.

Nik felt an odd sense of guilt edge up his spine. He had slept fairly well due to the powder he'd smoked. But he couldn't deny his pleasure from the vivid dreams, even when looking at the exhausted faces around him . He couldn't resist taking a subtle sniff of his shirt, expecting and hoping it would still smell like Jack.

"Will we have enough fuel to keep the wall?" Mona interrupted his thoughts. She was anxiously tapping her fingers across the back of her hand.

"Nevermind fuel, it's falling apart! Those damn sentries don't know their asses from their heads," the man across from Nikolai rumbled bitterly. "No offense."

Nikolai ignored him. "I saw a few of them repairing it. It happens. They'll make sure any breaches are secure." Though even he knew it would only be a temporary fix. Many of the engineers who actually knew more had already moved to the larger cities on the coast, or died in the war.

"Forget the wall," One of the few remaining female hunters was also at their table. She leaned forward on her elbows. "I hear Caelan and the others are meeting with an Imperial ambassador."

Nikolai and those gathered around them all turned to her in shock. The last time Imperial forces had traveled this deep in the mountains was when they were enemies. The fact that they'd sent someone now to meet with their village leaders was ominous.

Mona squeezed Nikolai's arm, "What could they possibly want from us?" "Maybe they came to finally put us out of our misery."

"Watch it!" Nikolai snapped. Anger spiked his blood. Jack didn't die so they could wallow in their own despair. The man across from him pressed his lips together but matched his glare. All had quieted at their table. The huntress was watching them both with interest.

Nikolai flicked his eyes to Mona looking up at him. "The war is over," he amended. "No one is coming to kill us."

A sudden commotion drew their attention to the entrance of the pub. A tall, middle-aged woman had entered with two men flanking her. The crowd went silent as Caelan's eyes passed over them all.

There were a few moments of heavy quiet before the chief leader drew herself up and began to speak.

"As I'm sure it's gotten around, we met this hour with an

ambassador from Korvos," She paused, and took a breath. "Seeing as most of you are here, I figure now is as good a time as any to announce that an Imperial force will be arriving in Zievon within the next two days. They will be assisting us with relocating South to Lockport—"

A rise of protests rose from the sparse, gathered crowd, but Caelan pushed on "--so we may survive the winter! You've seen that we no longer have the resources to properly fuel and maintain the lightning barrier. There is too little game for us to sustain ourselves, and there are not enough hunters eligible to take down more dangerous quarries."

Nikolai's stomach twisted.

"Do not think we made this decision lightly," she continued. "Do not think we have forgotten all Zievon has sacrificed so that we may live." Caelan looked down then and sighed. One of the male leaders behind her placed a comforting hand on her shoulder.

The third leader stepped forward and his voice boomed over the crowd despite his wiry stance, "Be prepared to evacuate in two days time. Only bring what is necessary. Those who are not prepared will be left behind."

That stirred the crowd. Many stood and began shouting, some anger and others fearful. Nikolai had jumped up too, his hip protesting just as loudly as those around him. He stared hard at the leaders of his village and balled his hands into fists. Caelan elbowed her way past the wiry leader again. "*No one* will be left behind!" She tried to shout over the din, but it was too late now. She started backing away, herding the two behind her with her. "Two days time to prepare! We will meet in the square tomorrow."

The leaders fled and nearly everyone was on their feet now, all talking over one another. A few sobs broke over the cacophony of noise. Nikolai's ears were ringing. He knew he'd never make it through the crowd to chase after them. He hopped over the bench, banging his knee with a curse and nearly falling. He made his way toward the kitchen and pushed past Hestia's cook to the back door.

By the time he limped into the cold and rounded the side of the building, he saw Caelan hoofing past, snarling at the wiry leader in her wake.

"You got to be *fucking* kidding me!" he shouted at her before she could get away. She turned and frowned when she saw him coming.

"Not now, Nik."

"We don't need them!"

"You know I can outrun you."

"You're going to let them destroy what's left of us! Zievon is going to *die*." She stopped and rounded on Nikolai just as he reached her. "They're not destroying anything," Caelan's voice was crisp as if she was explaining stringing a bow to some idiot who just wasn't getting it. "They're *saving* Zievon."

"Is that what they told you?" Nikolai scoffed and shifted onto his good leg. Caelan spread her arms, exasperated, "Look around Nik! We can't afford to feed them, much less protect them. Our people are *starving*."

"We can train new hunters," he argued, righteous

desperation spurring him a step toward her. "Our people survived without the oil before."

"Yes, but now they're all dead."

The words hung in the air. They stared each other down, the men behind her not daring to say a word. Caelan finally released a breath that made it seem like she was deflating. "I'm sorry, Nik. I know everything you've done for this town and its people, both during the war and after." She looked tired. "But if you truly want what's best for them, you'll see that they need to move on."

Nikolai said nothing. He knew she was right, and knew she could see that what was left of heart was breaking. The cold air stung his face and eyes.

Caelan made a face of sympathy, then nodded her goodbye and turned to leave. Nikolai's eyes never left her as she began to walk away.

"There's no way," Nikolai said suddenly. Caelan stopped and turned her head to listen. "There's no way Korvos could get here in two days when you just made this decision, right?" The leader of Zievon said nothing and turned her head away again. Nikolai's fist clenched and fury tempered in his gut. "You made this choice for us a long time ago, didn't you? *You never said a word.*"

When she didn't answer Nikolai took another step toward her. Suddenly the two other leaders stepped between them. The concerned one moved closer to Caelan, and the wiry one stepped forward as if to intercept Nikolai.

His eyes finally slid to them as if he just noticed they were there. Nikolai also finally saw there was a fourth person with them, someone he hadn't noticed hiding behind the leaders in the pub, who looked at him now with guilt and sadness in his eyes.

Arman opened his mouth and closed it again. "Nik–"

"I should have let you fall." The former sentryman said. Pain arced through his hip as he turned from them all without looking back.

The long walk home did little to cool his blood. Nikolai's physical pain only fueled his righteous anger. He wiped flurries of snow from his eyes, moving on instinct while the day's events churned in his mind.

He practically broke open the door to his cabin and immediately kept pacing. He kept beat with the throbbing in his hip. It felt like if Nikolai stopped he would collapse and never move again.

After making four laps through the main room, cursing and spitting once into the hearth, pain had spread like fire from ribs to his thigh. It was unbearable.

He stumbled into the table where he'd left his pipe. Nikolai loaded it quickly with the powder and lit it with little thought.

He inhaled deeply, more prepared for the burning sting. Nikolai blew the smoke out harshly, looking as close as one could to an angered fire-breathing beast. He took another hit off the pipe, the action calming him somewhat.

It wasn't until his eyes flicked down again to the packet of powder that he remembered where he'd gotten it. Anger and sorrow closed his throat. Nikolai then snatched up the open packet and strode easily across the room to throw it out into the snow.

He slammed the door, seething. It occurred to him that the aching all down his side had stopped, the medicine having done its job. Nikolai felt all his raging energy leave him suddenly through the bottom of his feet.

He let his forehead fall against the aging wood door. Sadness was the only thing left in his mind. The thought of leaving the home that his family had lived in for generations was untenable. Worse still, he wouldn't be here if Jack ever came home.

In his gut, he knew he never would. The thought burned like acid in his stomach and he screwed his eyes shut against the wretched feeling. He'd hated himself for letting Jack return to

the war without him. Nikolai's injury had prevented him from fighting any longer, so he'd thrown himself into the resistance effort to distract himself, serving at home in any way he could. He helped convince townsfolk to give up their forks and metal plates to melt into ammunition. He and Hestia organized rations and helped Caelan train hunters to be sent as soldiers to the larger cities. He rallied any and all to fight for Faragara and maintain their independence.

But he hadn't been there to protect Jack. Nikolai had never known what happened to him. The war ended and their country was annexed into the Empire of Korvos. Jack never returned to the gates of Zievon.

Nikolai stood there until his knees started to buckle. He weakly moved and lowered himself into his chair by the empty hearth. The rifle was on the floor where he'd thrown it when he'd arrived home.

He dragged it closer. Nikolai didn't have the energy to clean it. The metal was a cold bite under his chin.

He looked at a small piece of wood on his mantel. Eyes had been added to it, and they stared straight through him.

Then, he heard a voice.

"Kolya."

"You're not really here," Nikolai said quietly to the carving.

"Look at me, Nikolai."

He closed his eyes. The side effects of the powder must have been kicking in. "I'll see you soon." He rested his finger on the trigger.

"NO!"

A force hits him hard from behind, a hand shooting out and yanking the rifle forward out from under his chin. Nikolai's ears were ringing.

Another arm then wound around his neck and squeezed him into a chokehold.

"What the fuck do you think you're doing?!" The voice snarled in his ear. "Drop it, *now!*" Nikolai gasped for air, one hand clawing into the arm around his neck. It was solid and incredibly strong.

His mind raced. He hadn't fallen asleep, he was sure. *This wasn't a dream.* "I said, *let go,* Nikolai," Jack tightened his grip.

Nikolai released the rifle instantly, still in shock. Jack yanked it out of his hand and released his hold.

Nikolai leaned, trying to catch his breath, and turned in his head to watch Jack empty the chamber and start disassembling the rifle. His expression was stern anger and anxiety furrowed his brow.

"How...are you here?" Nikolai wheezed.

"A whole forest full of ghosts around you and you didn't consider I could be here with you?" Jack asked dryly.

"I didn't consider you were actually dead."

Jack looked up at him then and stared, hard. His eyes ticked between Nikolai's. After a moment, he turned away from him and tossed pieces of the rifle into a standing bucket of water, rendering the gunpowder useless.

He returned to kneel in front of Nikolai and took his hands into his own, stroking his thumb over his skin.

"What were you thinking?" Jack asked gently.

Nikolai shut his eyes, unable to bear the soft and sad look of him. Icy shame squeezed his lungs and he took fast, shallow breaths as he spoke, "Zievon...they're moving South. I...I didn't want to... couldn't live somewhere else. Without you,"

Jack tightened his hold on him. "Of course you could, Kolya. It'll be alright, you'll adapt, just like always–"

"I'm tired of...of the pain," Nikolai finally opened his eyes, stinging tears building and nearly blurring his vision. "It hurts, Jackie."

Jack's expression crumpled. He surged forward to wrap around Nikolai's waist and pressed his face into his chest. Nikolai could stop the sob that escaped him then and he pressed his face into Jack's golden hair.

When Jack pulled away, his eyes were red and wet. He placed a warm hand on Nikolai's cheek.

"Life is pain, Kolya," Jack said sadly, "That doesn't mean you should–"

"You don't get it!" Nikolai slapped his hand away, suddenly angry, "I can't hunt, I can't run–I can barely walk! Every day is *agony*. What's the point if I'm miserable every single fucking day?" He was breathing hard. "I might as well be dead."

"You don't know *anything* about dying." Jack's voice cracked and he pulled away from Nikolai completely.

"There's nothing," Jack went on, crying freely now. His eyes had a wild, far-away look. "I don't even know how I died. I was frightened, there was–pain. Then...nothing." Nikolai stared at him. Before he could make any move toward him, Jack spoke again, his voice softer than ever.

"Then suddenly, you." Jack looked up at Nikolai, eyes shining. "I had you again. And I almost watched you take that away from me."

Nikolai swallowed. He didn't know what to say. Could barely meet his eyes. Jack sighed and stood. As he moved, his foot accidentally caught on the tin bucket near his chair. They both looked down at it.

Nikolai realized it was the first time in a long while he'd

actually observed what was inside. His unused bullets filled it almost halfway, missing only the one Jack had disposed of.

Jack looked back up at him, confused. It only took him a beat more to work out their significance. He closed his eyes, a pained expression on his face.

He went to the window, arms folded and a hand turned over his mouth as he stared out into the freezing darkness. "I'm sorry, Nikolai," Jack said, "I'm sorry I left you to suffer all alone." "You have nothing to be sorry for." Nikolai replied fiercely.

Silence sat between them for several minutes. Neither of them moved, both staring into space and putting themselves back together. Nikolai's eyes fixed on Jack's carving on the mantel. He had to swallow again before he could speak.

"Why have I not been able to see you before now?"

Jack turned to him, looking thoughtful. He then crossed to the table and picked up Nikolai's pipe. He turned in his hands and sniffed it before returning his gaze to Nikolai. "Dream smoke. Not only good for pain but also good for communing with spirits." "Huh."

Jack raised a brow at him. "You haven't tried it before now?"

Nikolai sat back in his chair. "Could never get it, until...it was brought in from elsewhere," he trailed off, taking his turn to stare out the window as guilt and self-loathing filled him up. When he looked back he found Jack watching him again. They stared at each other for a while, then Jask said, "Let me make you something to eat."

J ack somehow was able to scrape together a meal from Nikolai's meager larder. "How do you live like this?" Jack's tone was exasperated but fond.

"Not well, obviously," Nikolai replied, gesturing to himself.

Jack gave him a withering look and stood to clear the table. He hadn't eaten himself but was more than happy to watch Nikolai, one elbow propped up on the table and chin in his hand. Commons 31

Nikolai's eyes followed him. Jack didn't look like he'd changed much from when they'd said their last goodbye at the lightning barrier years ago. Nikolai wanted to ask about what happened to him, he wanted to know what he'd seen and felt, but it didn't feel important now.

He leaned forward and rested his head on his arms. Jack turned back to him with a smile that warmed Nikolai from the inside. The younger man's eyes drifted over him as if he too were taking in the details he'd missed when they were apart.

"I'm tired," Nikolai said suddenly.

Jack's smile was knowing. "Come on, then."

Jack helped Nikolai stand and limp to the bed. Although his pain had dulled significantly, his strength seemed to have drained out of him.

When he was settled, Nikolai turned on his good side and patted the bed beside him. Jack huffed a laugh, but stripped off his sweater until he was down to his undershirt and shorts. Jack lays his back carefully into Nikolai's chest, allowing him to throw his heavy blankets over them.

Nikolai then puts his arm over his waist, pressing his lips into the back of Jack's neck. The younger man sighed, cocooned in warmth, and melted back into Nikolai's arms. After a long time of laying together did Nik's hands begin to wander. He ran one down his side and over his hip, slowly sliding back up until they rested under Jack's shirt. Jack hummed as if he'd been dozing. *Can ghosts sleep?* Nikolai thought with a chuckle as his hand traveled higher to brush over Jack's nipple.

The younger man's sharp exhale only made Nikolai laugh more, nuzzling affectionately against Jack's neck.

"What?" Jack huffed.

"Nothing." Nikolai squeezed a handful of his chest.

"I'm still mad at you."

"Let me make it up to you."

He tweaked Jack's nipple. The younger man jumped with a sound caught between pain and reluctant pleasure.

Jack threw a glare over his shoulder. "Dirty old man."

Nikolai laughed again and let his fingers move to splay over Jack's stomach, resting there as he pressed himself closer to Jack's back.

Jack arced into the touch, letting his ass settle back into the hollow of Nikolai's hips. "Jackie," his voice was rough.

The younger man leaned forward, and Nikolai grabbed his hips so he couldn't get far. He watched Jack dip over the side of the bed and return with a bottle of vegetable oil. Nikolai laughed, "I forgot I had that."

Jack passed it to him with a small smile. He settled back down and stretched like a cat. Nikolai kissed his shoulder-blade. "Are you sure this is okay?"

"Yes, Kolya," Jack blew out a breath and wriggled impatiently against him. Nikolai smiled down at him. He pulled at Jack's shoulder until he turned enough so Nikolai could kiss him. His teeth were gentle on his lower lip as he slid his tongue against Jack's. They settled together, Jack relaxing completely into him now, his mouth increasingly pliable as Nikolai kissed him over and over.

While he was distracted, Nikolai popped the metal cap on the bottle of oil. He cupped the opening and tipped it so it poured into his hand.

"Hold this," Nik then purred into Jack's ear, placing the bottle loosely in Jack's open hand. The younger man took it without thinking, opening his eyes and making a sound of confusion.

Nikolai then reached into Jack's shorts to grasp his cock with a slick hand, stroking up and squeezing around the head. The younger man jolted underneath him at the sudden touch. "Fuck!"

He puffed a laugh against Jack's ear and scraped his teeth along the sensitive skin behind it. Nikolai stroked his cock in long, slow passes, occasionally rocking his hips in time with his hand. Jack moaned quietly, letting his head rest against Nikolai, his fingers squeezing tightly around the bottle he held.

Jack then turned his head and searched for the older man's lips. Nikolai obliged him, and they exchanged long, searching kisses. They relearned each other's mouths, tongues running along teeth. They shared several breaths and Jack reached back to grasp Nikolai's hair, thrusting up into the firm hold around his cock.

When Nikolai pulled his hand away, Jack groaned and thrust his hips uselessly after him. He tugged at the older man's hair in protest. Nikolai grunted, nipping at Jack's jaw and held his wet hand expectantly in front of Jack.

He released Nik's hair to bring the hand closer to his mouth. He licked along his fingers, drawing them into the wet heat of his mouth. He reveled in the older man's groan and felt him twitch against his ass.

Smirking, he released Nikolai's fingers and poured more oil into his upturned palm. He then leaned forward out of his reach to place the bottle out of the way.

As Jack stretched, Nikolai slid two fingers between his cheeks and began working them into the younger man's hole. Jack moaned, falling back and bracing his arm on the mattress as his body trembled.

Nikolai slid his free arm under Jack and drew him back to his chest. He left a trail of wet, open mouth kisses along his neck, nipping at his skin and trying to memorize the taste and feel of him.

His fingers worked slowly in and out of Jack. Nikolai grunted a little with the effort, the pull on his fingers making him lose his concentration. Jack's head fell forward, a hand gripping tightly onto Nikolai, his nails digging hard into the skin and sending sparks of pleasure up his arm.

Nikolai lost himself in every sound his lover made. He admired the other man, watching his bones and muscle strain and release as he breathed through pleasure, sweat making Jack's skin glisten.

When the slide came easier, Nikolai thrusted his fingers hard and twisted, pressing deep. The strangled cry Jack made made his own cock twitch.

Jack tipped his head back again. He caught Nikolai along his jaw, kissing and biting fervently. "Enough," he moaned, "Kolya, enough."

"I could do this all night," Nikolai curled his fingers on the next thrust.

"*Please.*"

He kissed Jack deeply as he removed his fingers. "I could never resist you for long." Nikolai shoved his own shorts down around his thighs, letting his cock spring free. He used the remaining oil on his hand to stroke himself, looking up and catching Jack watching him hungrily. He shifted down until they were aligned and slowly began to press in. Jack moaned, low and rough, his hands clenching hard on the blanket around their hips. Nikolai pushed slowly forward, the tight heat making him dizzy. He wrapped his arms tightly around Jack, rolling his hips up into his ass, the younger man pushing back to meet as best he could.

"Come on, lovely," Nikolai panted in his ear. He seized Jack's hip and removed himself to the head of his cock in one, slow pull. The younger man's eyes shutter closed, a groan from deep in his throat sent heat straight to Nikolai's gut.

He snapped his hips, burying himself almost to the base. A shock of pain raced up his spine and vanished just as fast, but it didn't slow his rhythm.

Nikolai fucked Jack with as much as he can manage. He buried his face in Jack's neck and licked across the salty skin there. He lost himself in the small sounds, gasps, and moans from the man underneath him.

He reached over Jack to stroke his cock in time with his thrusts, but he batted Nikolai's hand away. The older man slowed his pace, lifting his head to look at him. Jack's face was apple red. "I want–together," he ground his ass back onto Nikolai's cock. "*Please, Kolya,*"

His tone weakened Nikolai instantly. He let his forehead fall to Jack's shoulder. "Alright! Alright..." he huffed, picking his pace back up. "We'll...make it work."

Jack moaned his name again, drawing out the sound and raising his lips to the ceiling. He made a small choked noise when Nikolai hit just the right angle inside him. Nikolai adjusted to fuck against that spot, hard and close. Jack squeezed him so tight, he didn't hear the younger man's babbling stream of words at first.

"...of you every day. Had to come home to see–you. Feel–*god!*" Jack gasped. "Always you," Nikolai's voice was rough and hot against Jack's ear. "Yours forever. *Jackochka.*"

Jack turned his head and surged up to kiss him, scraping

their teeth together as his whole body tightened impossibly around Nikolai.

Nikolai breathed in his relieved cry, licking into his mouth. "That's it," he whispered against his lips, "Easy now, I've got you."

"*God.*" Jack gasped. His head lolled against the pillow and he was breathing hard, "M'sorry. I know I said, I wanted–"

"Forget it, Jackie," Nikolai's voice was warm with laughter. The younger man turned his head again to meet his eye. Nikolai rocked his hips, his cock still buried in Jack's ass. "Help me out if you're so sorry."

Jack kissed him then, biting hard on Nikolai's lip. When he released him, his eyes were dark with lust. "On your back." Nikolai eased himself out of Jack with a groan, Jack hissing when he pulled free. He rolled onto his back, his spine and hip releasing tension as he melted against the pillows.

Jack rose up on his knees and pulled Nikolai's shorts the rest of the way off. He wrapped his hand delicately around Nikolai's cock, stroking it as he straddled his thighs. Rising up, Jack aligned himself and slowly sank onto him.

Nikolai groaned, seizing Jack by the hips and resisting thrusting up into him. Once he was fully seated, Jack leaned forward, covering Nikolai's body with his own. He began to move, rolling back and up again. Nikolai met him thrust for thrust, though Jack held all the momentum to keep pressure off his hip. The younger man spread his hands along Nikolai's ribs and leaned in to kiss him deeply.

"My Kolya," Jack drew his lips across Nikolai's jaw until

they were pressed against his ear. "So good, so strong. I'll always come home to you, Kolya. *You're mine forever.*" Nikolai seized upward just as Jack sunk his teeth into his neck. He dug his nails into Jack's hips, his world blurring for a moment. When he could hear his thoughts again, Jack was peppering his face with kisses, looking amused.

～

When they'd cleaned up, Jack lay back down on his back with Nikolai draped along his side, one leg thrown over his to relieve pressure off his bad hip.

They were nose to nose, Nikolai half-lidded and memorizing the details of Jack's face. Jack was pulling fingers through his hair and looked like he wanted to say something but wasn't sure how.

"I can hear you thinking," Nikolai said lightly. "Spit it out."

"You should go south with Zievon," Jack's tone was concerned despite his bluntness. Nikolai closed his eyes, "Jack—"

"You need people, Kolya. Please. You can't live your life in the past like this. You can only move forward. You need to *live*," Jack tightened his grip on his hair to make Nikolai meet his eyes. "Do you understand?"

His gut twisted, and Nikolai ran their argument through his mind and knew Jack would win. He finally replied at length, "Yes."

"Good." Jack leaned in to kiss him lightly. "I love you, Kolya."

Nikolai's heart squeezed.

"I love you, Jackochka."

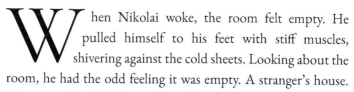

When Nikolai woke, the room felt empty. He pulled himself to his feet with stiff muscles, shivering against the cold sheets. Looking about the room, he had the odd feeling it was empty. A stranger's house. The warmth had bled out of it without Jack there.

He saw Jack had finished his carving and left it for him on the small table by his bed. Nikolai picked it up and turned it over in his hands several times. It looked like a dog, or a small fox. It had four eyes that stared up at him knowingly.

He closed his fist around the trinket and looked around his cabin again. *This is the last time I'll ever see this place.* The thought hadn't seemed so unbearable now, but sadness still ached in his chest. Nikolai realized there wasn't much here he wanted to take other than his rifle (fishing it out from where Jack had dismantled it), hunting supplies, a few trinkets that fit into a tin box, his good coat, some clothes, and a blanket his grandmother had knit when he was very young.

Nikolai packed all of it away onto his backup sled. He went through the motions like he was in a daze. He thought about his night with Jack, what he had made him promise. It didn't stop the bitter feeling in his throat.

Walking out he turned to look at the cabin one last time. It was like he'd never seen it before. It looked aging and worn against the tree surrounding it. *How had he lived here alone for so long?* A lump formed in his throat. Memories of when the cabin had been full swelled behind his eyes and slipped down his cheek. He scrubbed at his face with one arm before turning in the direction of Zievon, plucking a few protective stones from his circle of wards, and began the walk through the snow.

When he arrived in town, only two or three sentry men were pacing the high wall of the lightning barrier. Their faces were grim. Nikolai asked the man at the gate why there were so few of them.

"They all quit," The man sounded vaguely disgusted. "They said there was no point in manning the wall since they'd all be leaving soon anyway." Disturbed, Nikolai went on to the center of Zievon. The Imperial convoy was already there. They'd brought wagons and huge six-legged beasts to haul them. The soldiers wore clean uniforms in the colors of Korvos. Nikolai noticed with some interest that a handful of the convoy were Faragara citizens from Lockport, here to assist with their countrymen's move. A small crowd was gathering around Caelan and an Imperial officer. As he got closer, Nikolai heard him speak their language in short, simple sentences. Arman was there as well, listening and translating to the officer whatever he couldn't understand.

"We appreciate your cooperation," the officer was saying. "The sooner we can leave before the winter storms, the better. I see you do not have much here, so load your things quickly and bring only what is needed."

All around him, people grumbled. Some were listening intently, but most stood defensively and stony-faced, glaring at the Imperial soldier.

"When we reach Lockport, you will be counted and issued identification sanctioned by the Empire of Korvos," The officer continued as if bored, "You will then be proper citizens of the Empire and receive the benefits as such."

There was more fervent muttering from the crowd. The officer fixed them all with a hard stare, "Failure to comply may result in consequences, including but not limited to imprisonment."

Caelan stepped forward, shooting a warning glance at the officer. "We are still of Faragara," she assured them. "It is only a formality."

The Imperial officer cleared his throat, "We brought your fellow countrymen from Lockport to assist you. We will start packing your things in the caravan, but you are responsible for keeping track of what's yours."

He droned on about other details of the move. Nikoli felt dread pour down his spine and settle in his stomach. His hip seemed to pulse with his rapid heartbeat. The world seemed to narrow, the soldier's voice becoming a ringing in his ears. *It was all happening too fast.* He clenched his fists. *I'm sorry, Jack.*

Nik started to struggle his way through the crowd but struggled. A few people saw him trying to pass and gripped his arm to propel him along. When he reached the gathering he saw

Caelan's wide and angry stare. The officier barely regarded him, looking at Caelan and studying her reaction.

"I would like to speak." His voice was clear and strong; Zievron quieted immediately to hear him. Caelan opened and shut her mouth in shock. Before she could stop him, Nikolai turned to face his townspeople.

"These Korvos soldiers are not here with saving us in mind. They're here to manage us. Moving us is *convenient*," Nikolai could hear Arman translating quietly behind him. "Our ancestors lived here for centuries without the lightning barrier, before we needed to rely on their oil, rely on the Imperium! There are ways we can protect ourselves without the wall." Nikolai put a hand on his chest, "I've lived outside of the barrier for *years*." "Did we fight for our independence for so many years just to let Korvos take us away from our homes?

"We lost!" a dissenting voice came from the crowd. Eyes turned back to Nikolai expectantly.

"We lost," Nikolai admitted after a pause. "But we cannot give up our spirit. We have not lost ourselves as people of Faragara! We can't abandon our home like this–" Another voice snapped from the gathered citizens, "Maybe you can't, but what about those of us who cannot feed our families? Will *you* hunt for us?"

There was silence then. The townspeople shifted uncomfortably, already knowing the answer. Nikolai stared out at them, his heart pounding, at those who had rallied behind him so long ago. But they were different now, watching him with defeated eyes. Everything was different.

So am I, he realized sadly. *As much as I didn't want to be.*

Nikolai flinched when his arms were seized firmly on either side. Two Korvos soldiers had him by the arms. The officer beside Caelan spoke sharply to them and they began to push Nikolai out from the front of the crowd.

"Let go!" He snarled and tried to yank out of their grip.

The booming voice of the officer stopped any from the crowd who may have stepped in to assist him. "You have one day to collect your belongings. Be grateful we came to aid this town that cannot afford to even trade bread." The people seemed cowed by this reality, and watched as Nikolai was dragged off a distance from the gathering. He twisted and hissed as they pulled him, the steps too fast and jostling on his hip. Nikolai finally managed to jab an elbow into one of the soldier's ribs. He let go, as did his companion. They were far enough away now there was no need to restrain him.

The injured soldier growled and lunged at Nikolai, but his comrade stopped him with a hand on his shoulder. He spoke quickly to him, and turned away to return to the town meeting. The offended soldier glared at Nikolai and spit on the ground. "Beast-fucking *savage,*" the soldier muttered and began to leave.

Nikolai's fist connected with the soldier's jaw before he knew what he was doing. The man stumbled, pressing a hand to his face. Distantly, Nikolai heard gasps from the gathered townspeople followed by shouts and footsteps.

The soldier snarled and lunged at Nikolai. He tried to twist out of the way, but a shock of pain made him stumble, and the soldier tackled him to the ground. They wrestled for a moment,

Nikolai trying to shove the man off him, but the soldier dug a knee into his bad leg.

Nikolai yelped, his hands automatically moving to grip the man's thigh, and he's unable to stop the blow that caught him across the cheek. Nikolai's head whipped to the side, momentarily blinded by stars and his ears ringing. A moment later he felt the weight lift off him and shouts from over his head.

He couldn't hear anything, and the last thing he saw was Caelan's face before his vision went black.

The first thing Nikolai noticed was how unbelievably dry his mouth was. It closed his throat and felt like he was trying to swallow his tongue.

He heard voices talking around him. Nikolai struggled to crack open an eyelid. He was staring at the underside of a canvas roof. "Ah, you're awake." A woman's head appeared in his field of vision. She spoke his language in a foreign accent, and it took him a minute to decipher what she was saying to him. "You've been asleep for a whole day! Lucky you, skipping all the hard work." He grunted.

Another face appeared over his head. "I should've let them arrest you," Caelan said to him. "Thankfully it was easier just to treat you like cargo." It was then he realized they were in a covered wagon.

Nikolai smacked his tongue against the roof of his mouth.

"What–*ow!*" He turned his head and saw the woman sticking a needle into his arm.

"Not to worry! I'm a physicker," she told him cheerfully. "This will help with the pain, and should help keep you comfortable on the journey.

"What–?" He tried again.

"All your things have been packed here. Though I had to trade away the rations you left at Hestia's," Caelan continued. She placed a hand on his shoulder. "I'm sorry it had to be this way, Nik."

He looked up at her and finally got a good look at her face. It was the first time he'd really looked at Caelan in a long time. She looked so worn, and he understood then that she felt the same things he did.

"I have to go now," she said, squeezing the hand on him. "I'll come check on you later." He listened to her climb down from the wagon, and exchange words with someone outside. There was another dip in the wagon, and Arman's face popped into view. His surprise must have shown on his face, because the boy smiled sheepishly at him, then exchanged a few quick words with the physicker. She left shortly after, leaving them alone. Arman looked him over. "You okay, Nik?"

Nikolai swallowed, and his voice sounded rough and worn. "I've been better." They sat silently together for a minute, and Nikolai could start to feel the familiar effects of the painkiller making him hazy. He looked blearily toward Arman. "You have to know," Nikolai said finally, "what I said, I–I didn't mean–"

The young man took his hand and squeezed. "I know,

Nik." Arman pulled the blanket that'd been thrown over him a little higher under his chin. "Get some rest." Nikolai almost didn't feel the hot tear roll past his temple as he blacked out.

Someone was still holding his hand when awareness floated back to him. "Why can't you learn to behave yourself?" Jack chastised.

"Never learned how," Nikolai coughed. He looked up into soft brown eyes. "I thought I wasn't going to see you again."

"I'm afraid you're stuck with me," Jack whispered. He raised the small wood carving of the four-eyed creature into Nikolai's field of vision. "I tried sticking my soul to this. I won't always be...in sight," Jack gestured vaguely at the space around them. The dead man had added a cord to the wooden trinket and slipped it over Nikolai's head, settling it on his chest. "But I won't leave you again."

Tears suddenly welled up in his eyes again. "Jackie, I'm sorry. I'm so sorry–" Jack shushed him, leaning over to kiss his forehead. He pressed his lips to Nikolai's cheeks, kissing away tears, then kissed the corner of his mouth. "It's okay, Kolya." His voice seemed to settle over him, soothing his frayed nerves and warming him from the inside. "I'm scared," Nikolai's voice felt so small. "I don't know if I can..." He trailed off, more hot tears escaping.

"I'll be with you," Jack swore. "Even if you can't see me." He kissed Nikolai fiercely then. Nikolai opened his mouth desperately, letting Jack seize his bottom lip and run his tongue over his teeth. It felt like Jack was trying to brand himself into his skin, and Nikolai managed to raise a hand to fist into his hair.

He breathed in the air from Jack's lungs and tried to commit the warmth of him to memory. Nikolai would need him for the winter ahead.

When Jack pulled away, his eyes were shining with unshed tears. He pressed Nikolai's palm to his face and nuzzled into it, his gaze never leaving his face.

"Promise me you'll keep going," Jack's voice was strong but heavy with emotion. "You have to live. If not for yourself, then for me. For *me*, Kolya."

Nikolai nodded silently, drawing Jack down to kiss him again. "I will," he rasped, "I'll try."

Jack laid beside him then, lending Nikolai his warmth. He stroked his lover's face with calloused fingers, raking them up into his hair to massage his scalp.

"It will be alright," Jack whispered. "Sleep, now."

Nikolai closed his eyes and let the exhaustion wash over him.

A sudden bump made the wagon hitch, jolting him awake. His head thumped back against the wooden floor. Nikolai groaned and rolled to sit up.

He breathed carefully through the dizziness before he

realized he was moving. Nikolai felt sick. They had already left his home behind. The yawning chasm of an unknown future opened before him and threatened to swallow him.

Nikolai raised his hand to grasp the wooden figure that had been tied around his neck. He took several deep breaths, and crushed the feeling down again. He then crawled past boxed goods and stacked sacks of grain to the opening of the wagon.

When he stuck his head out, he saw a tall blonde woman was driving the beasts hauling the wagon along. She turned her head as he made his appearance. "Ah, he lives." She said dryly.

Nikolai climbed out so he could sit on the driving bench beside her. The road before them was dark, only the swinging lanterns over their heads offering much light. He could see the distant pinpricks of the caravan's lights in the distance.

The woman nudged a bag of oddly shaped fruit toward him with her foot. "Eat." His stomach growled loudly. Nikolai didn't protest and fished out a fist-sized fruit and bit into it without ceremony.

The woman spoke again, "You are Nikolai?" He turned his head to look at her. She met his eyes. They were sharp and focused on him, but could see her thinking behind a solid wall of stone. Nikolai nodded to her.

"I am Casta," she continued. Her hard gaze looked him up and down. "You had a man once, named Jack, yes?"

At Nikolai's surprised look her lips twisted into an imitation of a smile. "I heard you talking in your sleep."

"I knew a Jack too, once," Casta faced the road again. "He

was a fine man. Strong, but soft-hearted. Quick and quiet. One of the best snipers in our unit."

Nikolai stared at her. "You knew him?"

Her stare was even. "I was his captain."

They rode in silence for a long time. The fruit had turned to ash in his mouth as Nikolai processed what he'd heard. He blinked and returned to the present when he noticed Casta holding a small envelope toward him.

Casta held up the note. "We all wrote them, in one form or another, in case we didn't make it back. Our agreement was for the living to deliver them when the dead cannot." Nikolai hesitated, then took it while trying to suppress the slight tremor in his hand. His faded name in Jack's rough print stared up at him. The wind seemed less chilly. "Thank you," he said, his voice sounding far away.

She nodded, and looked forward once again. Nikolai slides his thumb until the catch, carefully unfolding the note. He tried to hold it steady with the bumping of the cart, and began to read.

Kolya,

Reading this, I am either sitting embarrassed beside you now, or I am dead. (It's strange to think of you reading this when I'm not there. Will my corpse know? Can you hear my voice in your mind?)

I'm not sure what to say. Picturing myself not at your side, unable to tell you these words myself, I can hardly bear it. I can hear you so clearly, telling me how foolish this exercise is since I'll be home soon anyway. I want to see you. I'm so tired.

But if I were to not hear your voice again, I can't waste this chance to tell you that I love you. We don't have much ink left, but even an endless supply would not be enough.

Please live on, my Kolya, and keep our precious heart alive.

Jack

Nikolai folded the letter again quickly so his tears wouldn't land and smudge the writing. He sniffed quietly and tucked the note into his coat. It felt warm there. Tipping his head back, he stared up at the ever-present stars and the giant moon above them.

Casta remained silent, occasionally adjusting the course of the oxen with a squeeze of the reins.

"What will you do now your letters have been delivered?" Nikolai asked eventually. Her steel gaze never left the horizon. The glow of the bioluminescent foliage around them and swinging lanterns cast her face in harsh shadows. Her eyes held no light. "I will go east," she said at last, her voice soft, "I will go hunting."

"Hunting?"

"For the one that is responsible for their deaths." Her voice was cold steel, "For Jack's death. To root out where she is hiding."

Casta turned her cutting eyes to him. "Will you come?"

Nikolai reeled. There was someone who had prevented his lover from coming home. Had been the cause of the misery he'd been steeped in for years.

Fire bloomed in his chest. Nikolai felt like he'd just pulled his head above the black water of the sea, taking a life-saving breath. He clenched his fist around the wooden figure swinging from his neck.

Nikolai met Casta's even stare with purpose in his eyes. "I will."